Drunk On YOU

Jen

A Hope Town novel

Shane sends
his love.

HARPER SLOAN

Drunk on You
Copyright © 2017 by E.S. Harper

ISBN 10: 1542756715
ISBN 13: 978-1542756716

Cover Design by Sommer Stein with Perfect Pear Creative Covers
Cover Photography by Sara Eirew
Models: Tiffany Robinson and Mike Chabot
Editing by Jenny Sims with Editing4Indies & Ellie McLove with
LoveNBooks.com
Formatting by Champagne Book Design

To Contact Harper:

Email: Authorharpersloan@gmail.com

Website: www.authorharpersloan.com

Facebook: www.facebook.com/harpersloanbooks

Other Books by Harper Sloan:

Corps Security Series:

Axel

Cage

Beck

Uncaged

Cooper

Locke

Hope Town Series:

Unexpected Fate

Bleeding Love

When I'm with You

Loaded Replay Series:

Jaded Hearts

Standalone Novel:

Perfectly Imperfect

Coming Home Series:

Lost Rider

Kiss My Boots

Cowboy Up

Playlist

"Home Alone Tonight" by Luke Bryan
"Sexual" by NEIKED
"That's My Girl" by Fifth Harmony
"Starboy" by The Weeknd
"Closer" by Nine Inch Nails
"Shape of You" by Ed Sheeran
"Play That Song" by Train
"Simple Things" by Miguel
"Shameless" by Sofia Karlberg
"Remember I Told You" by Nick Jonas
"Lights On" by Shawn Mendes
"No Promises" by Cheat Codes
"Torn" by James TW
"Ruin" by Shawn Mendes
"Bad Reputation" by Shawn Mendes
"Does It Feel" by Charlie Puth
"Come Running Back" by Us The Duo
"I Can't Fall in Love Without You" by Zara Larsson
"Yeah!" by Usher
"Sex You" by Bando Jonez
"Pony" by Ginuwine

Link to playlist : open.spotify.com/user/1293550968/
playlist/26V91S6dPfTM3UZHmvVRKD

Note about Shane ;)

Shane, my sexy little control freak, likes to throw in some of his
fluent French here and there … these have all been translated
by my amazing helper Barbara Hoover – while all are correct,
sometimes the translation from French to English gets a little
sideways. So, I've included a link with each phrase to take you to
the translation, knowing that Google won't always get them spot
on. I hope that this helps and that you enjoy Shane's delicious
words as much as I do.

Dedication

To Gel. You, my friend, are a gem. You bring my books to life
with the most breathtaking teasers and never fail to knock me
on my rear with your ... Tempting Illustrations. ;-) I'm so blest to
have you in my life, friend!

Chapter 1

Nikki

I'M GOING TO SNAP.

I'm not going to *just* snap either. It's going to be so glorious; it'll put the Britney Spears head shaving incident of 2007 to shame.

For real.

Maybe.

I should've seen the giant pile of hot mess coming today, seeing how it started and all—with the ex who just won't stay gone. And if I'm being honest, I probably should have just parked my butt at home and watched HGTV on repeat.

Each one of my kids can tell I'm in a mood, as much as I hate to admit that, but there is just no shaking it at this point. I stupidly thought I would be able to at least shake it off for the kids—all twenty-two of them—but no, not even the best kids in Hope Town can make me happy today. Usually, all it takes is stepping foot in my classroom, and I'm instantly happy—but no matter how big of a dream job I have teaching twenty-two of the cutest second graders around, they're just adding to the stress of what has become my day.

See, even with ignoring the whole before I got to work part of my day, there hasn't been a single hour during school that hasn't been a challenge. Bobby Lords showed up with a stomach bug, which wouldn't have been *that* big of a deal ... until he threw up all over his desk *and* Stacey Johann's lap. Not being able to handle the vomit erupting from the desks near her, Laurel Matison went all exorcist meets angry Kardashian and threw up not only on herself but also the two girls standing near her.

If two puking kids, more surface area than I care to remember being covered in vomit, *and* the lingering scent left over from *allll* of that wasn't enough, lunchtime surely had been the tipping point.

And the return of the whole dang reason I'm in such a mood.

Seth.

My very, *very* ex-boyfriend. Only, it seems he was the only one who didn't get the memo about us being over. It's been like this for months; ever since I caught him cheating on me over a year ago—and ended it—for whatever reason, Seth recently decided he doesn't want to accept that I really do mean done. And by done, I mean I hope he plays in traffic.

"Come on, Nik," I grumble to myself, tidying up my desk before pumping out some hand sanitizer. With one last disgusted look at where the puke party of 2017 happened earlier today, I all but run out of my classroom to the faculty parking lot.

Thankfully, Seth decided *not* to corner me as I left the school. Small favors, that jerk. Why couldn't he give me the same respect this morning when he showed up at my apartment *or* when he showed up at the school office wanting to have lunch with me?

I grab my phone and make quick work of shooting off a text to my best friend, Ember Reid, letting her know I'll be ready for our weekly wine Wednesday a little later than normal—the last thing I want to do is take my foul mood out on Em.

Saying a silent prayer that Seth has stopped his stupid quest and won't be waiting at my place, I take a heavy breath and put the car in drive to head home for a bath and reboot before my date with Ember. In all honesty, I have a feeling that if he is there, I might be starring in the real *Orange is the New Black* instead of that promising bath.

Thankfully, by the time I get home thirty minutes later, luck appeared to have shifted to my side. There wasn't any sign of his SUV being here when I pull into my complex parking, no weird notes taped to my door begging me to forgive him, and—best of all—no sign of Seth whatsoever popping up like a poorly placed Where's Waldo. I know it's too good to be true. I'm not stupid enough to believe that today is suddenly going to be the day he buys a clue, but I'm hoping I at least get a little break from his annoying stalking.

I place my schoolbag by the door, rolling my eyes when I realize I dragged it home even though I do not intend to work on my lesson plans at all tonight. My schoolbag—it's huge. You never know when you're going to need something, and on top of the bits and pieces of random things I *may* need, it holds all my planning and grading books, laptop, and the huge container of fish food I forgot to leave at school. Basically, it's heavier than I care to lug around. Big boobs give me enough back, neck, and shoulder pain without adding a million-pound tote bag.

The ringing of my cell has me pausing halfway to my bathroom. I had just started pulling my top off, so I rip it the rest of the way off and jog back to my bag. Grabbing my phone, I answer with a breathy hello.

"You sound like you did that one time I called and you were watching porn."

I smile at my best friend's voice, roll my eyes, and laugh. "I wasn't watching porn," I exclaim in mock outrage.

"You were totally watching it, Nikki!"

Balancing my phone between my ear and shoulder, I unsnap my slacks, slide them off, and then kick them into the corner. Reaching behind me, I unsnap my bra on the way to the bathroom.

"I wasn't *watching* it; I was studying it. There's a big difference, Emberlyn."

She snickers. "The way I see it, it's basically the same thing, girlfriend."

"It's not even remotely the same thing. If I was watching it, I would have been unable to answer the phone because I would have been enjoying it. I wouldn't answer the phone while watching porn."

I hear her daughter's squeal of laughter in the background

followed by Ember's husband mumbling something closer to the phone, making her giggle. My heart swells, happy as pie for my friend and the man who has always held her heart.

"You seemed on edge when you texted me. Everything okay? Do you need to skip this week's wine night?"

I scoff, kicking the thong I just pulled down my legs to the side and turning on the bath. "You could tell I was on edge from a text?"

"You're my best friend, Nik. I could probably tell you're on edge with less."

"I'll fill you in later. Wine night is never off, Em."

"Well, in that case, let me know if I should bring ice cream or an extra bottle."

"Probably both, just to be safe and all." I laugh, pulling the phone from my ear. Pressing the speakerphone button, I place it down on the vanity and pull my long blond hair up into a messy bun. "Just kidding. All I need is my bestie and that amazing Moscato we found last month."

"Then you've got it. I'll be over around six. I'm going to help Nate bathe Quinnly, and then I'll head out."

After disconnecting the call, I set the alarm on my phone for an hour from now before prepping my bath. Arbonne relaxing bath salt and flickering fragrant candles—the perfect cocktail for relaxing my mind and body. Now all I have to do is settle back and pretend I have a clue as to what to do with Seth and his persistence. Something's got to give because I need—for my own sanity—for him to disappear from my life.

"Yoo-hoo!"

I jerk awake in the bath, lukewarm water splashing more out of the tub than in, as I blink the sleep from my vision.

"What the hell," I grumble, reaching out to nab my phone off the closed toilet seat and frowning at the time. "I know I set the alarm."

"You probably set it for a.m. instead of p.m. like you always do, chick." Ember follows her voice into my bathroom, sitting down on the toilet and crossing her legs with a smile.

"You're literally the only person who has ever walked in on me in the bath and not snuck a look at my lady mountains. Also, I don't *always* screw my alarms up." One dark brow arches higher than the other as she gives me a "you've got to be kidding me" look. "Let me rephrase; I haven't done that since me and Siri made friends, and he stopped ignoring me."

"Siri isn't real, Nik. And your phone wasn't ignoring you … You just couldn't stop screaming long enough for the phone to actually hear your prompt."

"Same thing."

"I have a whole bottle of your favorite wine waiting. How about you get your pruned ass out of the tub and come fill me in on what happened today?"

I smile up at her. "Are you going to sit there while I climb out naked and get ready?"

With a roll of her eyes, she looks away and down at her hand, holding it up in indifference. "Your naked body lost its shock value years ago, Nikki. It's not like you have anything I don't."

Looking down at my chest before glancing at hers, I frown.

"Yeah, keep telling yourself that."

Ember gets up before I finished talking, snickering to herself while leaving my bathroom and bedroom. I look back at my phone, groaning when I realize how well my bestie knows me, and cancel the alarm for six *a.m.* tomorrow morning. The bath went a long way in easing the knots of tension in my body, and I know, by the time we're drunk calling her husband to come get her, the rest will be just a memory.

Twenty minutes later, with the AirPlay finally connecting my laptop to the TV mounted across the living room from us and a pile of junk food—and wine—on the coffee table, we're finally ready to begin wine Wednesday.

"We missed the beginning," I whine under my breath when the live Facebook video we're after pops up on the screen, and our friend Angie's voice fills the silence. I say our friend, but we've never met her, and aside from these live feeds, we've never seen her. But there isn't anyone who can watch Doodles of Pearls and *not* feel like they're long-lost friends with the crew.

"We wouldn't have if you wouldn't have been soaking yourself to raisin status. I was on time."

"We'll just have to watch it later when she switches to the next video."

"And miss an opening? I don't think so."

I'm fully aware that we sound insane, being this amped over a pearl party ... yes, a *pearl party*. We had stumbled across them late last year when a mutual Facebook friend had shared her video. What started as a "wtf is this" quickly turned into hours of rapt attention as we became friends with Angie *and* collectors

7

of pearls in no time. And hey, at least watching someone open oysters to reveal beautiful pearls isn't anywhere near as weird as watching pimple popping videos.

"I'm dying for one of those pink pearls, Nik," Ember says with a sigh, watching raptly as Angie inserts the shucker into the oyster. "Did you see that neon looking pink one last week? I almost called you, but Nate threw my phone across the room and said, I quote, 'This pearl shit is out of hand.'"

I turn my head from the TV and gape at her. "I hope you denied him sex that night."

"Have you seen my husband lately?" she smarts.

"So you let him come between pearl time *and* rewarded him?"

Her head falls back on the couch cushion behind her as she laughs maniacally. "I'm pretty sure I was the one being rewarded."

Joining in her laughter, I lift my wine glass up toward her. "That might be so, but seriously you went to Pound Town over Doodleville?!"

"Nothing in this world would have me turning down my husband and his wicked promises."

I snort, having just taken a sip.

"Plus, I watched all three of her videos that I missed the next day, so in reality, I *really* won."

I nod my head in understanding, having watched missed parties the next day myself, but my smile slips when I realize the biggest difference in Ember's situation and mine. She has an amazing husband who keeps her from our obsession with these parties while I have no one.

"Tell me," she says, instantly picking up on my change in mood.

"Seth."

"You've got to be kidding me! Still?"

I exhale, long and full of frustration. "I'm starting to think he's never going to stop."

"It's been over a year since y'all broke up. Why on earth would he be so persistent now?"

A humorless burst of laughter escapes. "Probably because, for the majority of that time, he still thought the grass shined with emerald dust on the other side. By the time he realized it's not any better, I was still alone, giving him the illusion I've been pining after him all this time. I mean, it is so like that son of a Bieber to think I would actually be waiting, let alone pining for him."

"How does he know you haven't met someone?"

"Oh, come on, Em. It's Hope Town. We might not live in some teeny tiny town, but we do live in one that isn't nearly big enough to keep the whispers from echoing around. We both know I haven't dated, but the difference is, we know the truth those whispers keep from his ears. I don't date because I'm hung up on what he did to me; I don't date because I don't want to give another man a chance to hurt me like he did."

"That isn't exactly any different, babe." She nods with sympathy, almost spilling her wine when she attempts to sip while still nodding.

"Uh, how so?"

"The common factor in both is that you, my friend, are still letting *him* affect the way you live your life. While not in the same way, of course, but either way, he's the one keeping you single. Not you being single because you want to be."

"But I do want to be single."

Ember's nod turns to a very emphatic shake. "No, you don't. You're the most loving person I know, Nikki, but you're also someone who loves *being* loved. Relationships, platonic especially, are something you thrive on. You're happier when you're not alone. Why do you think you love being a teacher? Why do you think you lasted so long with Seth when you stopped loving him a long time ago to begin with? Before Nate, I probably wouldn't have seen it so clearly since I spent years before finding my way to him in self-imposed solitude, but because of my relationship with him, I see right through you."

I swallow what feels like a mouthful of heavy air. "And what, my drunk friend, do you see?"

She leans toward me, narrowing her eyes. "I see someone who's letting a douchebag rule her life because she's too afraid to have some fun."

"That's …" I trail off as I think about what she's saying. I can say it different ways, but she's right. He's been keeping me from moving on. While it might not be because I'm pining away—as he would appear to wish—being afraid another man will cheat on me and hurt me might as well be the same thing. "Exactly what I'm doing." I slap my free hand against my forehead. The sound of my palm meeting flesh a loud snap in the room around us. "Stupid, stupid, stupid girl."

"Nah, Nik. You aren't stupid. I would have been more

surprised if you had been able to move on without a little nudge. You aren't stupid *because* you're protecting your heart. That is never a stupid thing to do."

"I guess it's hard to want to open myself up, to be honest. I spent four years of my life with Seth, and I probably would still be stuck in a dead relationship if he hadn't cheated. When I find another man to try with again, how do I know he is going to be worth giving myself over to—worth losing myself in the process again?"

Her pixie face scrunches up. The freckles across her nose look like they're dancing as she twitches her nose at me in confusion. "You didn't lose yourself."

I nod, my face washed clean of emotion. "Yeah, I did. I didn't do anything for me for years before we split. It was all about what would make *him* happy. I spent so much time afraid he would leave if he wasn't happy that I didn't even realize I *wanted* him to leave."

"So learn from it! Open yourself up to the idea of moving on, but do it on your terms. Start tomorrow by living for Nikki and making sure no one doubts your happiness when they're on the outside looking in."

Long after Nate had come to pick up Ember's drunken self and I had punched my pillow to try to get comfortable, her words filter back through my mind. She's right. I'm in limbo, and I don't really want to be. I've lost something I loved by keeping myself from getting close to someone—the happiness I feel knowing I'm the reason someone else feels that way. I miss the connection I've deprived myself of. The chemistry between a man and woman.

Companionship. What better way to prove to Seth that I'm serious about us never getting back together than to jump back in with both feet. No one says I can't sate my desire for some extra friendly friendship with some no-strings fun.

It's a win-win that even sober me would agree with.

I think ...

Chapter 2

Shane

"FOR THE LAST TIME, LACEY, it's not gonna happen."

She pouts. Something I used to find adorable now makes me grind my teeth instantly. In the year since breaking up, I seem to have a laundry list full of things I used to like about her. Fuck me; I'm not even sure there's anything left about her that I still like.

"But Shane," she starts, but I hold my hand up to silence her, the beginnings of a migraine already clawing at my temples.

"No more of that 'but Shane' bullshit. You want to jump from licking pussy to riding dick because you can't decide which you like the most, that's cool, Lace, but you won't be doin' that shit with me. I'm not judging this new life of yours. I couldn't care less what type of genitals you want to poke around with. But you need to do it anywhere fucking else than right here."

"We love each other!" she whines. The pounding in my head continues to grow.

"You don't know what love is, Lacey. You don't fuck around on someone you claim to love. I would've given you the world a year ago, but you ruined that when you fucked around. Now you don't just not get my world; you don't get a single fucking piece of me."

Her chin quivers and she blinks rapidly. I know her well enough, though, and she isn't fooling me. When Lacey cries because she actually is upset, she is the ugliest crier I've ever seen. Messy, loud, and hysterical. But this Lacey uses that delicate image of a woman against my protective nature. The one who fakes whatever tears she can muster to get me to cave.

That right there is the kind of woman I never saw because I liked her pussy too much. I let her use me, but I'm not stupid enough to let her back in.

Seeing that her one measly tear isn't going to work, she switches gears, and it's so swift and obvious. I have no clue how I missed this before now. Her chin stops, her eyes still for a beat before fluttering slowly, and I'm sure, she means to be seductive. Her tense posture melts slightly as she walks around my desk with a sinful strut.

"Don't even, Lacey." She stops abruptly, and I can only imagine she's confused as fuck now that both of her go-to manipulations have failed her. "I've got too much shit to do tonight, and we're down two bartenders. The last thing I wanted to do even before all that shit landed on my plate was explain to you, again, that we're not ever going to be together again."

"You don't mean that," she hedges.

My neck cocks back a twitch, and I laugh out a frustrated breath. "Woman, are you dense? You fucked off on me and picked your lover of two months over the man you had been with for years. You decided you wanted to lick some cunt and be wild and free, babe, and that's what you can have. When all that you did came out, that was the day you became no one to me."

"Shane," she huskily murmurs, going back to wounded and tearful Lacey.

"Seriously, get the fuck out. I haven't banned you from Dirty yet, but don't mistake my kindness for weakness. When it comes to you, babe, there are no weaknesses because you. Are. Nothing."

She frowns, I think—I really can't fucking tell anymore now that she's a little too close to her Botox injector friend. I see the spark in her brown eyes the second she decides to, yet again, convince herself that nothing I just said happened.

Fucking hell, I want this bitch out of my life.

"I'm going to run because I know you're busy. I'll call you tomorrow, honey."

And it takes every ounce of self-control for me not to snap. I hold my body still, my face emotionless, and my words to myself. Lacey walks out of this office only because I've had years of practice at keeping myself in control. Inside my head, though, I've got that skinny giraffe neck of hers between my hands and I'm whipping her around like a ragdoll until she can't fucking slither her way into my fucking life anymore.

She's not going to go far. I know she's downstairs below my office within the club. She'll hide in the shadows, but she won't leave while I'm here. Watching from the outside to make sure no one moves in on me—a man she lost a year ago because she got busted fucking another person—another woman—in our bed.

What I need to do is blacklist her from Dirty Dog, the club I'm part owner of with my buddy Nate. I hadn't wanted to do that, but no matter how much bad-mouthing Lacey will do because of it, I can't have her pulling that shit again.

I walk from behind my desk and over to the edge of the room, toe-to-glass with the window that covers the whole back wall. My eyes roam over the room below. Bodies undulating to the music, laughter and yelled conversations hitting my mind like a phantom echo of what I know it sounds like down there in the thick of it. Each of the bars in the vast club are swamped with bodies, and it isn't even time for the dancing.

Business is damn good. Another reason I can't have my ex bringing drama and bullshit to stink up that good business.

With a deep sigh, I rock on my feet and study the room. Two years ago, I moved to Hope Town on a whim when Nate called to let me know of his plans to open a club in his hometown. At the time, I was just managing Dirty and hadn't become business partners with him yet, but I believed in this place just as much back then as I did today.

Dirty Dog is that club everyone buzzes about. Everyone. It doesn't matter if you live here in Georgia or in the middle of the Pacific on the Hawaiian Islands. We're all over the internet. Celebrity gossip magazines almost always have some celeb coming or going from here. And with our recent decision to add-on to the building and make Dirty even bigger—the talk of Dirty being "the place" to be doesn't appear to be slowing down anytime soon. Or ever, I hope. What I had been working my whole fucking life to find was a stable job doing something I love that put money in the bank and food on my table. I was completely in control of my life now. Nothing would change that.

Letting Lacey lead me around by my dick is the last fucking thing I'm going to let happen. She must have had her brain sucked out of her pussy while she was getting to know her scissor sister because not one time did I let her call the shots when she had my cock.

Control.

As long as I keep it, I don't have to deal with bullshit like Lacey that I finally washed myself clean of.

Three nights later and I'm still short staffed, exhausted with Lacey's persistence, and so busy I've forgotten—again—to fill Nate in on what's happening with her showing up here. I figure, between the two of us, we can figure out how to detach her from me.

Nate took this shift working the bar, something the two of us rarely do but always alternate when they're shorthanded. If I'm being honest, though, I don't mind working the bar. And I know Nate doesn't either. My lips turn up when I see Nate jump on the bar and grind his hips in the woman's face in front of him. A laugh bursts from my mouth when that woman—his wife—shoves him away with a laugh lighting up her face. I'm happy he's found what he has with Ember. She's a damn good woman and the rare breed who doesn't mind what her man does for a living. Something I had thought—at one time—that I would have with Lacey. In my experience, when you're in a sex-driven industry *and* a relationship, it never ends without jealousy infecting things. Nate and Ember, though—they break the mold. He found his diamond in the rough. Sure, more women like Ember are probably out there, but I'm not willing to sift through all the other bullshit women on the way to find one of my own.

When I was stripping, I knew the chance of finding the 'it' girl was less than none. While Dirty isn't a strip club, all the men who work for us—and ourselves included—were once strippers. We used what we learned early on while stripping. Exploiting people's obsession with sex leads to immense profitability. We started with the base, the bar, and sprinkled in the rest. Damn good music, strong drinks, lines out the door every day from lights off to lights on, and … our ability to dance.

When Nate opened Dirty Dog, it was popular right out of the gate, gaining even more notoriety for being the male version of Coyote Ugly. The men danced for the sex-obsessed patrons to a tune so filthy the only difference from our days of stripping was that we didn't take anything off anymore. Well, not always.

Because of those not always nights—which really, we have some who touch a little too much every night—it was clear to me that a relationship with anyone other than a woman like Ember would never work, and I was sick of wasting the energy to find it.

I turn and walk back to my desk, the mountain of paperwork I had been putting off for a week looking a little thicker than it did two nights ago when I was here. Which only served to amp the migraine that had been building in my head for the past three nights. What I need is to release some fucking stress. Find someone who knows how to play without getting attached.

Maybe tonight … the thought filters through my mind, and I glance out the window looking into the dull light of the bar below. "Who knows," I mumble to myself, not dismissing the idea of finding a good old-fashioned one-night stand.

I stretch, looking over at the clock to see two hours have passed since I started doing payroll. My back tenses as I stand to work the kinks out of my body, reminding me how long it's been since I went to the gym. With a look at the still thick-as-fuck pile of work, I huff a breath.

"Fuck it." Taking off my suit jacket, I toss it on the back of my desk chair and start walking. I'm wound up tighter than hell, and I'm not going to get shit done if I don't go work out some of that pent-up energy. No better place to gain back some of that lost gym time *and* work out that energy than by working the bar at Dirty Dog.

"Well, well! Look at how lucky the bar is tonight," Nate booms when I jump over the bar top and land next to him. His arm drops over my shoulders, and he turns us both to face the excited crowd around us. "You are the luckiest motherfuckers in this whole damn place because not only do you get this sex god …" He pauses and waves his hand down his own body, moving me with him as he does some thrusting of his hips because his arm is still around my neck. "But you all get Shane, too. Now, I'm a happily married man who can recognize a hot thing when I see it, and you don't want to miss this stud muffin when he gets a hankering to be … fucking … DIRTY!" He bellows out the last word, and screams erupt around us. Nate grabs the opposite side of the bar and pulls himself over on his belly toward Ember. Her laughter stops the second his mouth crashes against hers.

I smile at the two of them and shake my head, turning from them to get to work. That is when I notice her. No fucking idea how I missed her before now.

Nikki.

Blond goddess with a killer ass, legs begging to wrap me up, and the sweetest pair of tits I've ever seen.

The first time she blinked up at me with those dark blue denim eyes, I knew she was trouble for me. A temptation on every level. She screamed at me to take her while my real life warred. She tempted me when I was with Lacey, making me feel guilty to desire someone other than the woman I was with. But it was what I discovered when I saw past her stunning looks. She was so much more than the fake type of woman I had originally thought. The vapid users that I had always seemed to attract.

Nikki was hilarious, smart, and driven in her career. She's only happy when those around her are happy. I'm not even sure she has a single vindictive bone in her body.

And worst still, she was dating a sonofabitch.

Until the day that changes, I'm going to keep doing what I've done since the day she crashed into my life … ignore the twinge inside me that demands I claim her.

Chapter 3

Nikki

THE MUSIC POUNDS AGAINST MY body, cascading a series of chills down my spine and across my skin. Almost like a physical touch. Of course, that probably has a lot to do with the dress pant covered ass shaking everything God gave him right in front of my face. Let me tell you, having so much sinful perfection in front of your face like that isn't the fun you would think it was. It's pure torture to sit here and act like I'm not affected by the show in front of me. Hell, I'm not even sure why I try to hide it anymore.

Didn't I just decide the other night to be all wild and free and enjoy my life as a single woman who dances with others ... naked ... in bed? There's no one to hold me back—I'm a free woman.

I laugh at myself, my eyes still not able to look away from the erotic show before me, and I almost spill my drink when I blindly reach for it because of his intoxication. Playing it off, I place the straw between my lips and drink while my chest heaves. The cold chill of the liquor racing down my throat does little to cool my overheated system.

My eyes roam down from his face and over the hard ridges of his naked chest now that he's unbuttoned his dress shirt all the way. The tails flapping as he dances. His hands move into view when he hooks his thumbs in his suspenders and pulls them from his taut muscles … then he lets go. The loud snap when they hit his chest through the shirt, dancing above the music, occurs at the same time a zap of lust shoots through my body. My eyes continue to trail over his hard torso until I reach his hips. Then my eyes widen and I almost choke on the sip I had just swallowed.

Is he … hard?

Oh, my. He totally is. Son of Bon Jovi with Meatloaf on top!

How long have I thought of what it would be like to be on this end of Shane's dancing? It burns me alive from a distance; so unbelievably hot, I knew it would be just as strong up close and personal. I just never imagined the heat would be so scorching that it literally takes my breath away.

I gulp, my eyes unable to look away from the man who's invaded my mind for way too long. Watching the solid bulge behind his zipper as it becomes more pronounced, I admire the way he rolls his hips in tune with the beat of the music in the most delicious of ways. There is no way he's missed where my attention is stuck either. He takes a step closer, his black dress shoes framing the spot in front of me where my drink had just been. When he's this close, there is no doubt he's not dancing for the crowd anymore. My pulse speeds up as I start to lift my gaze. He towers above me, his tattooed forearms peeking out from his rolled-up sleeves when he raises his arms above his head, holding on to the large bar that runs parallel to the bar top, his face tilted down as he winks and pulls his bottom lip between his teeth as the beat drops and the music gets that perfect sex rhythm.

That's when he starts moving. And I mean *realllly* moving. I've never seen him dance like this, but I know one thing for sure, I want to see him do this naked and between my thighs.

"Should be illegal, right?" Ember says in my ear, loud enough to be heard over the pulsing music around us but still just for me. She keeps her head close but leans back to look at my face.

I nod, incapable of doing much more, and glance back up.

"Starboy" by The Weeknd continues, a song that never really seemed as sexual as it does right now, and still, I just stare.

Good heavens, I might start drooling. My eyes widen, and I bring my hand up to pass over my chin … just to make sure and all.

His shoe makes a loud boom when he slams his foot against the thick bar top, right in front of me, and I startle with a tiny jerk. I trail my gaze up his legs, pausing on that hard crotch again. Clutching my drink to my chest, I realize I'm feasting on the poor man again and continue my perusal upward. Then, I see the sinfully handsome face of Shane Kingston. One of his thick, dark brows goes up in a way that I just *know* he's daring me. For what, though, I'm not sure.

This man, this ridiculously sexy man, knows he affects me. Heck, he's probably always known.

I watch as one heavily tattooed arm reaches behind his back, and before I realize what he's doing, he's maneuvered his shirt off while keeping his suspenders in place. Then he's tossing it in my face. I jump with a gasp, my nose filling with a scent that's all Shane—sweaty man and expensive cologne. Ember laughs, and I know she's enjoying seeing me speechless because that's a rarity.

Am I going to let this man get the best of me?

No.

Hell, no.

I'm ready to be wild and freaking free!

Tossing the shirt in Ember's general direction, I say a silent prayer that she holds on to it because I'm stealing the damn thing. My drink goes next, my hand shooting toward her until she takes it from me. The whole time, Shane continues to dance on top of the bar with the rest of the bartenders at Dirty Dog. I couldn't tell you what came over me next; all I know is I was a new woman after finally seeing what my cheating, no good, son of a nutcracker ex was still doing to me long after our breakup.

No longer was I going to let a man intoxicate me with his allure. Not when I know I can give just as good as he can. And boy am I planning on giving it real good.

I crook my finger up at him, smoothing my face out until I just know I look fierce and in control, and I step back just enough to allow a small gap in front of me. He places his hands on a bar above his head and lifts his muscular bulk up then swings his legs back, getting the momentum he needs to launch his body off the polished wood and into the narrow space between me and it.

I step up to him right after he lands, so close that my boobs press against his sweaty, rock-hard chest. He doesn't move, letting me invade his space. Even with my four-inch heels, he's still a giant. I look up, meeting the eyes that are too hard to read in the dim lighting, and wing it. Trailing my fingers down each strap of his suspenders, I smile at him.

"You enjoy that, starboy?"

His jaw flexes. The spot near his ears that ripples with his clenching motion makes me shiver—I couldn't help it if I tried. Something is extremely sexy about that part of a man.

"I think you enjoy it a little too much. Turning women on while knowing you're just a big tease because of it."

"You think I'm a tease?" he grunts on a laugh of disbelief.

I step even closer at the same time I press my hands against his abs, the muscles flexing under my touch. The second I roll to my toes, my face is at his throat, and the scent of him fills my nostrils again. I close my eyes—thankful my new position doesn't afford him the knowledge that I'm becoming lust drunk on the scent of him. His hands clasp my hips tightly, his fingertips biting into the skin before he gives me some help by literally lifting my feet off the ground.

"Unless you plan on taking me right here, I think, by definition, you *are* a tease."

His hold on my hips gets tighter, the bite of pain making my eyes roll back in my head in pleasure.

"You couldn't handle me, chèrie."

"Sherry?"

His chest moves with his silent laughter.

"Chèrie," he repeats, this time his mouth at my ear, and I hear a subtle French accent to the word that I remember from my high school days. But I failed French so badly I can't even remember how to count to ten.

"Someone's cocky," I joke, curling my toes to keep my heels from falling off as he continues to hold me off the ground. "I could *so* handle you."

His head tips, and his nose trails from the base of my neck up to my ear before his lips are back against my skin. My hands, braced on the corded muscles of his shoulders, jolt, and I tighten my grip until my nails bite against his skin. His chest vibrates, and I wish I could see his face. "You couldn't. A man like me … I would ruin you and have you begging to be ruined all over again once you'd recovered."

"Don't underestimate me, Shane Kingston."

He lifts his head until his face is just a breath away from mine. My heart speeds up so rapidly that I'm convinced he can feel it against our pressed chests. Praying he doesn't call my bluff, I raise a brow and dare him to turn me down.

"You still dating that idiot?" he questions in a deep, rasping tone.

"You still dating that bitch?" I return, shaking my head mirroring him, both of us silently confirming we're single.

"You want to play, Nicole, make sure you understand what you're asking for."

Lifting one of my hands off his shoulders, I look up at the thick hair mussed on top of his head, dark raven strands falling against his forehead. With a whisper touch of my pointer finger, I push them back before raking my fingers across the top of his head. The thick locks feeling like damp silk as they move through my fingers. His face is unyielding, until that moment, and I lift my other hand up to one shaved side of his head, my fingertips just kissing the thick upper part of his stylish cut. My other hand is placed against the other side of his head. I rub my palms against the short buzz until I'm framing his face with his ears resting on the webbing of my thumbs.

Then I tilt his head slightly with my hold and take his mouth in a deep kiss.

I feel, rather than see, him turning us until the bar top is biting against my back. His hands move at the same time he opens his lips and his tongue starts sliding against my own. His hands shove under my short skirt until my bare ass is in his hands. Those strong fingers flexing against their hold in a way that makes me think Shane Kingston is definitely an ass man. His hot breath fans on my cheek when he groans loudly, deepening the kiss and trying to take control.

Oh, no way.

My legs wrap around his hips, and I suck his bottom lip into my mouth before biting it. A raspy hiss escapes him before I swallow it in another dueling of our lips. I roll my hips, using the bar as leverage, and I mentally cheer when he shivers.

Wishing we weren't in the middle of a very crowded club, I break away from him and press my forehead against his to catch my breath. "Do *not* underestimate me," I repeat myself.

He nods, lust and need written all over his face. His eyes

are leaden, betraying the unaffected nature he would like me to believe.

"How about *you* let me know when you're ready to pick this back up somewhere a little less … crowded?"

He doesn't move. Still holding me against him silently between the bar and his hard body. That sexy tic back in the edge of his jaw.

"Let me down, Shane. Let me down and dig out your phone so you can grab my number. You want to show me just what you think I can't handle, you give me a call. If not, well … your loss, not mine."

His hands release my ass, slowly trailing back out from under my skirt, and I unhook my legs—reluctantly. He doesn't release me until my feet are firmly on the ground. His face is so unreadable I kick my ass for assuming he was just as into that as I had been. Guess that's what I get for being out of the game for so long.

I shrug and try not to let the disappointment get the best of me. Well, at least the kiss was hot. He doesn't move, making me squeeze out from where he has me pinned. I smile awkwardly at a slack-jawed Ember, noting that she's still holding Shane's shirt. Good; I deserve it after the free show we just gave the bar.

"You ready?" I ask her, still breathless from that kiss.

Her mouth opens but snaps shut a moment later. At the same time, a firm hold against my arm stops me from moving. My eyes widen when I feel Shane press his front against my back, the thickness of his erection instantly clear against my body. His lips close around my earlobe, and he bites down. Thankfully, his arm snaked around my stomach at the same time because that alone took every bit of strength out of my legs. His free hand comes around my other side, and through one hell of an aroused haze, I see a phone dangling in front of my face.

His mouth releases the sensitive flesh, and in a tone deeper than I've ever heard from him, he commands, "Think real hard about taking this, Nicole. If you put your number in there, you're as good as mine for however long we decide to … handle each other. I'm not the kind of man you want to be playing games with."

Ember's eyes are ping-ponging from the phone to my eyes to Shane's direction so rapidly I'm a little worried my best friend might get dizzy and pass out.

If I was smart, I would have taken heed of his warning. Lord knows there are other men I could be wild and free with, but I've always wondered what kind of man Shane would be in bed. Even when it was wrong to think those thoughts. He's just got that effortless thing about him that invades your mind with dirty images. But I don't want to find some other nameless man. I don't want easy. I want Shane. I'm sick of playing life safely, afraid to move on with my life. I'm over living like that. I want to be wild, free, and confident. Like I said, if I was smart, I would have done what the old, safe Nikki would have done. But that Nikki had been with the same cheating bastard for years and never felt an ounce of what I just experienced with Shane. That Nikki was gone, drunk on this man, and desperate to feel that high more and more.

So I snatched that phone from him and quickly plugged in

my number and called my cell. Not only did I give myself his number—but him mine as he requested. Then I ripped myself from his hold, grabbed Ember's hand, and hightailed it out of Dirty Dog so fast, I'm convinced I found the speed of light.

With his shirt.

Holy moly.

What the heck did I do now?

Chapter 4

Shane

FUCK.

Fucking fuck.

"What the fuck was that?" Nate, my best friend, hisses.

Yup, pretty much took the words outta my head.

I close my eyes and press my palms against the one-way glass lining the upper offices to get some control over myself before turning to look at Nate.

I can still smell her.

I can still fucking taste her on my lips, some mix of the drink she had been nursing and something that must be completely and uniquely Nikki.

"Do you hear me?" Nate says, frustration mingling in with the earlier shock I heard in his voice.

"Hear you," I confirm.

"And?" he continues, not backing down.

"What do you want me to say, Nate?"

"Well, shit, I don't know. How about give me a little hint to what the hell just went through your head. I've never seen you act like that. With years of practice, you've become a robot to the women throwing themselves at you like bitches in heat, and the one chick I would prefer you kept your dick away from makes you turn into some sort of live porno foreplay for our whole fucking club?"

"Shit," I say under my breath.

"Look, man, I love you like a brother, but that's my wife's best friend. I don't want you fucking with her and making things tense. Since I promised I would never let my lady lose her smile when she isn't happy, I'm definitely not happy."

"She was giving just as good as I was, Nate. Don't make me out to be the bad guy who is after corrupting the innocent. That was two very consenting adults, not a monster and his prey."

I hear him grumble under his breath, and I turn from the window to look at him. He's standing on the other side of the desk—my desk—gripping the back of the chair placed in front of it tightly. It's weird to see him on the other side of the desk, but ever since I became a partner here at Dirty—and we converted his office from one big as hell space into two private office suites—it's moments like this that finally let it start to sink in that Dirty is just as much mine as it is his.

"Don't start this shit unless you're going to treat her like more than just a piece of pussy you toss away when you're done," he finally says after a long stretch of silence.

"Not really your place to request that of me, Nate."

"I know it isn't, but she means something to Ember, and what's important to my wife is important to me. That girl's been through some shit with her ex, and she doesn't need to find herself with another man who's going to keep his options open, if you know what I mean."

I narrow my eyes. "You make me sound like a fuckin' chump."

"You've been fucking your way through Hope Town since you finally split with Lacey. I'm not *making* you sound like jack shit. I'm speaking the truth, and you know it."

"I enjoy my life, Nate. Nothing wrong with that. Something you used to do too before you settled down. Don't judge me because I enjoy casual sex."

"When casual sex occasionally turns into fucking a different woman every night, that's doing a lot more than just enjoying your life."

I take a sharp breath, trying not to get pissed at my closest friend. "It's been six fucking months since I stuck my dick inside any woman, Nate, so I'd appreciate you not assuming I'm turning into a whore." I narrow my eyes and add, "And don't fucking point fingers at me."

His head jerks, shocked by my words. "Jessa?"

Guess he's not going to believe my recent celibacy that easily. I roll my eyes as I remember carrying the drunk-out-of-her-mind woman from Dirty last night. "Gave her a ride home because I knew she would try to drive herself if I didn't. Cock stayed in my pants. Cock didn't even *think* about coming out of my pants."

33

"Could have called her an Uber, Shane."

"Could have, yeah, but she's friends with my sister, so I didn't."

"Claire?"

"Another of Libby's friends," I tell him through clenched teeth.

"Are all the women who you conveniently help friends of Liberty?"

"She's a popular girl." I shrug, moving to drop down in my chair and shift next month's work schedule around.

"Bethany?"

"You're going to keep this up, aren't you? Even when you run out of names, you'll just keep making shit up."

He doesn't move, waiting for me to answer and ignoring my aggravation.

Jesus Christ. "Yeah, that one I fucked," I admit.

"That was..." he trails off, thinking back.

"Almost nine months ago. Must have been harder than you thought to come up with some names."

"Well, shit, I could have sworn she was recent."

"You've built me up to be one hell of a slut in your head, Nate. It wasn't too long ago when I could have been standing in your shoes, 'cept my guessing game wouldn't have been such a struggle, seeing as you actually did fuck *everyone* before settling down with Ember."

"Jesus Christ, Shane. I don't mean to sound like a hypocritical bastard, but this is Nikki here. She's been around since we opened the doors here almost two years ago. Why now?"

"Did you ever think that maybe I haven't made a move on her because I wasn't ready to *not* be a fucking slut?"

Nate laughs, the sound not even close to humor. "You finally scraped Lacey off, Shane, but she's still barking after you. She's here every fucking night, still, after almost a year. If it weren't my worry that you're still fucking everything with a willing body, I would still be concerned about that bitch."

I get angry at just the mention of my ex. "I don't exactly invite or welcome her shit, and you know it."

"So you're telling me that you're going to start something serious with another woman while your ex is still coming around constantly?"

"Didn't say that either," I grumble, feeling more and more like a kid getting in trouble with Daddy for being out past curfew.

Nate tosses his hands in the air and makes a show of his exasperation.

"Look, I respect where you're coming from, but shut the fuck up, Nate. You're not my daddy, and you damn sure aren't hers. If she calls, I'll figure it out then, but right now, I'm not even sure what the fuck just happened. Honestly, all I know is that felt like some strong ass shit. A lot stronger than just getting my rocks off with easy pussy."

"Don't fucking hurt her," he says with a resigned sigh. "Just try not to make things awkward as hell when whatever all that is, ends. My wife likes you, for whatever reason, though if you fuck with her friend, I'm thinking that's going to change."

"Go home, Nate."

"Yeah, I'm going. I have a long night ahead of me."

"Quinnly still teething?" I ask about his daughter, hoping this means the subject of Nikki is closed. He's made a lot of noise about how much his tiny daughter has been keeping him on his toes for the past two weeks, so I'm thankful we're done talking about other things.

"Nah, gotta fuck my wife."

I laugh, feeling lighter than I have since Nikki rushed out of Dirty, not even fazed by his crass.

"Just think about what you're doing, okay?"

I nod. "I always do, Nate. Always."

He leaves even though he's still not convinced I'm not going to fuck up his perfect fucking life by sleeping with his wife's best friend. It's written all over his face, but thankfully, he's whipped by his desire for his wife more than he cares about who her friends are fucking because he doesn't argue anymore. When the door snicks shut, I rest my head against the seat and think back to the hot-as-fuck woman who just blew my mind with a simple kiss.

I would be opening a whole can of fucking worms if I gave in to what my body wants when it comes to Nikki. Especially with Lacey still trying to get her claws back in me. But maybe that's what she needs to finally get a hint that it's over between us and has been for a long damn time. I can look past a lot—her bitchy attitude and hankering for expensive handbags being some of them—but opening her legs for another *woman* damn sure isn't one of them.

"Fuck," I groan, running my hands through my hair.

I pick up my phone and send a text to Dent, our full-time manager, and let him know I'm taking off for the night. I send another to my sister to let her know if any of her friends end up drunk and stupid tonight, it's on her and not me. Then I grab my car keys and get the fuck out of here.

As I make the whole drive across town to my house, I still feel the heat of Nikki as if she's pressed against my body. My cock still throbs for release with each pull of air through my nose that continues to carry her scent. I'm not sure if I'm praying she calls or not, and for a man who prides himself on control, this isn't a position I care to be in.

Fucking hell.

My house is dark when I pull into the garage, which isn't a shock since there isn't anyone waiting for me anymore. I spend more time at Dirty than I do at home anyway, so I hardly notice the loneliness anymore, but tonight it is almost oppressing in its obviousness. The silence around me thickens when the deep purr of my engine cuts off. I trudge into the house, still shirtless from earlier, and walk through the darkness to my bedroom. My shoes are kicked into the corner, and my pants follow behind them. By the time I'm in the shower, with warm jets of water pounding my skin and my cock in hand, only one thing is on my mind … release.

It isn't until later, the sun just hours from coming up, that I realize it was Nikki's name I barked loudly as my come shot from my cock.

Jesus Christ. Either I need to get her under me, or I need to find someone else to get over this shit with. My cock's been in hibernation for six fucking long-as-hell months—since the last time Lacey showed up at my house with another desperate attempt to worm her way back in my life on an unfortunate night when I had been drinking. I haven't had an issue with my cock being stuck in the on position in a long damn time, and now I can't get it to go fucking down.

I wasn't joking when I told Nikki I was no good for her. Every relationship I've ever had turns to shit because the women get jealous-as-fuck about what I do for a living. Lacey being the last and, shockingly, longest relationship I had. Even when I was still stripping, she had been there, but for whatever reason, things at Dirty made her more jealous—but for fuck's sake, my clothes stay on there. Even if I wanted something more than casual, I can't bring another woman close only to have them start their bullshit about my job or them—because if a woman can't support what I enjoy doing, she isn't worth my time.

My phone chimes from across the room, and I toss the covers back before climbing from my bed and over to where I tossed my pants earlier. Swear to God, this had better not be Libby with more bullshit for me to clean up. Or worse, Lacey.

Unknown: I just made myself come thinking about you.

"What the fuck?"

Me: Who the hell is this?
Unknown: Ouch. Guess that wasn't as memorable of a kiss as I thought it was.
Me: Nikki?
Unknown: Got it in one, starboy.

My lips form into a smirk at the stupid-as-fuck nickname. I back out of the text and quickly store her number, walking back to my bed before replying to her.

Me: Didn't think you would be this quick, chèrie.
Nikki: Oh, I wasn't. I made sure and played with myself for a long while before I finally came.
Me: Jesus fucking Christ.
Nikki: Yeah, I think I might have said that a few times, too.
Me: You're playing with fire.
Nikki: Good thing I prefer my fun hot.
Nikki: Tell me, what would you say if I had a mutually beneficial offer for you?
Me: I would still say you have no idea what you're getting into, but I'll hear you out.

I lean back and watch the stupid fucking dots dance at the bottom of the screen while she types, reading back her words while stroking my hard cock with my free hand. Jesus, I bet she did fucking get herself off too. She had been seconds away from coming in my arms earlier and I hadn't even gotten my hands past her hips and ass. My hand speeds up, and I lean back against the headboard while I wait for her to respond, my mind bringing up an image of her from earlier. Long blond hair cascading down her back, her angelic face free of the heavy makeup most women who come to Dirty wear. The black skirt she had on so fucking short if she would have bent over, I bet I would have gotten a perfect shot of her pussy. Her heavy tits straining the black top she had on, some kind of lace shit that showed her skin and the fact she was only wearing a red bra underneath.

And those shoes. They had been the first thing I noticed. All I thought about during that dance in front of her had been what those heels would feel like digging into my ass while I pounded into her.

I was so lost in my mind that when my phone went off, it surprised the fuck out of me, my orgasm just seconds away, retreating briefly.

Nikki: I'm in the need of some help getting rid of a little problem I have, and judging by the chemistry we so clearly have, I think you're just what I need, Shane. You pretend you can't get enough of me, we enjoy some fun between us, and hopefully that little problem gets a clue. The mutual benefits come in terms of you fucking me so hard I forget what my name is. All I could think about while I came all over my fingers was how much better it would have been with that hard cock I felt earlier. So what do you say? A little role playing?

"Oh, fuck." My abs clench as I come, thick jets shooting from my cock and all over my stomach from just her fucking words alone. "You've got to be kidding me," I tell the darkness around me as the thick load starts to roll from my body to the mattress. I drop the phone on to the bed and jump up before I get my own fucking come all over my bed. I'm not against sleeping in sheets wet from a release, but only when it's a woman I've been working over for hours, not my own shit stickying them up.

When I get back from the bathroom, my stomach clean from my release and my cock finally going down, I almost choke on my tongue when I see the numerous texts from Nikki.

Nikki: Maybe I shouldn't have had that bottle of wine after I left Dirty.

Nikki: Or the one after that.

Nikki: Oh, son of a Bieber, you probably think I'm nuts.

Nikki: Can you just forget … all of that?

Nikki: Can you unsend texts? I should just stop. And Google. OMG. I swear, I'm not crazy.

Nikki: Just one more question. Is your cock as big as it felt?

Nikki: Oh, holy Hanson. Forget that too. OMG.

Anddddd there goes my cock again. I look down, seeing it standing at full attention again, and groan. Without thinking about it, not even giving one fucking shit if this is a good idea or not, I turn on the light next to my bed and bring up the camera on my phone, snapping a picture of my cock and sending it to her all in mere seconds.

Nikki: OMFG. Is that … if your last name was Princeton instead of Kingston, I could have a lot of fun with the jokes over that piercing. Hey, how do you fit that monster inside your man panties?

Me: What the fuck are man panties?

Nikki: Boxers. Briefs. Whitie tighties. Banana hammock.

Man panties. Whatever!

I roll my eyes and laugh despite the corny as shit temptress.

Me: I don't wear them.
Nikki: I'm going to die. Scratch that, I think I AM dead.
Me: Exactly how drunk are you, Nicole?
Nikki: On a scale of what to what?
Me: From meaning what the fuck you're saying to me and forgetting this conversation happened until you wake up and read it back in the morning.
Nikki: Somewhere in the middle, but closer to the meaning what I'm saying. Definitely closer to meaning what I'm saying.
Me: You want my cock?
Nikki: Are we sexting now?

I laugh, deep belly laughter that booms through the silent room.

Nikki: Am I supposed to send you a picture too now? Is that how this works?

My cock jerks. God, she's refreshing.

Nikki: I'm not sure if I can get a picture as good as yours, though. You don't even have to work at it, do you? Just pull that monster out and snap a pic. I have to contort my body

to get all my jiggly bits in there and then it's just not hot. You know what is hot, though? Me after I take a million pictures just to get ONE good enough to send back.

Me: God, you're a nut, Nikki.

Nikki: Plus, you're an ass man. I can't exactly take a good picture of my own ass.

Me: I'm a man, chèrie; there isn't a single part of a woman I love more than the other.

She doesn't respond. The little dots don't appear. Shit. I read back my words and realize she might have misunderstood me. I sound just like the slut Nate was accusing me of earlier. She isn't wrong, though; I'm definitely an ass man. But I'm a legs man, a tits man, a sexy brain man … there isn't a part of a woman I don't enjoy the fuck out of.

I was just about to text her back when she finally responds. Only, this time she really does suck the wind right out of my lungs. I don't even look at the keyboard as I type back, my eyes riveted on the screen.

Me: You're getting my cock. Fucking hell. Now I just can't decide if you're going to get it in your pussy or between those tits first. I'll be at your house at lunch, and we'll discuss how much we're going to mutually enjoy these benefits.

She doesn't respond, but I wouldn't have paid any attention if she had. I was too busy looking at the picture she had sent. Lying against her gray sheets, she has one dainty-as-fuck hand between her legs with her fingers buried deep. Her bare and full tits just begging for my attention so powerfully my mouth waters.

All I can do now is pray that she meant what she said because, one way or the other, Nikki Clark will be mine.

Chapter 5

Nikki

"UH," EMBER SPUTTERS.

"Uh, what?"

"Did … uh … Nikki!"

"Jonas on a stick, what is wrong with you?" I question, rubbing the sleep out of my eyes and starting to climb out of her deep-set couch. Bam, her huge beast of a dog, grunts when I move over him to get off their couch. "Move, you hulking monster."

Quinnly squeals her happy baby laughter when she sees me from her spot in the middle of the living room surrounded by toys.

"Hey Quinnie-Q-Moosie-Moo," I sing to her, gaining an adorable smile as she drools all over herself. "How the heck did I end up on the couch when I went to bed in your guest room?"

"Nikki!" Ember yells in a high-pitched squeak.

"It isn't normal that you can even get your voice that high! Do you not remember polishing off that bottle of wine last night?

Chill yourself, woman."

"Chill myself? *Chill myself?!* I just pried your phone out of my daughter's mouth, thinking I was doing you a favor, only to have a dick slapped in my face!"

"Whoa. I do not need to hear about your and Nate's kinky bedroom games. You can probably get eye infections that way too. You should Google that."

"It wasn't Nate's dick that slapped me in the face, Nicole Clark!"

A throat clears behind me. "You know, when I heard you two yapping women, I was thinking I should back away slowly, but now I want to know who is slapping my wife in the face with their dick."

I jerk my head around to Nate's booming voice, a mixture of confusion and hilarity, and narrow my eyes.

"Here! I'm sure you've seen it before anyway," Ember says before holding the phone out in his direction, her eyes twinkling with mischief. I'm too busy wishing the floor would open up and swallow me whole to do anything to stop her, though.

His eyes get weird, and he hesitantly reaches out to take my phone from Ember. His eyes search her face before looking down at my phone like it's a snake about to attack.

"I've got a dick; doesn't mean I want to see another dude's. You know, just because I used to strip doesn't mean I went around staring at other men's cocks, baby. Not my thing, you… motherfucking hell, is this Shane's junk?"

Oh. My. God.

My face flames as the early morning drunken-fueled activities come back to me. I see Nate's thumb move at the same second I remember what other picture was sent on the heels of that glorious one from Shane. And if he moves his thumb, he's going to see a whole new side of his wife's best friend. Oh, my *God*.

"Don't you dare swipe that screen left, Nate! Son of a biscuit, NATE! Do. Not. Swipe. Left!"

I'm moving at the same second I realize he saw the picture. His eyes going so wide it looks like they're about to bug out of his head, and his jaw drops. Thankful for any sliver of luck, I almost breathe a sigh of relief that—even in his shock—he doesn't look *back* at the picture. I catch my phone on a dive as he drops it like it might come to life and bite him. Quinnly laughs her cute baby laugh when I land hard on the ground with a huff.

"You will forget that happened right this second, Nate Reid."

"What *is* happening right now?" Ember asks, no longer frantic about the dick slap to her face.

"Seriously, nothing seen. Nothing … Christ."

"I'm never drinking again."

"Will *someone* tell me what's going on?"

Nate looks at me for a second, and I watch in horror as his eyes give him away. "Did you know your friend got her rack pierced?"

"You jerk face!" I yell, grabbing a pillow off the couch and smacking him over the head with it. He laughs hysterically, not even attempting to stop me.

"Well, yeah, Nate. Who do you think took her? She even tried to get me to do it," Ember answers, not even the least shocked that her husband knows about my nipples being pierced. Or how he knows, for that matter.

Nate stands, to his full height at that, and looks at his wife over my head, ignoring the pillow I'm still thumping him on the head with. "You thought about doing that too, firecracker?" he asks her huskily.

"Arghh!" I toss the pillow down and stomp over to my purse. "You two … this never happened. None of it. None! You hear me?"

"Oh, come on. My wife saw Shane's pocket rocket, so it was only fair I got something out of this morning too."

"You're a pig," I yell.

Ember giggles, and I look over at her. She holds her hands up in a mock surrender but keeps laughing. "What? It was a nice penis."

"Cock, baby. Dick works too, but don't call a man's pride and joy a penis. Little boys have a penis; a man has a cock."

"You two are the weirdest couple ever."

"Maybe, but we're also the weirdest couple who now knows what each other's best friend's naughty bits look like. What do you think about *that*, Nikki?" Nate laughs, reaching for his wife and pulling her into his arms. "I think we need to discuss this piercing thing a little more, firecracker."

"I'm out!" I yelp the second his hands start to reach for Ember's chest.

By the time I got back to my apartment, the embarrassment had *somewhat* faded. Okay, that's a big honking lie. My best friend's husband just literally saw me naked. Not just naked *naked*, but a picture that might as well have me halfway to Pornville. If it had just been Ember, I wouldn't have even blinked. You aren't friends with someone as long as we've been friends and *not* seen each other naked a few times or twenty.

The day I met her—years ago in middle school—had been in the middle of dressing out for gym. A horror story for any teenage girl just discovering her growing and changing body. I hadn't given it much thought to change in the middle of the room. Even at a young age, I didn't care what other people thought of me. Em, my sweet bestie, had been hiding in one of the shower stalls waiting for all the girls to head out before getting undressed. Even now at almost twenty-four and married with the cutest little princess you've ever seen, she's still not one to flaunt what she's got.

So even though she might be used to my lack of cares when it comes to that sort of thing, that doesn't mean I want her to see me with my fingers shoved inside my body. We've never crossed *that* line—friends don't masturbate together.

"Good heavens above, I'm never going to live this down," I grumble to myself, climbing the four flights of stairs to my top-floor apartment.

Thankfully, none of my creepy neighbors are outside when I get to the top landing. Four other apartments occupy the top level with mine, and each one of them houses a red-zone creeper. I've affectionately named them Thing One, Thing Two, and Thing

Three—the single men living in apartments C2, C3, and C4. I might have known their names at some point, but since I do everything I can to avoid running into any of them, I couldn't tell you what they were to save my life.

Even with the early morning sun shining bright, my apartment is dark and gloomy when I step inside, locking the door behind me. It's a small place. I don't need much more than a living room, kitchen, bedroom, and bathroom. When I had been dating Seth, he had been here more often than not, making my tiny little place feel like a cardboard box. But now that he and all his crap are out of my life—it's not so bad.

I hook my purse on the doorknob of the closet next to the front door and walk the four steps to my living room. I don't even bother to open the blinds of my balcony space before I plop down on the couch. Taking a deep breath, I pull up my phone and read through the texts from last night.

"Oh, boy." I sigh, seeing that drunk chatty Nikki was in full force.

With each text, my eyes get bigger and bigger. Then I get to *that picture*, not mine … but the one Shane had sent. Hell, I can't blame the wine on my reaction because even if I had been dead sober, I would have said the same thing. He's tan *everywhere* with a buzzed thatch of dark hair manscaped in a way that only highlights the huge, thick, *pierced* penis between his legs.

I lean my head back on the couch, dropping my hands to my lap. Even without the phone in front of my face, I can still see that picture clear as day. I've been with a few men, but never one working with something like that. Hell, I had been with Seth for almost four years, and I'm pretty sure I had grown back my hymen from his lack of endowment—a man like Shane is going to rip me in two.

God, what a way to go, though. My lips curl in a devious grin at the thought.

Clearly, he had been into the idea of my stupid, wine-fueled texts. He didn't shoot me down, and if that last message from him is anything to go by, I'm going to find out what being with a man like Shane feels like real soon. The question is, can I go through with it?

I wasn't kidding when I said it would help me with the Seth problem. Ever since we broke up and he realized the grass isn't greener on the other side of Slutsville, he's been getting increasingly persistent in his attempts to rekindle our relationship—something I have no interest in. He seems to take my lack of dating as a sign that I'm still pining over him. If I could get Shane to play along, there was no way Seth would misconstrue things anymore. Shane turned me on brighter than the sun with just a kiss—I can't even imagine what it would feel like to take things further. All I know is chemistry like that can't be faked.

"God, Nik. Shake it off and stop worrying about things you can't control." I pull my tired body off the couch, looking one last time at my phone and that beautiful cock. "I wonder if it would be weird to make this my wallpaper?"

I continue to contemplate the pros and cons of putting his dick pic as my phone's wallpaper when a text comes through. Chiming loudly in the silence around me, it causes me to jump. My phone goes flying across the room before I can stop my arm from moving, and I press my hands against my chest, breathing deeply.

"I'm going to die of a heart attack, and it's going to be Shane's cock's fault," I complain, walking over to where my phone landed and picking it up.

Starboy: I'll be at your place in 30. Be ready to talk, chérie.

Oh, hell.

In all the craziness of this morning, I had completely forgotten he said he was coming over. I look down at the paint-covered sweats I stole from Ember and groan. I'm sure the rest of me isn't a pretty picture after the amount of wine we polished off. I can't even remember if I took my makeup off last night.

A burst of excitement hits me when I see his message again, and before I rush to clean up, I move my fingers over the screen to bring back his picture ... then press a few more buttons before I toss the phone down on the coffee table with a smile on my face. Might not be my wallpaper, but at least I can still find it when I want to see it—often. I rush down the tiny hallway into my bedroom, stripping as I go until I'm standing in the shower. Not even waiting until the water is warm, I rush through a quick rinse. I have thirty minutes to make it look like I didn't just wake up, flash my friends, almost scar a baby for life, and proposition a man I hardly know to let us use each other.

But ... that cock.

Yes, that makes all the craziness that brought his visit to fruition worth it because I want that ... a lot.

Ten minutes later, I'm pulling my long blond hair up on top of my head in a wet, messy bun. I've got on a pair of my favorite yoga pants—the ones that I know make my ass look amazing—and a tight tank top. I wasted five minutes wondering if I should wear a bra or not, but I decided Shane would get me how I usually look on a Saturday: no work, no makeup, no fuss.

I look down at my chest and regret skipping the bra when I see my nipples poking through the cotton material.

"Well, that's one way to say hello." I giggle, turning back to go lock these bad boys up. Or that had been my intention until a quick but strong knock sounded on the front door.

My eyes widen, and I turn woodenly to stare through my apartment, half convinced my overexcited mind imagined the sound. When it repeats, I jolt, rushing through the living room area until I've got both my palms against the door and my face pressed against the peephole.

Even through my fisheye view, he's the most handsome man I've ever seen. His artfully shaped beard looking a day past a five o'clock shadow, something that I just know he spends time making sure looks good daily, makes the strong features of his face more pronounced. His long nose is perfectly symmetrical to his face, straight and as perfect as the rest of him. Thick brows that aren't too thick or too shaped, as dark as the locks on the top of his head, make his eyes look lighter than the moss green I know them to be. And those lips. Those sinfully full, pouty lips that just make a woman want to drop down and thank the good Lord he made such a perfect man.

"I am in *so* far over my head," I whisper.

As if he heard me, he looks up from the spot on the door he had been studying right in the peephole, smirking one side of those lips up in a grin that makes me think he can see through the door and right into my damn soul.

"So. Damn. Far."

I glance down at my nipples one more time and sigh. Well, might as well just go with it. The disengaging lock sounds louder than I've ever noticed. The only thing louder is the pounding of my heart. I take a deep breath, open the door, and look up, swooning the whole time, and pray I don't look as nervous as I feel right now.

"Hey," I wheeze, clearing my throat as my cheeks heat.

His smile widens. He's clearly enjoying my awkwardness just as much as I like what he looks like on my doorstep.

"How did you know where I lived?"

His lips part and his white teeth bare as his smile grows even more.

"It's really not fair that you're so hot. I actually think it's frying my brain cells."

His chest moves as he laughs; slow and deep grunts of what can only be described as a manly chuckle make goose bumps dance across my exposed skin. "Let me in, chèrie."

"Oh, fine," I exasperate sarcastically, rolling my eyes and stepping to the side so he can enter.

He doesn't even attempt to be polite and use the space I've given him to pass into my apartment. He steps into my space, crowding me instantly with his eyes downcast and only giving me enough space to shut the door behind us. He reaches up, and before it registers what he's about to do, he's got the hoops of my piercings pinched between his fingers, pulling them just enough to give me a bite of pain. With the thin material of my shirt not offering much protection, I feel the burn of his heat tango with the pain smarting my nipples.

"I liked these when I saw them last night," he whispers in a deep rumble of pure seduction. "I think I like them a lot more now that I've got my hands on them."

I whimper. Shameless and pleading. My shoulders roll back and forth with a dance that begs for a partner when my nipples pinch from the movement and his hold.

"Tell me, Nicole. On a scale of drunken mistakes to fuck me now, how much of last night did you mean?"

I lick my lips, whining deep in my throat when he tweaks my piercings again.

"I don't like repeating myself," he continues, releasing another bite of pressure from his fingertips when he pinches me again.

"Whe-where does fuck me until I can't walk fall into that?"

His eyes shoot to mine, and I watch in fascination as his control slips for the briefest of seconds, the play behind his eyes making them look more honey brown than moss green.

"Ça va être mon plaisir de jouer avec toi, chèrie." [1]

"Holy shit," I gasp, eyes wide and panties soaked. "What was that?"

"A promise."

---

[1]   It's gonna be my pleasure to play with you, darling

Chapter 6

Nikki

"IF YOU KEEP SAYING … well, whatever it is that you're saying, I'm pretty sure I'm going to make things crazy awkward and lock you in my bedroom for the rest of eternity."

He laughs again, clearly not understanding the state of my hormones as he shakes his head and bends to kiss my cheek. "Talk first, eat first, or let me eat you while you talk?"

My skin burns where his lips had touched briefly. Hot Hunnam on a stick, I'm going to combust. "Actually, I take that back. I'm not even sure I care if it makes things awkward, to be honest, because if those are the kind of options I get … I might just keep you." I continue even though his words make my whole body go into overdrive.

"Eat first, talk second, and I'll eat you last," he decides, ignoring me completely. His eyes study my face for a small second before his smirk grows, and he silently walks around the cut-out bar top area and into my galley kitchen. Without even touching me as he struts past me, the jerk.

He makes himself at home. Opening the fridge, he rummages through the contents, not saying anything else while I stand there shocked and horny. I'm not capable of doing much else besides just gawking without even budging. I'm too close to melting into a puddle to be bothered with something as mundane, let alone asking the guest currently helping himself, if I can be of assistance. I'll tell you what I would rather be assisting him with.

"Not sure that's going to work," I finally say breathlessly.

All sounds from his raiding of the fridge stop and I wait, watching his grip on the fridge door tighten before he lifts his head and looks over the open door with a brow raised in my direction, silently questioning me.

"Even if I were hungry, I can't eat like this," I continue, waving my hands wildly in a sweeping movement from head to toe before waving them some more—and maybe a little more enthusiastically toward him.

He shuts the fridge, standing to his full height—again, silent. I should have worn shoes. At least, had I done so, I wouldn't be craning my neck to look up at him when he is so close. I would also be able to use that little height I gained to pretend he doesn't intimidate the crap out of me. But I didn't, and the second he moves from the fridge, taking the few steps needed to be back in front of me, I'm a ball of nerves two seconds away from going out of my mind. I keep my eyes level with his chest, watching the hard muscles flex under the black cotton T-shirt he's got molded to his skin. It's stretched tight against his muscular build, his pecs flexing with every single movement he makes.

I just resist fidgeting with my own shirt, knowing there is a massive difference in his hard and my soft. I take pride in keeping my body in shape, but nothing like he does.

His body is a work of art. Every inch of him, I bet.

Oh, shit. I'm doing it again. I mentally berate myself for ogling him for the hundredth time, shameless in my desire for him.

"I make you nervous," he mumbles, reaching one hand up to trace a slow trail from my temple to my chin. "Why?"

The silence ticks around us as he moves his fingers down my neck and over my shoulder before reversing his path. My heart pounding with each whisper touch of his. A finger. That's all it takes to make my core start to ripple with needy anticipation—and it's a finger that isn't anywhere near where I would love it to be.

He steps closer; my vision fills with the blackness of his shirt and my nose with the scent of his cologne when I take a quick—albeit nervous—breath. I need to get a hold of myself. I'm the one who started this craziness, and now, here he is, ready to take what I'm offering, and I'm freaking out instead of taking what my body so clearly wants.

His fingers pass behind my neck, tickling the soft wispy hairs that had fallen loose at the base of my skull. I never thought the annoyingly small strands could be such a turn-on, but when he trails back, brushing over them again, I shiver.

"Si timide. On va s'amuser," [2] he whispers huskily.

---

2   So shy. We will have fun.

I shiver, wishing to everything holy that I would have paid better attention in French class. Two years in high school and I've got nothing.

"What happened to the fearless little vixen who sent me a picture with her fingers deep inside her pussy? Hmm?"

"Oh, my."

"I won't bite," he continues, his low and husky voice tinted with humor. His tongue snakes out, the tip trailing up the shell of my ear before pulling away and pressing his stubbled cheek against mine; his mouth is so close to my ear his breath chills the wet trail he just created. "Unless you want me to, that is."

Good God, what about this man makes me mute and docile? I have *never* been that type of woman. Until this moment, I never would have guessed I had a docile bone in my body, but there is no doubt Shane dominates every single part of me.

Body and mind.

And even more confusing, I *want* him to. I need to get my head out of the books I love to get lost in.

"Why do I make you nervous, chèrie? Is it because you're not used to the type of man I am, or because you aren't used to the way the type of man I am makes you feel?"

"May-" I clear my throat. "Maybe I'm just nervous about that giant cock you're working with."

"Now isn't the time to use your humor to shield yourself, Nicole. I asked you a question; now, answer it."

"I've never felt anything like this," I tell him softly and honestly with no hesitation. I couldn't have kept the words in if I had tried. He just has this sort of power over me that I can't explain.

He makes a noise of agreement but doesn't vocalize it; he just continues the light brushing of his fingertips over my skin.

"My brain just stops working when you're near," I continue, the words still flowing without pause. My eyes widen, unable to stop them. Now that I've opened the gates, it seems the mute button is finally clicked off. Too bad the nerves won't vanish as well.

"That's because your body knows who is in control here."

I snort. "My body hardly knows you."

His fingers fall from the glide they had been making up my neck. Before I even have a second to miss his touch, he's fisting my bound hair tightly, and with a gentle yet firm twist of his wrist, he's forcing me to look at him. His touch isn't painful or menacing, but it isn't forgiving either. I have no doubt I'll be in this position until *he* wants me to be free. Huge jolts of awareness start to shoot off inside my already overwhelmed body, and I find myself melting even more. My legs wobbling as I sway toward him, I reach out to brace my hands on either side of his torso with wide eyes.

"Your body burns for me, Nikki, and all I've done is tasted your mouth. You think it matters if we know each other past that to fuck? I barely touch you, and you come alive."

Wetness dampens my panties, and I swallow a lump of arousal before speaking, fighting the intoxicating allure of his dominance. "I'm not a slut," I hiss, hoping to hide the edginess I feel if I were to attempt anything other than that. "Just because my body is reacting to you doesn't mean that."

His eyes narrow, and his hold on my hair jerks, tipping my neck back a little more. He takes a step forward and presses our bodies together. My head remains in his control, tipped perfectly to look up at his handsome face. His head bends as he moves, our fronts rubbing together and enticing a moan-like whine from my lips. His eyes brighten, looking more golden brown now. I wonder, briefly, if his eyes are like some sort of mood ring to his soul.

"Don't insinuate that I would think you are, Nicole."

I gulp, the sound loud in the silence around us. "We both know you're only here because of that text I sent, Shane. You also know from that text that I'm a sure thing. You don't have to play games to get me there when I've already *been* there for a while now."

His eyes flash, darkening until the gold is all but gone and only brown remains. I'm thinking, if they *were* a mood ring, brown definitely isn't a good sign. Not with the hard set of his jaw accompanying it.

"I don't play games like that, Nicole. It might have been that text that got me here today, but that's because it was an opening I had been waiting for, not because I want to get my cock wet. You might not know everything about me, but you know enough. We're not strangers."

"You don't seem like the kind of man to sit around and just wait for an opening if you want something." If my arms could move, I would pump my fist in the air for being able to form a complete sentence without sounding like I'm burning alive on the inside from his nearness.

"Until last night, I thought you were still with that asshole. I'm not the kind of man who's going to move in on another man's woman—no matter what I think of that man or how badly I want that woman. I might be a lot of things, but a cheater isn't one of them."

"I haven't been with Seth in over a year."

"He's been around, so you see where one might assume differently." His voice is cold, and his eyes are narrowed.

"Yeah, that's true, but that isn't because I want him to be, jeez!"

He studies me, and I take the time to calm myself down. Or, at least, attempt to.

"You'll explain that," he demands.

"Not now, but yes."

"Good girl."

For whatever reason, those two words turn me on more than they should. My body zings with an odd mixture of excitement and anticipation. I know instantly that I'll do whatever it takes to hear those two words again and feel *that* again.

"Regardless of what happened to get me here, Nikki, don't doubt that I very much *want* to be here." He presses his hips tighter against my body, his erection pressing into my stomach with heavy undeniable awareness. "As I said, I'm not a cheater, but you've tested my control at every turn. Since the day I met you, it feels like it. Even before I became unattached, you had me thinking thoughts that no man in a relationship should have for a woman who wasn't the one he was with. I didn't even know you, and I craved you when she was sleeping in my bed, and for that, Nicole, I'm going to punish you now that I'm finally free to do something about this attraction between us."

"Punish?" I question, gasping while I sway slightly. My legs wobble, and for the first time since he fisted my hair to control me, his other hand touches me. His arm wraps around my back, hand clasping me tightly at the hip to support me in a way that makes me a prisoner to him. I love it.

"I tried to warn you, but I'm thinking I was wrong about you, Nicole. I didn't *think* you could handle me, and that was a big part of why I denied allowing myself to act on this attraction. But I was wrong, wasn't I? All I have to do is look at you, and you're ready to drop to your knees and do what I command, aren't you?"

My mouth flounders, but words don't come, my mind not knowing how to handle his words combined with the way I'm feeling. I've never felt anything like this. My sex life hasn't ever been anything special. I always felt like something was missing.

Desperation.

I've never felt that overwhelming need before. I've never had someone make me feel intoxicated, drunk, and craving the only thing that can keep this high buzzing through my system.

Desperation, for him.

Any way I can get him.

Shit, he's right. I really would do anything he demanded of me. I can't even understand it myself. I have never reacted to a man the way that I am, right now, to Shane.

He drops his hand, releasing my hair and *me* so swiftly I almost lose my footing as I try to clean the cobwebs from my head. I reach out, grabbing the breakfast bar corner to steady myself at the same time he reaches out to steady me, but otherwise, I don't move. And neither does he. I'm not sure if he was trying to steady me or keep me in place. I'm struck immobile by the truth of his words. My body at his complete control without conscious choice. His eyes trail over every inch of my face. Waiting for what, I'm not sure, but it only amps up that damn desperation.

I hear a door slam in the distance, and my senses heighten while I wait to see what he'll say or do next. Footsteps on the landing outside my front door break the silence. People talking. A car starting down in the parking lot. All of that sounds in stereo as if he's unlocked my body and I can sense everything that much stronger.

I open my mouth to tell him so, only to gasp—sucking in a hard, frantic pull of oxygen out of reflex alone. He's right, and there's no doubt about it. If this is a hint of what he can give me, I know I'll do anything he wants if it means I can continue on this euphoric high. My eyes wide in shock, I search his face for a clue to where his thoughts have gone while I've been lost in my mind, but he just studies me with a stoic, almost bored expression.

That free hand, that same devilish hand that had been forcing me to stay still minutes ago with a grasp on my hair, moves until it's wrapped tightly around my throat. Not firm enough to cut off my air, but constricting enough that I know he could do just that if he wanted to. His fingers flex, biting a little more forcefully into my skin but only long enough to show me who is in control— as if I could forget—before he relaxes them. The movement not enough to leave a mark, which I'm sure is his intention. I'm not sure if I'm happy about that, though.

As the images of his handprints on my body invade my brain, I feel as if I could pass out. I'm dizzy, my head spinning with something I've never even thought about experiencing. Not fear, as one would expect, but pure excitement. I shouldn't want that. I've never had a man put his hands on me like this, but it just makes me want more—badly.

"Who's in charge here?" It comes out as a question, but he must not actually want an answer. When I try to open my mouth—fully intending to give him some attitude—he gives a sharp shake of his head "Think real hard before you answer that, or I'll be punishing you for lying to me on top of teasing me with what I couldn't have for years."

Years? Holy moly. I swallow, testing the hold he has on my neck before speaking. "You are, Shane," I offer meekly, feeling an odd need to look away from him to prove my words are true. To submit to the hold he has on me.

"Dominer³," he says under his breath.

I try to shake my head, to let him know I don't understand, but then his hand tightens again, just briefly.

"All in good time. First, I think we need to get a few things clear before this goes any further. I don't share, Nicole. Ever. While we're taking some time to get to know each other, whenever and wherever I want, there will be no other men in your life."

"Wherever?" I squeak.

He ignores me, powering on with his speech. "I won't give you hearts and flowers or any of that other bullshit. Don't start dreaming of white picket fences and two point five kids because I'm not that man for you. Bottom line, if you're hoping for a relationship here, you won't find one with me."

"Sex only?" I whisper.

3   Control

"That's what you want, isn't it?"

I don't speak as I weigh his words. It *is* what I want, but can I really keep myself detached from this kind of attraction? Already, I crave his touch, and he hasn't even gotten my clothes off. I've never had sex with someone who I wasn't in a relationship with, so I'm honestly not sure, but after Seth, I would like to think I'm capable of taking what I want and nothing more. The last thing I want is to get hung up on someone else who will never want a future with me.

"Don't fall for me, Nikki—it will only end badly," he continues, driving home his warning.

His words give me a flash of defiance. How can he be so sure I would be the one to get attached? "Maybe *you* should be worried about falling for me, Shane."

Molten. That's the only way to describe the heat boring into me—his eyes even darker now with his pupils dilated and a hint of brown just peeking around the darkness of them.

"You either respect that I demand exclusivity from you, or we stop this now, Nicole. I've warned you not to look for anything more than what I'm willing to give because I respect you too much to give you false promises. If you choose not to listen to me, that's on you. I won't be responsible for breaking your heart because you didn't heed my warning."

"If you're going to demand exclusivity from me, then I'd better get the same respect from you," I stress.

His forehead drops to mine, and his fingers flex again at my neck. "You're fucking lucky I'm feeling forgiving of that attitude, or you wouldn't be able to sit for a week."

"I wouldn't bet on that." Did he just say I wouldn't be able to sit? And more importantly, why does that turn me on so much?

"You won't have to."

"I mean it," I whisper, his confidence in answering without wavering not what I expected. "In order for me to get what I need *and* want out of this, exclusive is the only way this will work. I meant what I said last night—about us receiving mutual benefit from this attraction, but that means you give me just as much as I give you. I'm not asking for a relationship, Shane, but just for it to look like one from the outside."

He mulls over my words before giving me a small nod. "You have my word that I won't touch another woman."

"And you have mine that I won't touch another man."

"Or woman, Nicole. Man *or* woman," he adds oddly.

I wrinkle my nose. Weird, but whatever. "Do I need to worry about you slipping the tip in another man too?"

"Humor me," he says, his tone losing some of that alpha male he's been rocking and taking on one that seems … worried. Something I never would expect from a man like Shane.

I shake the thought from my mind. "Or woman," I agree. "I'm exclusively yours for however long this goes on, and my heart will not be broken by your inability to have a relationship. We give the world a fake one that I won't twist around in my head to believe is real. How's that?"

He doesn't look away. Nor does he call me on my attitude. Joe Jonas on a stick, whoever put that in his head really did a number on him.

"You'll tell me everything later, Nicole. I want to know what made you need to have a fake anything when you could have any man you want. Damn sure you could have someone who could give you what I won't, but right now, I can't think straight with the way my cock is begging for your pussy. Tell me again, who is in charge here?" He repeats his earlier question and waits with a stoic mask of pure power-driven domination across his handsome face.

"You are." I gasp softly with strength in my tone even at just a whisper.

With his hold around my back, he lifts me, dragging me up his body with little effort. At the same time, he releases my throat. When he has me high enough to look into my eyes without bending his neck, his free hand grabs my hair again and turns my head. His tongue licking a path up my neck. I clench the cotton of his shirt on both sides of his torso, panting shamelessly as my eyes close.

"Then, Nicole," he whispers with heat, "get on your knees and suck my cock."

I look from his face down to his crotch. Oh, my God, this is really happening. Blocking out the nagging feeling of doubt from my mind, I suck in a deep breath and do what he wants, dropping to my knees and praying I'm able to keep this strictly physical. And if I can't, that I'll be able to recover after the dust settles around us.

Chapter 7

Shane

*I*T STARTED AS A WAY for me to test her. To see if she really was the submissive I had always pegged her to be. I figured if I had been wrong about her, I would know with just a few carefully placed questions and demands. What I hadn't planned on, though, was taking it past working her up with those demands alone. But the second she surrendered to my touch, I knew any talking would have to be after she came with my cock deep inside her body. Maybe she's used to letting a man control her in bed. I wouldn't be shocked if that was the case because all it took was one assertive hand to make her passive, waiting for my cues.

What I fucking need is to take off this edge she's built up. I've wanted to fuck that sweet mouth for far too long, and after last night, I'm finally getting it. I've suffered through nights and nights of her sitting at the bar at Dirty, teasing me with her innocent intentions. She would just smile, and I was hard. She spent hours there—dancing with Ember, drinking at the bar, and playing with the straws in her drinks. Even if she didn't do anything intentionally, she did it all the same. Fuck me, there was never anything more than watching me with a smirk on her beautiful face and hesitant desire behind those blue eyes. So wickedly sweet and unaware of the power she holds just by being her. No damn tricks or games. Nikki is the type of woman who, when she wants something, gives it her all or nothing at all. Just as she did last night when she made her move. As attracted to her as I've always been, knowing just how sweet and innocent she is was another thing that kept me at bay. All that discussion about not being dumb enough to fall for me might as well have been a big warning to myself, too. No doubt about it, she's the kind of woman who would steal your heart, and you'd just beg her to fucking keep it.

I expected her to argue with me, or maybe be offended by my brash demand.

I've misread her. I could kick myself for being so wrong about her because who knows how long ago I could have gotten my hands on her. According to her, we've both been single for about the same length of time. Time we could have been having a lot of fucking fun if I just would have gotten my head out of my ass and embraced the feelings I had been so accustomed to denying.

She's wiggling against my hold the second my words leave my mouth. Not trying to get away but to get *down*. Right where I told her … right where I want her.

One thing is for sure … with her, I won't ever get bored.

I drop my arms to my sides at the same time her knees hit the ground so hard I know it had to hurt. My palms twitch to get my hands back on her and fuck her face instead of letting her have a small, brief taste of control.

Her hands immediately go to my jeans, fumbling in her rush to unfasten my belt. She mumbles something sharply under her breath, and I take pity, pushing her hands aside to undo the leather from the buckle myself. She keeps her position with her face close to my crotch and waits with patient hunger for me to pull my belt free of my jeans. My mind already making plans for it later. As soon as the belt drops to the floor with a clatter, she has her hands right back up there, releasing the button and zipper with careful efficiency. Her hands push in under the denim at my hips. Her warm, soft fingers blaze a trail over my naked skin, and she pulls my jeans down until they're bunched at my knees. My heavy cock springs free without the confines of underwear and almost takes her fucking eye out. Still, she waits. Something moves inside me when I realize I'm not entirely sure who is really in control at the moment. Not when she's kneeling before me, looking up at me with a mask of innocence and trust. And if I'm honest, I'm not sure I mind that it might not actually be me.

She makes a humming noise deep in her throat when I don't move—a cross between a moan and a purr—causing my cock to jump. Her eyes widen when she realizes the sound escaped her. Fuck, if that isn't the hottest thing I've ever heard. I watch, waiting for her to make the next move even though everything inside me is screaming to grab her head and shove my length so deep she gags. She won't get a moment like this again, so I should let her enjoy a taste of control and use this time to shake myself of these foreign feelings.

Nothing is timid about the way she takes hold of me when she finally moves. One hand curls around the middle of my shaft as the other presses against my thigh, moving up my leg at the same time as her head moves forward. Her warm breath teases my sensitive flesh then she closes her lips around my cock. Her tongue swirls around the sensitive tip, tugging at the ring piercing it and zapping a shock of pleasure through my whole body. The hand on my thigh moves up even more to cup my balls, and the other wrapped tightly around my cock starts to stroke in tune with her head's descent.

The knot she had her hair bunched into when I arrived is now more loose than it is bound, causing more hair to fall free with each frantic bob of her head. I reach down to brush a fallen piece of hair away, ignoring the slight tremor in my hand as I clear her face. I lock my knees the second I feel her relax her throat, and it was just in time because when she pulls me deeper, I feel like my head is spinning.

"Goddamn," I hiss through my teeth. My hand freezes in the air as keeping her hair free from her face becomes a mission long forgotten.

Nikki makes that humming sound again; only this time, it's with my cock deep in her throat, and I swear to fucking Christ, I see stars. I can't even remember the last time I fucked someone I didn't demand silence from, but with her, I hope to Christ I hear more of those sweet-as-fuck sounds coming from her.

She continues to suck my cock like a pro as I fight to hold back the beast inside me. For the first time ever, I don't even give a shit about control. My need for it is nowhere to be found.

With just her hands and mouth, she fucking owns me.

And I'll gladly let her.

When was the last time I gave up enough of my control to allow a woman to take this much from me?

Never.

The answer is immediate and shocking. What is it about Nicole Clark?

Hell, I've never wanted to give a woman this power, but this one has me running in circles, and I haven't even fucked her yet.

And then? After you've had her? If you are both this combustible now, there's no way it won't explode in your face. Are you still willing to give her control when that blast goes off and complicates things?

Fuck. Needing to get a little of that dominance back, I grab her hair with both hands, the rubber band flying free as I fist her thick locks. Her eyes shoot up to look at me, her eyes a dark blue shining with the same drunk lust that I feel. Then she uncurls her lip from her teeth and gives me a soft but *very* noticeable and intentional bite, hitting me right at the sensitive base of my tip.

"Motherfuck!" I bellow, that tiny bite of pain almost making my come shoot down her throat and flood her mouth. She looks positively giddy at my reaction, and I mentally promise her a punishment for teasing me—one that I had only been halfway joking about earlier just to see her reaction. No doubt about it now, her ass will be so tender she won't be able to sit for a month without remembering just who is in charge.

"Keep my cock in your mouth but remove your hands. Now.

Place your palms against my thighs, Nicole, and don't fucking move them."

She instantly complies, her eyes never leaving mine. Her chest heaves and the color pink is high on her cheeks as she waits for me to continue, squirming her hips.

"If you get to where you have had enough at any point, you tap my legs twice, and I'll stop immediately. Right here, Nikki." I pat her fingers with mine, showing her how to notify me. "You have my word on that. You won't be able to use words if you get overwhelmed, so you tap me, and we stop immediately. If I'm too rough or you can't take the way I give you my cock, *you tap me*, do you understand?"

She nods but sucks against my cock to keep it from slipping free of her mouth. I feel her try to swallow, but the thick head between her lips makes it impossible, and she ends up drooling a little out of the corners of her mouth. The whole time, her eyes growing heavier with arousal and intoxicated by need.

"Do not let me lose your eyes. I want to see what having a mouth full of my cock does to you. How you feel as I stretch your throat. Begging me with those beautiful eyes to give you what you're thirsty for."

She blinks rapidly but, again, nods. With her willing submission to me, I pull her head forward and flex my ass in order to push my cock in deep. She gags the second my piercing touches the back of her throat, her eyes watering, but she doesn't tap. My hips move rapidly, and each time I pull her head down on my cock, she gags when they flex. The wet sounds of her mouth being fucked by my cock act as a soundtrack to my senses. I could keep this up for hours without coming, just using her for my pleasure, but I don't want her first taste of me to leave her with a sore jaw—especially since I plan to have her do this again after I've fucked her cunt.

"You want my come?" I hiss, feeling my orgasm start to coil around my spine—tightly and swiftly.

Her chest heaves, and I feel her through my hold of her hair and cock in her mouth as she tries to nod.

"Don't you dare lose a drop of me. Relax your throat, suck me deep, chèrie, and take everything I let you have. Every last fucking drop."

She hums again, and that's all it takes for me to lose my last shred of control. I yank her down and lock my legs while my balls pull tight. She gags for a second, her fingernails digging into the skin on my thighs, but then she remembers my words and relaxes her throat. Letting me slide just a little further down until the tip of my cock is resting as close as my piercing will allow to the back of her throat, she never looks away from me the whole time. When the first jet of my come shoots against her throat, her eyes flash with pleasure and she hums again, but she still never looks away, and that almost rocks me harder than my orgasm. The muscles in my body tense, riding out one hell of a release while I bark out a sound of completion and empty myself down her throat.

I release her hair, and she drags her lips down my shaft, kissing the tip before sitting back on her heels and resting her hands against her thighs. She continues to hold my eyes, licking her swollen lips, and breathing deeply. If I didn't know better, I would think she's already been with a man like me. And that move right there proves what I already knew—Nikki's a natural submissive, and the pleasure I get knowing I'll be the first man to show her how mind-blowing sex can be when she surrenders all control is one hell of a power trip.

"Good girl, Nikki," I praise, bending and catching the drop of my come on her chin that had been left behind as my cock fell from her mouth. "Every drop," I remind her, sticking my thumb in her mouth and pressing the pad of it against her tongue. She closes her lips before I can get free and sucks her cheeks in, sucking my thumb while licking it clean with her tongue.

"You keep that up, and I'll be fucking you before we finish talking."

She releases my thumb and gasps. "Please. Please, Shane. I need …" She shifts her body, and I realize exactly what she's trying to do when I see her knees press tightly against each other.

"Don't you dare make yourself fucking come," I tell her firmly, bending to grab my jeans and pull them back up, not bothering to button them after awkwardly stuffing my already hard again cock inside.

"I need … please," she continues, whining her broken plea.

"I know what you need, but you won't get it until I'm ready for you to have it."

She whimpers.

"Nicole, I can't fuck you until you understand what you're getting into."

"Will you beat me like Christian?"

My head jerks back. What the fuck?

"Who the fuck is Christian?"

Her cheeks flush. "From the book ... well, you probably would know the movie over the book because you don't strike me as a romance novel reader. *Fifty Shades of Grey.* Christian is from that series. He ... uh, well ... I think so at least, is like you."

"I don't get the reference, but no, I won't beat you."

She almost looks ... disappointed, and I swear to Christ, if I knew what I had done in life to get the perfect woman at my feet—literally—I would make sure I did it again and again to keep her here.

Keep her? What the fuck is that shit?

"But you said you would make it hurt to sit," she continues, still whining, and I'm not sure she understands how that conveys to me just how much she wants this.

"I'm not a sadist, Nicole. I don't get off on hurting women. I get off on *controlling* them. Not sure what your friend Christian was into, but I won't be beating you. While I might not get off on hurting you, certain aspects of my sexual preferences will be used to heighten your pleasure. I'll drive your body to places you've never even dreamed of, but I'll do that because *I'm* the one in charge. Will that cause your body some pain in the process? Without a doubt, but it will be controlled pain, and I will never harm you or give you more than you can handle. It's the only way I'm capable of being, and if you can't be the obedient partner I just witnessed you being at all times when I'm leading, then this ends now."

"How will I know when you're ..." she pauses and frowns.

"Leading? In control?"

She nods.

"Because my cock will be out, and you'll either have it down your throat or I'll be working your body up to take it. I need control, yeah, but I don't need it in all aspects of my life. Outside of what we do with our bodies behind closed doors—wherever that might be—you are free of certain things when we're not playing. But when I'm in the mood to play, I'm the master of your every move; you will obey me or you will be punished."

"Explain that," she breathes, the husky and heavy sound of her voice going straight to my half-spent cock. "The punishments, I mean."

"Do you trust me enough to show you instead?"

Her eyes widen at my question, and her body trembles visibly. She can say no, and it wouldn't make this end. I must earn the right to control her tempting body completely, and I know that— but if she can't handle a simple punishment, then this will never work. It's better that we know now if she can handle it. I pray I'm not wrong about her because it just might kill me to walk away now.

"I do," she says, soft but sure.

I nod, swallow, and breathe in deep. The familiar sense of calm fills my body as the beast that rides my sexual appetite drives forward. I ignore the thought to take her already—wanting to sink inside her so fucking bad even so soon after finding my release. I hold my hand out to her, watching silently as she reaches up with a shaking hand. She takes mine instantly, and I help as she climbs from the floor.

"Get naked," I stress, enjoying the flush that paints her cheeks instantly.

I turn, walk to where I threw my belt earlier, and wait with my back to her, giving her a chance to get used to the fact I'm in charge and see if she follows my direction. In the three steps that it took to get to my belt, I mentally prepare myself to leave and deny my cock if she isn't halfway bare when I turn back. Knowing she needs some time to work up to obeying me, I reach for the remote. After switching on the television, I find one of the programmed stations that plays only music, settle for a slow, instrumental beat, and turn the volume down.

I close my eyes, drawing from the power provided by my control, and turn. When I open them again and see her standing there—completely bare before me, displaying tan skin I can't wait to mark—the ability to hold back my selfish desires almost snaps. Her long blond hair falls around her shoulders, covering her nipples. A tiny dusting of the same colored hair on her mound is the only thing keeping her pussy from being completely shaved, thankfully, because I find a well-groomed pussy hot as fuck over a waxed bare one.

She stands there, letting me stare at her without showing any signs of being uncomfortable with my attention.

I leave her there, walking to her kitchen table and pressing my hands against it to test its sturdiness. The metal on my belt clanging against the wood sounds like a gun blast going off in the silence around us. I turn back, feeling the anticipation burning through my veins, and curl my lips in a smile when I see her facing the other way, obeying me as if this isn't the first time she's submitted to my control.

Wiping my face clear, I call her name. "Nicole."

She looks over her shoulder but doesn't move.

"Feet on the floor, tits on the table, arms above your head until your fingers are grabbing the edge."

Her lips part and that humming sound is back. Fuck, just my words do it for her?

She moves, bending over to lay across her table, and wraps her fingers around the edge, just as I directed.

"Turn your head toward me so I can see your face, chèrie."

Instantaneously, she does as I say.

I run my fingers down her spine, making her whimper. "Spread your legs a little more. Enough that your wet cunt can feel the air touching it and don't move again until I tell you you're allowed." I wait, watching her shift her legs apart a little wider as I calm my breathing. "You need a safe word, Nicole. A word that can easily be understood by me as your out when you can't take anymore. You speak it, and I stop. I don't care if I'm balls deep inside you about to come—that word leaves your lips, I won't be upset, and I will stop immediately. It can be a word of your choosing, or it can simply be red. You pick, but remember, do not use it unless you can't take anymore. And know that I will never be angry with you if you need to use it."

"Red is fine, Shane," she whispers quietly, her voice wobbly.

"Are you afraid?" I ask, needing to know if she sounds nervous from fear or anticipation.

"No."

"No, *Sir*," I add, letting her know how I expect her to address me when we're like this.

"No ... Sir."

"Do you remember why you're being punished?"

She nods.

"Words, Nicole."

"Because ... because I teased you ... Sir."

God, she really *is* a natural. How did I miss this for so long? Or better yet, how the fuck did I resist what I so clearly and ignorantly ignored.

"Is that all?"

"Yes."

"Yes, *what*?" I ask, grabbing the full flesh of her ass and jiggling it. Her plump flesh turning me on. She wasn't wrong; I might love all parts of a woman—but I *love* a thick ass.

"Sir. I think that's all, Sir."

"I should add to your punishment for teasing me again after having just sucked my cock dry, but since this is the first time, I'll give you a pass. What's your safe word, Nicole?"

"Red, Sir. It's ... red."

Stepping closer to the table, I continue to skim my left hand on her skin, watching the play of goose bumps dance in the wake of my touch. Her breathing changes, becoming more relaxed, but I still wait. Then right when I know she's given in to my touch and forgotten to be on guard, I bring the folded belt up in the air and then drop it against her lush-as-fuck ass hard enough to cause pain but not as hard as I would normally be. She jumps, her body bowing up, and she gasps, humming that purr that shoots straight to my balls and wraps around my rock-hard cock. I close my eyes for a beat and savor the sound.

"Do you need your safe word?" I ask, rubbing the redness

with my free hand while I wait for her answer.

"No, Sir," she answers, humming again as she settles back down.

"Then count. Every time you feel the leather against your ass, you give me a number. You need your safe word, you give me that, but until you get to ten, you'll stay on this table."

She wiggles her ass, and I could have fucking come on the spot. She fucking wants it. One taste of it, and she craves it just as much as I do.

My focus becomes solely to drive her mad with pleasure; her punishment being the orgasm she so desperately needs being denied until I'm ready for her to experience it.

"Count. And Nicole? Don't you dare fucking come."

She whimpers, a sound that quickly morphs into a cry when the bite of the belt meets her flesh again. But she opens her mouth and breathes out a shaky, "Two." This continues, each slap making her skin redder and her trembling voice hoarser. With each pass of the leather against her skin, I make sure to rub away the burn before continuing. By the time I've struck nine, I'm not sure who is being punished here anymore. Not with the view of her pussy I have, showing me that she is, in fact, loving the fuck out of this.

Smack.

"Ten." She gasps, sucking her bottom lip between her teeth and clamping down on it hard.

I toss the belt down, drop to my knees behind her spread legs, and take my first deep breath of her scent while I rub my hands over her cheeks to ease the burn, getting fucking high off it even more than I am off working her body. Fucking hell, if this is how turned on she gets by my belt, I'm going to have fun breaking her in, and goddamn, I'm going to enjoy the fuck out of it. So is she if the arousal wetting her thighs is anything to judge it by.

The last thought I have before I lean forward and bury my face in her pussy is that this woman might very well be my kryptonite because I could easily become addicted to this.

Chapter 8

Nikki

IS TONGUE LICKS SLOWLY ALONG my pussy, and I cry out, making him growl. Taking me with his mouth, he has a noticeable hunger to his touch, and my fingers gripping the edge of the table begin to cramp. I don't dare move them, though; not even when his hands grab each of my cheeks—burning against the tender flesh—and pull them apart with a firm hand. His nose presses against my ass, and I whine, wanting for the first time to feel what having a man *there* is like.

He continues his assault against my center, lapping at my wetness in a frenzy—only to get a renewed rush as his groans of pleasure make my core flutter quicker than before. The empty feeling in my pussy becoming something almost painful as he continues to lick every inch of me *except* the one place I need him the most … inside me. His nose butts against my asshole again as he presses his face even closer, growling against my wetness as he shakes his head from side to side slightly, moving his tongue wickedly against me. My eyes roll in the back of my head, and I open my mouth on a breathy wheeze when I feel him release my ass and move his hand between us then drag a finger across the lips of my sex.

"Please," I pant, my ass pushing against his face.

SMACK.

I cry out, and my eyes shoot back open.

"You don't call the shots, mon colibri. I'll give you more when I want to … after I finish eating your sweet pussy." His hot breath against my soaked center makes me even more desperate. I have never felt need with this sort of intensity before.

He continues to lick, bite, and suck at me, the sounds of him echoing and mingling with the ones coming from my own mouth and body. I almost come twice, him easing up before I can tip over the edge, before he finally pulls away, and I hear him stand over the drunken-with-pleasure roar rolling through my mind. I don't move, nor do I attempt to rise from the table. I might be brand new to this whole type of sex thing he's into, but something inside me that I don't yet understand is driving this show, and the only thing I can focus on is earning his praise. I'm finding the power of that praise almost as pleasurable as the feelings he's enticing from my body.

I hear a heavy thump against the floor, followed quickly by another, and it takes me a second to place the sound as his shoes falling to the ground. The anticipation of what's going to come next causes another wave of ecstasy to flood my system. If his shoes are coming off, I pray that means he's about to give me what I so desperately want.

Him.

I hear him move; my eyes stuck on the wall in front of me as I breathe rapidly.

And I wait.

And wait.

And wait some more.

Until the silence becomes so overwhelming, I could cry with the anticipation of something more … anything more.

"Are you on birth control?" he questions, his voice a low, throaty rumble that breaks the silence and caresses my mind.

I swallow thickly. "Y-yes."

SMACK.

"I won't remind you again, Nicole."

I blink through the fog, the firm hand smacking my ass quickly becoming something I *need* as much as air at this moment.

"Yes, *Sir*," I say again obediently.

"When was the last time you were checked?"

It takes me a second, but even if I had been in the right frame of mind, I wouldn't be offended by his question. In this day and age, you don't have unprotected sex without knowing these things about your partner.

"Right after Seth and I split. I hadn't been with him months before that, and I haven't been with anyone since." I shudder in a breath, my eyes widening when I realize I forgot again. "Sir. I'm sorry. What I meant was, I'm clean, Sir."

"Good girl," he drones, rubbing his palms down my back as

he steps closer, his thighs touching the back of mine. I shiver from his touch, but it's the feeling of his naked flesh against mine that makes me moan. "Si humide," he says, low and under his breath. "Such a treat, mon colibri."

"What did you just say?" I ask, remembering him saying that a second ago too.

He continues to tease me with his hands, running them up my back and ignoring me. He repeats his movements a few times before lifting his hands from my back, and then I feel his cock touch my entrance. He rubs the tip through my lips, coating himself in my wetness. It's too much to feel him like that, yet I need so much more. My eyes water as my core clenches, needing to be filled.

"Do you want to come?"

I nod my head, the wood under my cheek making a squeaky sound and tears filling my eyes.

He leans into me, pushing my thighs into the wooden lip of my table painfully, causing me to whimper. "Don't even fucking think about it, Nicole. You come when I tell you to. Do you understand?"

I nod my head, tears rolling free and onto the table underneath me. I don't even understand why I'm crying, only that the feelings firing through every inch of my body are so intense that I need a release of some kind desperately.

He steps back, and I gasp on a sob.

Then his hands are on my hips, and I'm being pulled off the table like a ragdoll. He's strong, so strong that he has me up off the table and flipped onto my back before I even have a chance to blink. His hands slam down on either side of my head and his face presses close, those eyes now such a unique shade of golden mixed with green. They're stunning, but it's the intensity roaring in them that makes the breath in my lungs freeze, all thoughts of what that mood ring color would mean vanishing.

"Why are you crying?" He turns his head, his eyes trailing all over my face as if he could find the reason.

I shake my head, and his eyes narrow.

"Did I hurt you?"

I lick my lips, still shaking my head.

"Did I hurt you, Nicole?" he questions in a hard tone that holds more concern than it does anger at my silence. "I want to push your limits and give you things you've never experienced, but I have to trust you will tell me when you're getting to the point where I might hurt you. That's what your safe word is for. I'll ask you one more time, Nikki ... did I hurt you?"

"I don't know!" I yell, gasping now that I've stopped holding my breath. "I don't know, Shane. Shoot, Sir. I don't know, Sir. I can't understand ... It's too much. I need ... I can't ... I don't know what to do with these feelings. I'm so drunk on them; I'm ..." I trail off, not knowing how to express my intense emotions. This is so much more than being horny and turned on. "I feel like I'll die if I don't get you inside me. Please, *please*, Shane. Fill me up and give me more. Everything."

His nostrils flare, and his body stiffens. Slowly, he lifts until the only part of me that feels him is at my knees where his thighs are touching. His hands go under them, hooking under the back of my knees and pulling my legs up, placing my feet flat on the table. His eyes never leave mine as his hands press my legs open, exposing my body to him. The gentle touch of his hands against my knees betrays the hard expression on his handsome face. If I could just wiggle my ass closer to the edge of the table, I could get closer to the part of him that my body needs the most.

His chest is heaving as he continues to look down at me.

I open my mouth, ready to beg again.

"Silence," he bellows, smacking a hand against my pussy so hard that my back arches off the table and I cry out from the smarting pain heating my core. He soothes my burning skin by caressing and rubbing the wet and abused skin. I can hear, even over my own heavy breathing, how wet I am as he moves his hand over my pussy. "You aren't in charge here, Nicole." His hand lifts then smacks my tender and swollen center again. "I decide when you get my cock. Not you. Remember that." Again, his hand pops against my pussy, and I cry out, a sob catching in my throat.

My vision goes hazy, and I fear I might pass out from the overwhelming desire he's brought forth with the painful pleasure of his hand.

"Who does this pussy belong to?"

"You, Sir," I gasp out immediately on a whimper, holding my legs open for him with not one care to being so exposed to him.

"No one else gets this. Fredonne pour moi, Nicole. Fredonne pour moi[4]."

I'm still blind with lust, unable to understand the words he is speaking, which has nothing to do with them being in another language. When he slams his cock all the way inside my body

4   Hum for me, Nicole, hum for me

without warning, I yell, screaming out so loudly that my throat burns from it. With being over a year since I've been with a man, even though he had me drenched, the shock of being so thoroughly filled stole my ability to breathe straight from my lungs. I reach my hands up, grabbing at his chest and digging my nails into his skin. I'm frantic to pull oxygen into my body but unable. He holds himself inside me, so deep inside my body, and leans down until I feel his mouth on mine. He doesn't kiss me, though. Instead, he opens my mouth with his lips and *breathes* for me. Pushing air into my mouth that I greedily suck in. He repeats the process twice more before he lifts and looks down at me. His eyes just as wild as I imagine mine are.

He continues to watch me, his face straining through his tightly held control, and my chest vibrates with a moan of pleasure as he pulls slowly from my body. The overwhelming shock of him filling me has passed, allowing me to climb back up the peak toward my release. He never looks away as he slowly thrusts into me, almost as if he's waiting for something. My nails dig into his chest when he bottoms out inside me, hitting a spot that has never been touched before and making me mewl from the white-hot pleasure of it.

"There it is," he says in a thick voice, betraying the indifference on his face and showing me he's just as lost in my body as I am in his. "Paradis[5]."

The sound leaves my lips again, and he closes his eyes and sucks in a breath. I might not understand the majority of what he says in French, but I have no trouble deciphering that last word,

---

5   Paradise

and it shocks me to the core. Surely, I misunderstood.

When he opens them again, I see the dominant Shane is back, no longer giving me that window into his feelings. He leans up, removing his hands from the table to grasp my wrists in his strong grip and pull my hands from his chest. He slams them down above my head and starts powering into my body. I test his hold on me, knowing I won't be able to get free, and he tightens his hands even more.

I'll have bruises.

Instead of being worried about how I'll cover those for work, I struggle again, *wanting* the pain just as much as I do the marks.

He narrows his eyes in warning.

I do it again.

"Nicole," he growls.

And again.

"Motherfuck!" he roars. He moves my arms until both wrists are being held by one of his large hands instead of both. The other coming to my neck and squeezing in warning. "Don't test me, mon colibri. You will not win."

"Hurt me," I gasp, shocking myself *and* him with words. "Hurt me, Sir. Please."

"Goddamn." He tightens his hand, cutting off my ability to breathe. It doesn't scare me; instead, I feel myself coating his cock with a rush of wetness. His hand jerks away from my neck, and then he's trailing it down until he's grabbing one of my breasts roughly. He squeezes so beautifully hard before pinching my nipple between his fingers.

"Mark me, Sir."

He shivers, his whole big body trembling above me, and I feel his cock jump inside me. He's done this, made me so dependent on his touch that I'm unable to silence the demands as they fall from my lips. Instead of reprimanding me, though, his hips start to power against mine, thrusting rapidly into my body.

The bite of pain in my breast from his hold becomes white hot as he gives me even more of his strength. He's fucking me so hard now that I hear the table protest under me. I'm not even aware of the sounds coming from my mouth when the pleasure inside me becomes too much to handle. The need to come becoming harder to hold back.

His head drops, his mouth hitting the skin between my neck and chest. The rapid gusts of air rushing from him dance across my breasts, and I again feel like I'll pass out if I have to deny my release any longer. He continues his rapid thrusts, giving me each thick inch all the way to the hilt before pulling out and repeating. Each thrust taking me higher and higher.

"Fuck!" I jump, his loud yell so close to my ear. "Fucking come, Nicole!" His mouth opens, his teeth touch my skin, and while I explode around his cock and my whole body feels as if it's being torn apart by the force of my orgasm, he bites my shoulder. His hips slam against mine one more time before he is groaning and twitching inside me, his hot come shooting deep into my body.

The last thought I'm aware of floating through my mind is that I've just been ruined for any other man.

I'm so royally and literally screwed now.

Chapter 9

Nikki

MY CHEST HEAVES, RAPIDLY SHUDDER-ING in an attempt to catch my breath. There's a ringing in my ear that I'm pretty sure is from my own screaming as I came—coming harder than I had ever come before. I blink, looking up at the ceiling only to close my eyes on a sigh when my vision is too fuzzy to focus on what's around me.

Can you be fucked blind? If so, I'm pretty sure that's what just happened.

I push the ridiculous thought aside and start taking stock of my over-sensitized body. The first thing I notice is the very empty feeling between my sore legs.

Shane isn't inside me anymore.

I pout mentally at the thought, hating that I missed feeling him pull his length from me.

"Clean yourself from my cock, Nicole."

My eyes snap open, and I jerk my head in the direction of his voice. He's standing next to the table, the tip of his cock pointing at my face as he holds himself like an offering to me. How the hell is he still hard?

"Don't make me say it again, Nicole. Clean my cock."

"But you …?" His eyes narrow, and I think back to feeling him come. I know I felt him fill me up. I know it as sure as the sky is blue. There's no way he should still be hard. "You came already … Sir."

"I want to watch you lick your wetness from my cock. I don't want you to use that wicked mouth to drain me fucking dry again. Later. For now, give me that mouth and clean. My. Cock."

Oddly, the thought doesn't gross me out. With any other man, it probably would, but that foreign need to have Shane's praise drives me to distraction. So I roll and rest on my side, looking up at him as I open my mouth. He steps closer, pressing his thighs into the table, and pushes himself into my mouth. He controls it all. How much I take, how fast I'm given it, and all I can do is get lost in him.

"Such a good girl, mon colibri."

I purr. Seriously, I purr from his praise. There's no other way to describe the sounds I'm making. What kind of power does this man hold over me? He starts to pull out of my mouth, and I whine around his thick head, trying to suck him back inside when it becomes clear he's trying to deny me. My teeth capture his piercing and I give a slight tug to keep him in my mouth. He carefully pulls free, and I watch as he slowly strokes himself, needing him once again even more than before.

"Greedy. Mon colibri is so greedy for my cock." He doesn't wait for me to speak, dropping his hold on his cock and hooking his arms under my arms to lift me up and into his chest. "Which way to your bathroom?"

"Hmm?" I question in a daze, quickly remembering myself. "Sir?"

"Shane, chèrie, just Shane."

"But?" I rub my head against his chest. "Your cock is still out."

He chuckles, the rumble against my ear sounding like heaven. "That it is, Nikki. That it is."

He doesn't say anything more, and I don't press him to clarify my confusion. I imagine it'll take me a while to get used to this whole dominant sex lifestyle, but one thing's for sure—I'm going to enjoy the hell out of it. And if that's the kind of treatment I get for being punished, I have a feeling getting used to this kind of sex from Shane is going to be worth it.

He takes us into my bedroom and gently lays me down on my bed, bending to press a sweet, chaste kiss to my lips so unlike the man I've started to know. Silently, he turns and walks into the bathroom. I hear the water start to run and the telltale sounds of my tub filling. I nestle my head against the pillow and sigh contentedly. While my apartment is small, that tub makes up for it, and after that workout, I can't wait.

I must have dozed off because when Shane picks me up again, the sound of running water no longer permeates the air. A calm silence has taken over not only my apartment but my mind as well.

He steps next to the large garden tub and bends down, placing me in the tub with a gentle ease so unlike the man who just savagely took my body. His face is calm, somewhat peaceful, as he meticulously submerges my body in the warm bubble-filled tub. His arms glide out from under my wet body, his fingertips trailing slowly while he makes a satisfied noise deep in his throat.

Holy crap.

Then he kneels next to the tub, picks up a washcloth, and starts *cleaning me.*

"Uh … I can do that," I whisper, not actually making a move to take the washcloth from him.

"I know."

"So do you want to let me do it?"

"Hell no," he answers with a steel-like conviction that leaves no room for argument.

"I'm not really sure what to do with this, Shane."

He looks up from the soothing pass he had been making of the washcloth over my breasts and smiles a tiny smirk at me.

"Just relax. It's my job to take care of you."

"Oh," I breathe, not sure what to do with him now.

"Stop overthinking, Nikki. I worked you hard, and this is part of it."

Good heavens, this man talks in circles. "Part of what?"

"Caring for you," he says, not looking away from my body, a small frown wrinkling the skin between his dark brows.

He continues washing me in such a soft and soothing way, and I don't know how to handle this side of him. He's such a contradiction. One moment, he's holding himself back with that control he drives himself with as if it's more an armor, and the next, he's gentle and almost sweet. Despite the fact I've known him for close to two years now, I feel like he really is a stranger and I'm nowhere near finding out who the real Shane Kingston is.

"What are you thinking?" he asks, running the soft cotton down my stomach and over my sex.

"That I have no idea who you are."

He makes a sound in his throat, a small and deep laugh that isn't from humor at all.

"I mean, I know you, but I don't, do I?"

"You know me, Nikki."

"I didn't know you would be like this. You're hard but soft. You don't want to give me all of you but want all of me. You're used to ... this," I say, shrugging and letting him decipher what I mean by *this* since I don't think I can come up with the right words.

"It's not that I'm used to this, Nikki. It's what I need. That's all."

"That's all?" I snort. "You make it sound like what we just did was nothing more than a dance in the rain. That, Shane, was a monsoon we just tangoed through."

"And? You enjoyed yourself, did you not?" He stops cleaning me and wrings out the washcloth, draping it over the spout.

"You know I did."

"Then what's the big deal?"

I sigh. "I think you know I'm not used to that."

He nods.

"I'm going to be real honest with you, okay?"

Again, he nods his head, eyes open and focused solely on me.

"I don't know what to do with the things you make me feel."

The frown between his brow is back, wrinkling the skin. It only makes him even more attractive.

"Tell me why you made your move last night."

Well, bingo for the naked sex god.

"What about it?"

His expression turns to one that clearly says he can see right through me and my non-answer.

I exhale, long and drawn out and full of the frustration I've felt since the day Seth popped back in my life. Do I admit to this man that I let my ex railroad my life? I might as well; there's no point in keeping it from him when I've made it pretty clear that I'm using our mutual attraction to gain more than just one hell of an orgasm.

"Just as I said, we can both benefit from this attraction."

"Your ex," I start, earning another frown. "It's been how long since you broke up?"

"I don't know. Somewhere just over a year," he answers.

"Right, same as me and Seth. However, just as you assumed I was still with him, until last night, I figured the same about you and her. I'm at Dirty enough to know she's still around, Shane. But it's the same with Seth that pushed me to make my move."

"Explain."

"God, you're bossy."

"Wrong. I don't like surprises, Nikki. Having all the information means I can avoid that shit."

"Right." I shift, leaning forward, unplugging the drain and

letting the water out. "Hand me a towel, please?" I point over his shoulder at the closed linen closet across from my tub.

He stands, his erection still just bobbing around. It takes a lot to keep my hands to myself and not reach out for him, but somehow, I manage. He hands me a towel, and I wrap it around my body before taking his offered hand and stepping out of the tub. He follows silently behind me as I leave the bathroom and walk to my dresser. I pull out one of my sleep shirts; something I think I stole from Ember's husband the last time I crashed at their house. Shane steps behind me and plucks at the sleeve, standing close enough for me to feel the heat of him against my body.

"Who does this belong to?"

I arch my brow. "Probably Nate." His eyes go hard, and I hold up my hands. "Whoa there, tiger."

"The fuck are you doing with his shirt?"

Ignoring the hard bite in his tone, I roll my eyes and turn back to my dresser, pulling out a clean pair of underwear and stepping into them before addressing him. "Pretty sure I ended up with this when his daughter puked all over me and it was on the top of the laundry basket I had just finished folding for Ember. But who knows; maybe it was from the giant orgy I have with them twice a week and every other Sunday."

His grumbled complaint vibrates from his chest. "Take it off."

I turn and blink up at him with my jaw slack. "Pardon me?"

He studies me, his eyes volleying from eye to eye as his nostrils flare. I watch his hands move but just stand there in shock that he would be this angry over a shirt until his fingers push gently between my neck and the collar of the shirt. He holds my confused gaze for a beat before one brow arches; with a quick tug, he literally rips the shirt straight down the center.

"You did not just do that!" I exclaim, jumping back with the ruined shirt floating around me. I jerk it off my shoulders and toss it at Shane's face. He catches it before I hit my mark, his frown gone as a satisfied smirk tips his lips up. "First, I was kidding. Second, I enjoyed that as a sleep shirt, and now it's ruined. Third, what the heck!"

"Don't like you wearing my best friend's shit."

"Clearly," I huff sarcastically.

"I'll fuck that attitude right out of you, Nikki. Find something to cover yourself so we can finish our talk."

I continue to mumble my complaints as I jerk open my dresser and rummage around, looking for another baggy shirt but coming up empty. That's right, you big dummy; that was the last one because all the others had belonged to Seth, and you burned them in the apartment communal grill six months ago. With another heavy exhale, I jerk open my workout drawer and pull a tank top over my head. When I turn, Shane's eyes jump to my chest. The white tank is completely see-through; I know that for a fact after wearing a white sports bra with it the last time I went to the gym and unknowingly gave everyone a nice little sweaty wet tee shirt contest, party of one. I haven't worn it since, but seeing as how Shane hasn't taken his eyes off my boobs, it was a nice revenge choice for tearing my shirt.

"That isn't better," he groans.

"It's all I have since you just ruined my favorite shirt."

"Fuck me," he hisses through clenched teeth. He doesn't say

anything else before turning on his heel and stomping through the apartment. I follow behind much slower. He stops at his pile of clothes and grabs his shirt, walking back to me and feeding it over my head a second later. I stand there while he continues to dress me in his shirt, wondering what the hell is going through his mind.

"Right. What are you doing?"

"You want more, I'll let you know the next time I have laundry to do and you can steal all the shit you want, but any man's clothes on your body had better be mine."

"That's pretty possessive for someone who claims he doesn't want more than sex."

He shrugs. The confusing man just shrugs. Nothing more.

"I want you to be my boyfriend. And before you get all 'I don't do relationships, Nicole,' I don't mean a *real* boyfriend. We go out when you aren't working. I'll come to Dirty, and you'll give me some more nights like last night. For anyone watching, we look together, but for us, we're just good friends who have amazing sex."

"And why would we act like we're together?"

"Because, Shane, we both have needy and crazy exes. I don't know about yours, but mine seems to think I'm not serious about never getting back together with him because I have, in his words, not moved on."

"So you want him to see you moving on so he'll leave you alone?"

"Bingo, big man."

"What do I get out of this?"

"Aside from being able to finally scrape off the shadow I've seen leering around you every time I come to Dirty?" He nods. "I guess you get to keep having phenomenal sex with me."

"Phenomenal, huh?"

"You don't need your ego stroked just as I don't need to waste my breath when you know it was."

I almost lose my footing when his face goes soft. "You're right; my ego is fine."

"I'm glad we figured that out," I whisper, my body swaying toward him when he steps closer, taking me in his arms and pressing a kiss so unlike him to my temple.

"Let me ask you … when this is all over and both of our exes are done trying to get something they have no chance at, then what?"

I swallow, the heavy lump struggling to get down. "Well, then we go our separate ways."

He nods, but I can tell he wants to say more. I have a feeling he doesn't believe we'll just be able to walk away in the end. And, if I'm honest with myself, I'm not sure he's wrong.

Chapter 10

Shane

ANOTHER GLASS FUMBLES OUT OF my hold, slipping free from the towel I had been using to polish it and tumbling to the floor. The sound of glass splintering makes me flinch, and I brace for Nate's commentary. He's been giving me wide berth for a few weeks now, but I know he's just seconds away from not biting his tongue any longer.

When I look up from my mess and see Nate giving me a sideways glance, I ignore him and continue cleaning up the shattered glass. This stupid glass might as well be a metaphor for my week. A mess that's becoming my new normal ever since Nikki's bombshell proposition. Not that I'm counting, but it's actually been three weeks and a one fucking day since that Thursday night. Not one peep from her. She hasn't been in Dirty, she hasn't called, not a single text. Nothing. And I can't figure out if I'm more pissed about her lack of communication after that night or if it's that I even care at all.

"What the fuck, dude?"

Ah, there it is.

Ignoring Nate, I continue to sweep the broken glass into the dustpan with the broom we keep behind the bar. There's no way Nate's going to give up without pulling answers from me. Not since he's finally stopped looking at me like keeping his mouth shut is the worst thing he's ever had to deal with. Swear to fuck, I've never met a grown damn man who could pout better than a toddler. Surly bastard.

"What the fuck, what? Glass slipped, I didn't exactly want it to."

"You need to get laid. Maybe you won't have butterfingers if you work out that frustration that's had you acting like a moody son of a bitch for weeks."

I don't respond, but my mood sure does fucking sour a little more at the mention of getting laid, which only fills my brain with the memories of Nikki coming undone beneath me. I haven't even been able to think about getting laid if it wasn't with her. No one else will do. How fucked up is that?

"Seriously, Shane," Nate tries again, leaning in to nudge my shoulder with his. "What's crawled up your ass? Even when we used to handle all this inventory and prep shit by ourselves, we could fly through it, but today, it's like you aren't even fucking here."

"Nothing's up, Nate," I grumble, putting the broom and dustpan back under the bar and standing, placing my hands on the wood and dropping my head with a loud exhale to look at my booted feet. When I look back up, my eyes scan the empty room around us before glancing over my shoulder at my best friend. I sigh, shake my head, and hold his probing gaze. "Fuck, Nate, I'm not even sure I can explain it all without breaking more shit."

He drops his clipboard onto the empty bar top before turning to lean with his ass against the wood to focus on me completely. "Ember always tells me to just start from the beginning, man, so I figure you could go with that, and then we can muddle through it together."

"We sound like two chicks ready to paint our nails and gossip about the new cute boy in class."

Nate laughs, a deep belly laugh that echoes around the empty club. "The day you ask me to paint your nails is the day we break up. That is reserved for only my special ladies."

Easing the tension from my shoulders, I let out a burst of laughter before sobering. "It's Nikki." I open my mouth, ready to explain more, but close it when I realize I really just don't have the fucking words to explain further. With a sad as hell shake of my head, I just hold his gaze and offer him a shrug.

"Well, isn't that a relief. I figured as much, but Ember was all 'don't bring it up, honey' but waiting for you to bring it up would've taken years. Thanks for bringing that up, man. I'm so glad we have the kind of relationship where you feel like you can come to me and all. As annoying as you can be when you're acting like a pouting baby, it sure is entertaining to watch the mighty Shane Kingston crash and burn. Before I start enriching your love life with my words of wisdom, I feel like I need to tell you that if I ever see your cock again, I'm going to have to bleach my eyes.

That just doesn't sound like a fun time, so no more cock sharing, okay?"

"Nate, what the fuck?"

"Two weeks, one week, three? Fuck, I don't know how long it's been, but the last time Nik crashed at our house, Quinnie got her hands on Nik's phone, and man, I thought we were pretty close before, but that was before I knew what your dick looked like."

"Jesus Christ, you've been waiting this whole time to slip in that you saw that, haven't you?"

Nate's smile grows, mischievous little shit.

"She been around?"

"Nikki? Uh, yeah. She lives in Hope Town. Where else would she be getting around?"

"You're a pain in my ass, Nate."

His booming laughter rings out. "Saw her this past Wednesday when Ember went to her place for their weekly gab fest, but I haven't spoken to her since the day I saw your dick."

He wags his eyebrows, and I know instantly what he's implying. I ignore the anger that I instantly feel knowing he had to have also seen the picture Nikki had sent me that night. I don't like how out of control this girl makes me feel. Not one fucking bit. For fuck's sake, Nate's the happiest married man I know. There's no way he saw that and thought about her sexually, but just knowing he *did* see that part of her is enough to make me want to put my hands back on her … to mark her as mine.

Fucking hell.

"I feel like this is the part of our little chat when I point out you didn't deny you've crashed and burned over a woman."

"I haven't … what the fuck are you talking about?"

"Shane and Nikki, sitting in a tree," he belts out, moving his hands as if he was conducting a band to his silent tune.

"How old are you again?" I drone, grabbing the clipboard and picking up where he left off.

"So are y'all like a thing?"

"No," I answer.

"You gonna be a thing?"

"No."

"You sure about that?"

"Nate, seriously, shut the fuck up."

"We could double date. Don't girls love that kind of stuff?"

"I think we need to go do something manly, Nate. You're around too much estrogen at home. Clearly, you need more guy time."

"If you have a boy, you'd better keep him away from my princess."

"What the fuck? Who's having a baby?"

"You should probably just call her. Stop breaking shit around here and go get your willy wet."

"Something is *seriously* wrong with you," I tell him, wide-eyed yet annoyingly entertained.

"All jokes aside, why don't you just call the girl, Shane? I know I said a lot of shit about you starting something with her a few weeks ago, but if it's what you both want, go for it."

"I'm not interested in a relationship, Nate. You know the shit I went through with Lacey. It got so bad after we moved here and Dirty opened; she hired a PI because she was that fucking convinced I was cheating on her. Not sure why she didn't do that shit back in Athens, but something about this place made her go insane."

Nate laughs dryly. "Yeah, if that isn't the pot calling the kettle black."

"You've got that right." I put the clipboard back down and turn to lean against the bar, looking at Nate. "We're going to do this girl talk shit, aren't we?"

He holds his arms out wide. "Come on, girlfriend, tell Nate Dog all your troubles."

"Something really is wrong with you."

He shrugs. "My dad tells me that daily. Come on; we've got an hour before the crew shows. Let's get your love life settled so we can finish this shit and get out of here early tonight."

We share a look, knowing there isn't a chance in hell we're getting out of here early tonight. Not with Dent, our full-time manager and bartender, out sick, and five other employees down with the flu.

"How much do you know about her ex?"

"Seth, king douche?"

"I guess. I only met the guy a few times over the years, but the way he's still sniffing around, I didn't think they had split."

"Looks like we got another pot in the room," Nate sniggers.

"This isn't even close to the shit I've got going on with Lacey."

"Isn't it, though?"

"Explain, Nate."

"She scraped that fool off right around the time Ember and I got solid. I don't remember all the details. I was distracted by tears and a lot of ice cream. Not to mention, I was public enemy number one just because I had a cock, so I got out of that convo between her and Em real fucking quick. Something about him cheating, but if you ask me, he was treating her like shit long before that."

"And he's been around because she took him back?"

He reaches out and smacks my forehead with his palm. "No, dumbass. Just like you with that cheating bitch Lacey, she keeps trying to get the dude to leave her alone. Both of y'all have exes with their teeth clamped tight."

"Which is exactly why I'm not fucking calling her. Combined, we've got enough baggage to sink the *Titanic* … again."

"Or because you'd rather be a little bitch than figure out what is between the two of you."

"*Or* maybe because it's easier to crave something you got a taste of than deal with the stomachache that follows when you indulge your sweet tooth too much."

"You know, before Ember, I probably would have agreed with you. Shane, man, who's to say you'd have to deal with that kind of ending? Nikki isn't like most girls. Maybe you need to ask yourself if she isn't worth at least seeing what's going on between y'all, why she's been able to affect your life this much just by the silence coming from her end."

Nate drops his hand to my shoulder, giving a solid pat and a cocky smile before walking away from the bar. His words tumble through my head while I finish inventory. Long after the club opened for the night and I had finished the paperwork on my desk, I was still thinking about what Nate said.

Nikki might be different than most girls, but I haven't met a single one who could handle my job. Jealousy is a nasty bitch that taints everything in its path. Different or not, I doubt Nikki Clark is immune to it. If she makes another move, we can play, but play is all we'll do.

Chapter 11

Nikki

"LANDON, WHY WERE YOU POKING Tara with your pencil?" My knees cramp as I kneel, watching one of my favorite students as his face gets red with embarrassment. I peek around him, making sure the other students can't hear. "You're not in trouble, sweetheart. I just need your help to understand what happened."

"I like her," he whispers, big brown eyes wide. "And she looks really pretty today."

"I'm sure you do, Landon. She's a sweet girl."

He nods, looking like a pint-sized bobblehead.

"That's nice that you like her, but you shouldn't poke your friends with pencils. Maybe next time you want to get her attention, you can try using your words?"

"But that's not what Daddy does."

My head turns slightly as I regard my student. "What does

Daddy do?"

He takes a huge gulp of air. His little body rocking with the force of it. "When Mommy is pretty, she gets the tip. Daddy says so. He doesn't use his words with Mommy all the time either. He just pokes her with his finger and tells her she's gonna get the tip later. I didn't want to hurt Tara, so I just gave her the pencil tip kinda like Daddy."

Oh. My. God. This isn't happening.

"Landon, honey, how about next time Tara looks pretty, you just tell her. Leave all that other stuff to your daddy."

"So tell her she's gonna get the tip?"

"No!" I hold my breath and say a quick prayer for some kind of divine intervention. "Sorry, Landon. I didn't mean to raise my voice. I thought I would fall over." I wobble my balance, my knees still protesting while I keep myself at his level. "Maybe just say 'you look pretty' and leave it at that. No need to bring any tips into it."

I can't believe I just said that.

"Okay." He nods and smiles, but that smile quickly slips. "What happens when I wanna tell her I like her booty?"

Lord, kill me now.

"You know what? How about we color a picture?"

"Ms. Clark, you're really funny."

"Thank you, Landon. If it's okay with you, can I talk to your mom? I bet she would be able to tell you all the sweet things a girl would like to hear from a boy who likes her. I'm afraid I won't be much help, honey."

Please buy it. Please buy it.

"How come you wouldn't be able to help?"

"Well," I say with a smile. "I can't help because I haven't found my prince."

Landon smiles and nods. "I can catch you a big frog then! I'll get my daddy to help, and then you'll have your prince!"

"That's okay, honey. My prince is just waiting to hop his way to me, so we have to let him find his path."

"I guess."

"Thank you for thinking about helping me, though. That was very sweet."

Landon nods again, his shoulders straightening as pride fills his tiny body. I lead him over to a group of kids drawing silently and help get him settled before walking over to my desk. My second graders are the best kids in the school, no doubt, but this whole week, they seem to be possessed by little demons. Landon is the fifth boy to discuss what his daddy does. Carpool line hasn't been the same since. Just yesterday, sweet little Cara-May Jenner asked me what bum fun was, and I honestly didn't think it could get worse than that. Looks like I'm in for another awkward as it gets chat with another parent tonight. I scribble a note to myself in my planner to give Landon's mom a ring later. Thankfully, she's one of the parents I'm closer to, and it will ease a little of the tension, but regardless, it isn't a chat I want to have with any parent.

The rest of the day passes without incident, thankfully. I make quick work of tidying up the room and getting the following week's lessons in order before packing up. After a week of craziness at work, I can't wait for this weekend. Much like my past couple of weekends, I plan on spending time doing a whole lot of nothing. Only this time it's because my students have broken my brain and not because a man broke my body … deliciously. It was hard enough getting through the Friday after Shane's visit, but it took almost two weeks for me not to shift and feel like he was still touching me. I spent the whole weekend after he had shown up just lying on the couch with a sore body, watching reality television. His touch was as intoxicating as a drink to an alcoholic.

As much as I would love to have another round with Shane, I've had way too much time since that explosive night to think. About him. Just as I had worried, he's deeper under my skin after sleeping together than he had ever been with just a simple lust-filled crush. I would be a big fat liar if I said I didn't want another round with Shane, but is it worth getting hurt in the process? Plus, Shane's been keeping his distance as well, so maybe he wasn't actually interested in playing our little game anyway. *Or I was just as bad in bed as Seth had always said.*

Unfortunately, that reprieve I had just felt while packing my stuff was short-lived. The second I step out of the back door and into the faculty parking lot, I see him—Seth—leaning against my car with a stupid smile on his stupid face. And of course, he's here. I might as well have just conjured him up. This isn't the first time he's been here. Since I hatched my fake boyfriend plan, he's been annoyingly around—only without said fake boyfriend, he wasn't taking no for an answer.

"What do you want, Seth?" I ask in a dull tone, unlocking my car, popping the trunk, and dropping my schoolbag in before shutting it and crossing my arms, holding his gaze.

"Wanted to take my girl out."

I look around the almost empty parking lot, a trickle of unease making me fist my keys. "Unless you're waiting for someone else, I don't see your girl."

"Oh, come on, Nik! Stop playing hard to get. I fucked up; I know. I've said I was sorry, baby. Let's just put it behind us and move on."

"Sorry doesn't cut it. I don't know why you have such a hard time realizing that I'm not joking. You didn't just cheat on me, but you had been doing it for years, Seth. *That* isn't anything I would ever be able to forget. You made your choice, just as I did when I ended our relationship. I won't change my mind, buddy!"

His face goes hard, the carefree boy next door mask slipping off completely. "So you're just going to throw away years together because of my mistake?"

"Ding, ding! We've got a winner, ladies and gents. I'm so glad you're finally listening," I sarcastically exclaim.

"You don't have to be a fucking bitch," he forces through his clenched teeth.

"And you don't have to be a freaking stalker. It's over. It's *been* over. Give it up and move on."

"It's not over, Nik. If it was over, you wouldn't still be waiting for me."

I laugh, feeling a headache forming. "You think I'm waiting for you? That's rich, Seth, it really is. I'm not waiting on you. I wasn't the day I walked in on another girl—one who looked like she wasn't even close to eighteen, I might add—bouncing on your naked lap. I wasn't waiting the day I moved all your crap out of my apartment. And you'd better believe I wasn't waiting when my new man showed me just what I had been missing with you!"

Verbal diarrhea. I couldn't stop it if I tried, and now, with him giving me the nastiest glare ever, I can still feel more bubbling up, threatening to tip over and out.

"You're lying."

"Have I ever lied to you?" I ask. I might not have been the best girlfriend to Seth, but he never had to doubt my word because I had never lied to him before. So this is a massive stretch to say I'm not lying now, but Shane did kind of agree to a 'relationship'—even if it's been radio silence since—Seth just doesn't need to know about all the fine print.

"How come you aren't ever with this man of yours?"

"He's busy." *I've been avoiding him.*

"Nik Nac, baby, you don't need to lie to make me feel bad. I messed up. I know. Stop this and let's go have some fun." He reaches out, but I jerk my body away from his reach. "The fuck?"

"Seth … I've been nice about it. I've told you over and over that it will never happen. It's been over a year! Enough already. Respect that I've moved on and do the same."

"You say you've moved on, yet here you are, lying about it just because you want to play games and make me pay for my mistakes. We both know we'll get back together. Just cut the act."

"That will never happen. Look, I've had a long day, and I just want to go home. How about you pick your stalking back up tomorrow when I've had a full night's sleep and I'm better equipped to deal with your crazy."

I push past him, ignoring the nasty things he's muttering about me, and squeeze into my car with the little space he's allowed between himself and my door. I don't look out my window, but I do lock the door before fumbling with my keys. I jump only slightly when Seth bangs his hand against my window, but I keep my eyes forward and put the car in drive, thankful no one is in the parking lot to witness my ex spewing profanities.

The only thing I'm able to process on the drive home is that Seth must be dealt with. Clearly, he really isn't going to just leave me alone. Why, I have no idea, but months of this after almost a full year of having him out of my life is torture. Torture that I'm over. Not only that, but if he continues to show up at my school, acting like he did today, he's going to get me fired. It was one thing when he was just being an annoying texter and caller, but now, he's taking it too far. And quite frankly, it's getting a little scary. What's he going to do next? Show up during school hours and cause a scene? He knows just how much I love being a teacher, but he also knows that my position at Rosefield Prep came with a steep morality clause. Having an *ex*-lover's spat in public, in the school parking lot, well … you can guarantee I'll be packing my office up if that happens and someone witnesses it. I wouldn't put it past him to do it just to hurt me either.

Joke or not, it looks like I need to talk to Shane. At this point, he's my only hope in scraping off Seth before he does something that changes my whole life. At least with him, the chemistry between us doesn't have to be as fake as the relationship. No, that's something we definitely don't lack.

"Call him," I mutter to myself, pacing the small area between my coffee table and television. "Just pick up the phone and call him," I continue, thumping the remote against my forehead.

Since I got home a few hours ago, I've called Landon's mom about her tip-loving son and husband, took a long bath, threw on some lounge clothes—the shirt I stole from Shane that night he danced for me at Dirty—and cooked myself a pathetic dinner for one. Now here I am at ten o'clock on a Friday night, watching *Live PD* and talking to myself between random rants at the screen to unleash the dogs. This is where my life is. At least Seth didn't follow me home; that's about the only thing that could make my night worse. I could call Ember. I *should* call Em. Other than her, there aren't any other options, which means she is the sole bearer of my troubles when I need to vent. I'm not proud of it, but she's probably the only real friend I have. Even with the time that's passed since my split with Seth, he successfully drove a wedge between any friendships I had because those 'friends' got sick of seeing me stay with someone who treated me like crap. Ember was the only one who refused to give up and loved me despite the man I was dating. And I think he only really let her stay in my life because, at the time, she was dating his friend. It's pretty pathetic that I haven't at least gained another friend since the breakup.

My life really is sad.

Screw it. I'm better than this.

Tossing the remote on the couch, I stomp to my room where I left my phone charging and make quick work of sending off a text, not willing to let myself think twice about it.

Me: My place. Tonight.

I look at the screen then consider that might have been a little rude.

Me: Please. It's important.

Ignoring the shake to my hand, I palm my phone and try to calm the nervous flutters. Thank God I changed his contact picture from the erection picture he had texted me, or I imagine I would be even more nervous than I already am at this moment. My eyes remain glued to the television when I drop back on the couch, trying to listen to the words the hunky salt and pepper cop on the screen is saying, but all I can feel is the giant weight of my phone—the phone that hasn't gotten a response.

Another hour passes before I lie down and continue watching my show, doing a terrible job of ignoring my phone. The work-week doesn't take long to catch up with me, though. The second my head is resting on one of my many throw pillows, I'm out.

Chapter 12

Nikki

"JOE JONAS!" I SCREAM, RUBBING my head and blinking the sleep out of my eyes. The pounding at the door starts again, reminding me how I ended up on the floor after cracking my head against the corner of my coffee table.

Climbing off the floor, I glance at the clock hanging above the television. Three in the morning? The banging starts up again, spurring me into action and out of the zoned-out, half-asleep state I had been trapped in.

It doesn't take me long to throw all the locks and yank open the door. "What?" I grumble to the chest right in front of my eyes. I peer up, and the rest of the sleep that had been fogging my head clears.

Shane.

Here.

Oh, boy.

"Why are you bleeding?" he questions with concern lacing his words.

"Huh?"

"Your head, Nikki. It's bleeding."

"It is?"

His eyes narrow a split second before pushing his way gently around me. Taking my hand, he urges me to follow. Beyond over everything at this point, I slam the door shut and follow. He stops in the kitchen, moving around like he's been here a million times. Correctly opening the drawer where my towels are, he moves to the laundry closet to grab my first-aid kit before dipping the towel he grabbed under the faucet. Then he walks back to where I'm standing and places his hand against my stomach, pushing me backward with a tender touch. I sit, mutely, while he dabs my head with the towel. My eyes never leaving his face as he continues to care for me. I never would have imagined he was capable of such gentleness.

"You don't need stitches. The butterfly bandage should be enough."

"Uh, okay?"

He studies me for a beat before opening his mouth. "How hard did you hit your head?"

"I'm okay."

He doesn't look convinced.

"I'm fine, Shane."

"You might think you are," he mutters under his breath.

"What are you doing here?"

Again, his expression gets a little wonky before it visibly

washes clean, void of any emotion. "You texted me earlier."

"Oh, yeah. That."

"Yeah, Nikki, *that*."

"*That*, Shane, was hours ago."

He shrugs. "We were short staffed tonight at Dirty. I just walked out the door ten minutes ago, chèrie, and I'm fucking beat. You texted, I came when I could, so what's up?"

"Just like that?"

"Just like that."

"Oh."

"Nikki," he groans. "What's up?"

"I figured you would just text me back."

"Not a big fan of wasting my time. Your place is on the way to mine, figured I would stop by and see what you wanted."

"At three in the morning?"

Silence. His handsome eyes a murky brown, watching and waiting. However, it's the absence of golds and greens in those eyes that tell me more than his silence will.

"You're angry," I whisper with a frown. "Why?"

"It's been three fucking weeks, Nikki. I don't hear a peep from you until today, and after your text, I had to hear from Ember about some bullshit with your ex stalking you, showing up at your work scaring you, and then I get some short, curt message in a text and nothing else. You didn't tell me all that shit when we were together last, so yeah, color me fucking shocked. I couldn't leave Dirty if I wanted to, didn't have time to text you back, but my mind had plenty of time to imagine a million things you might need and not all of them were good. How do you want me to feel?"

"You were worried?" I don't call him on the fact we're actually a few days past three weeks even if I just want to be a smart-aleck. I have a feeling he's not going to handle my lame jokes very well.

He throws his hands up, making me flinch. His eyes get even darker. I'm having a hard time following him, but I can't imagine what I did to piss him and those damn mood ring eyes of his off.

"Yeah, I fucking was, and I don't like it."

"I'm sorry?"

With his hands on his trim hips, he glares at me. "Don't be fucking cute right now."

"I'm just being me, Shane."

"And that's the fucking problem!"

Needing a minute to wrap my head around his confusing behavior, I stand from my seat at the two-person kitchen table and walk to the couch. Clicking off the television, I toss the remote down and look at the man in my apartment. His head bowed, tension radiating off him, and his breathing coming in shallow pants. The silence around us uncomfortable, but I'm at a loss of how to break it.

"I left here three weeks ago thinking that you might have been serious, but then nothing. I figured if we were going to do this fake bullshit, you would at least reach out. I was game. But fuck, Nikki, you completely ghosted me. All I've thought about was what changed. Millions of shit-filled reasons going through my head, but it always ended with me fucking worried that something happened with that asshole ex of yours, and he was keeping you from reaching out. Then you finally do text, and I show up with you bleeding, and still, I fucking worry."

I open my mouth when he stops talking, but he holds his hand up.

"I don't like how this feels," he finally says. "I don't like surprises. I don't like to worry."

"I'm sorry I worried you," I offer, but he just narrows his eyes.

"I've never fucked a woman once and had her burrow under my skin as you have."

"Well, aren't you romantic."

"Tell me what made you text me tonight. Don't bullshit me either, chèrie. You've been silent, made it clear you were done, yet here I am. So, tell me, what's up."

"I'm not done."

"You've got a bad way of showing it."

"I've had a long past few weeks at work, Shane."

"Yeah? So have I, Nikki, but it didn't stop me from thinking about you."

The flutters in my stomach pick up at his mention of thinking about me. "I didn't know what to say," I finally whisper. "I didn't know ... I'm not used to this, Shane."

"That makes two of us."

"I'm sorry I didn't call you, but you could have called me too."

"Yeah, I could've."

"Uh, okay."

"Nikki ... chèrie, I'm begging you to just tell me what you need so I can get home and crash. It was just Nate and me on the main bar tonight; we had seven people call out or get sent home sick. I'm dead on my feet, but I knew I wouldn't be able to turn my mind off without seeing that you're okay with my own eyes."

"You're acting like a real boyfriend and not a fake one, you know."

"Nikki," he fumes, dragging those two syllables out.

I hold my hands up. "I wanted to revisit our talk from that night."

"You want to revisit our talk?"

"Yes. This time without our hormones muddling things."

He laughs. "You want me?"

My cheeks heat. "I think you know the answer to that." I cross my arms over my chest, hiding my stiff nipples from his view. The shirt covering them offers no help in masking how much it turns me on for him to talk in that low rumble of his.

My eyes follow his movements as he moves to drop his bulk down on my worn couch. A rush of air coming out as he drops his head back against the couch, looking at the ceiling. The silence continues as he blinks up at nothing. Now that he isn't scowling, I can see just how exhausted he is. His eyes have a shadow under each of them, his normal larger than life hard-as-nails persona isn't joining us. He's just Shane; stripped down and raw Shane.

"How about you crash here, and tomorrow morning, I'll cook you breakfast and we can talk. No sex, no touching, just sleeping and talking in the morning. If, when we wake up, you aren't interested in what I have to say, that's okay. But until then, we both get some sleep and table this conversation for after we've gotten some rest."

His head rolls on the back of the couch until his eyes clash with mine. There seems to be so much working behind his gaze, but it's moving too fast for me to decipher it. He silently stands and walks over to me, grabbing my head gently and pressing his lips to mine in a hard, closed-mouth kiss. Then he releases me and walks to my room. I lock up, turn off the lights, and creep down the hallway, my breath catching when I step into my room and see every rock-hard inch of Shane Kingston face down and passed out, completely naked with not a single tan line on his glorious body.

I walk back out to the linen closet and grab the huge quilt my grandmother made me years ago. Shane doesn't even stir when I settle on the bed and drape the quilt over both of us. In fact, he doesn't move once … until I curl on my side, facing the wall with my back to him, and fall asleep. Unfortunately for me—since I fell asleep—I missed him turning and pulling me into his strong arms.

And I also missed his whispered words.

"Not sure I can be your fake anything, mon colibri."

"How do you like your eggs?"

Shane looks up, his sleepy eyes hitting mine. "When did you wake up?"

"Uh, not too long ago," I answer, looking at the clock. I hide my wince when I see that it's not even nine yet. No way I'm going to tell him just how long I've been up. I woke up three hours ago, and I've been going insane since. I've never been one to sleep the day away, but the second my mind woke up and I felt Shane against me—holding me tightly in his arms with every inch of his body touching me from head to toe—I wouldn't have ever been able to get back to sleep even if leaving his arms was the last thing my still exhausted mind wanted to do. It took me longer to get out of his hold than I care to admit, but he looked so peaceful, so not like he did last night, that I wanted him to get as much sleep as he needed. I don't even allow myself to analyze why I was so drawn to stay in his arms.

God, I'm getting in so far over my head, and we haven't even started whatever this is.

"Right," he says gruffly. "You're a shit liar."

"I'm not lying!" I wave the spatula at him and narrow my eyes, heat hitting my cheeks.

He steps up behind me, his solid body hitting all my soft curves, and I sway, unable to hide my reaction from his touch. His lips ghost over my neck and up to my ear, warm breath bathing my skin as goose bumps chill my body.

"When you lie, your nose wrinkles. Just one side, cute as hell, but a dead giveaway."

"It does not," I retort breathily.

"It does. You also blush, right here," he whispers, his hand coming around me and his fingers swirling around the skin exposed between the open buttons of the shirt I'm wearing. "I bet, if I could see them, your tits would be the same light pink as your chest."

I click the burner off, move the pan of scrambled eggs to the back burner, and exhale loudly. "I'm not a liar."

"You aren't." His response instant and without doubt. "But that doesn't mean you won't stretch the truth when you don't want to give me everything." His touch burns when he grabs my hips and pulls me away from the stove. His body fits against mine more firmly now; his erection a heavy reminder against the small of my back. "Make a note, mon colibri; I don't give a shit about much, but when I ask you a question, I want the whole truth. No matter what."

I nod, not trusting my voice.

"Your ex, he didn't like it if you didn't say what he wanted to hear, did he?"

I'm beyond grateful that he can't see my face. The shame I feel knowing that I let Seth's short temper affect my life in such a negative way for years isn't something I will ever be able to get over. I can grow from it, but I will always remember how much I let a man dictate how I lived just because he was a big fat jerk. How to think. What to say. Who to be. Pure. Shame.

"Like you, he likes to be in control."

Shane's hands get tight, their hold on my hips pinching slightly. Before I can say anything or adjust my body, his touch eases.

"I'm nothing like him, Nikki. Don't ever lump me in the same likeness as a man who resorts to scare tactics to get a woman he didn't deserve in the first place."

"I ... that's not what I meant."

"I know," Shane interjects, stopping me before I can say anything more. "I want to make it clear, though, that the man I am, the control I need, isn't the same as what he used on you to make himself feel like a bigger man."

"Do you think we could have this chat with food and maybe less … erection? It's distracting."

Shane laughs, a short burst of gravelly noise that sounds rusty and unused. "Yeah, Nik. I think that's a good idea." His hands leave at the same time he steps back, and I instantly regret saying anything. "You look good in my shirt," he says with a smile to his voice, plucking at the collar, dragging one finger down my neck, and then hooking it around the top button. "I was wondering where this ended up."

"Sc-" I clear my throat, swallowing thickly. "Scrambled okay?"

"Yeah, scrambled is good."

I don't look at him while I move around the kitchen. I give him the majority of what I had cooked, piling the eggs and bacon on his plate before grabbing some toast and setting it to the side to grab a much smaller portion for myself. He takes both plates from me and walks them over to the table. I watch his back, the thick muscles flexing as he moves, and when I feel myself get wet between my legs, I shake the desire from my head. He shouldn't be allowed to be shirtless.

"Juice, coffee, or water?"

He turns, looking back at me. "Juice is good, Nik."

I nod, trying not to get sucked into just how handsome he looks sleep rumpled and half naked in my apartment. "Juice, got it. Two orange juices coming right up."

He smirks, and I narrow my eyes. Clearly, I'm not hiding my emotions as well as he can. I might as well have a big neon sign above my head that says 'hot, wet, and needy' at this point.

I grab the orange juice and make quick work of getting the cups down. I see him out of the corner of my eye sit and relax against the chair while he waits. The tiniest of things, him not starting to eat, makes me stop mid pour. My head turns, drinks forgotten, as I blink at him, unmoving, while I process his manners.

"What?" he asks, one brow arched, his one heavily tattooed arm resting in his lap while his ink-free one toys with the edges of the lesson plans I had dropped on the table yesterday.

"You can eat." My frown deepening when he shakes his head. "Really."

"I'll eat when you sit."

"But it will get cold."

I can still hear Seth screaming at me when I would get upset that he would be halfway finished with any meal before I even had a chance to fix my plate, let alone sit. The nasty words he would say. His lack of compassion for the woman who waited on him hand and foot, always wanting to make him happy even at my own expense. One thing he always spewed in my direction was that he couldn't stomach eating cold food. I heard it so much over the years when we were together that I'm not surprised a little anxiety over upsetting Shane with a cold meal is popping up. Boy, did Seth screw me up. Apparently, worse than I realized if he's invading my thoughts right now.

I'm not sure how long I silently freaked over the past, but when I look back up at Shane, he's as calm as always. His steady gaze seemingly too knowing.

"Then I'll eat it cold," he finally says, not looking away or hiding that he's taking notes on my reactions.

"But," I stutter. My eyes grow wide when Shane pushes his chair back and walks over to me, taking over pouring the rest of the juice before putting the container back in the fridge. I watch as he picks up both glasses, dips his head, and presses a featherlight kiss to my temple.

"We'll discuss why you look so scared about my food being cold later, but for now, let's eat, okay?"

I don't answer, but I do take a deep breath, grab some silverware, and walk to the table, pulling my chair out and dropping down in it. His scent fills my nostrils when his arm reaches around me to place my drink down, easing some of my nerves instantly. I pick up my fork and start eating, not once looking at him but seeing his hand move to do the same. We eat in silence—not uncomfortable but not exactly without a little strain. He wants to ask; I can feel it hanging in the air around us. The unspoken questions about why I would freak out over something so stupid. As embarrassing as it is, he deserves to know about my weird hang-ups. Fake relationship or not, we're a team until we beat our competition—meaning the exes.

"Seth wasn't a nice guy," I begin, but stop when Shane grumbles. When I look up, he waves me on and stuffs a huge fork full of eggs into his mouth. "Save the sarcasm, starboy, I doubt your ex was without faults."

"You've got that right, chèrie; she had more than a few."

"Right, well, as I was saying," I reply, keeping my gaze locked with his even though I want to look away. "Let's just put it this way; Seth liked to have things done a certain way, and when they weren't, he didn't shy away from using his words to let me know what I was doing wrong."

"And that has something to do with you not wanting me to eat cold eggs?" he questions, taking another huge bite. I look down, shocked to see that he's almost done eating.

"Just reminded me of some stuff."

Shane nods and then the silence stretches on. I continue to eat, but even with a much smaller helping, he's done well before I am. I look up when he picks up his drink, my eyes glued to his neck while he swallows. Who would have thought that a man drinking some juice out of a girly pink cup would be so dang hot, but as his throat constricts with each swallow, I find myself getting more and more turned on.

When the last of his juice is gone, he calmly places his cup down and rips a paper towel off the roll in the middle of the table and wipes his mouth. I put the last bite of toast in my mouth and wash it down with some of my drink, trying to calm my horny body down.

"I don't care if it's cold, hot, or some creation you slaved over that tastes like shit. If you make it for me, I'm going to eat it. My mama might not have been able to give us much growing up, but she taught us respect and how to give that to those in our lives. I'm not your ex, and fake or not, you'll have my respect without question."

"Uh, wow."

"Try not to be so shocked that I have manners, chèrie. I know how to treat a woman."

"Thank you," I finally say with a shrug, not really sure what to do with all that. "Your mother sounds lovely," I add awkwardly.

"She was."

"I'm sorry," I tell him, seeing how much he cared for his mother clear as day as a shadow crosses over his face.

He lifts his shoulder, not looking away. "She lived a hard life. By the time she got sick, there just wasn't any fight left in her. I miss her, but she's in a better place."

"Your dad?"

"Not in my life. Just me and Libby now. Her dad took off right after she was born." The frown lines leave his face, and a small smile curls his lips. "She's one of the greatest things I have. When I moved here, she transferred schools so we wouldn't be hours apart."

"I always wanted a sister. It sounds like you guys are really close. How old is she?"

"We are. She just turned twenty-one. Pain in my ass, but I would do anything for the brat."

My gaze roams from his eyes to his lips—now fully smiling with his teeth showing—and I don't think I've ever seen him so open. His strong jaw even more pronounced, the beard that he keeps trimmed short only emphasizing his features more.

"I like you like this," I blurt, groaning when I realize that my filter has once again failed me in life.

The corners of his eyes crinkle, his lips curving even more. "Like what?"

"I don't know … open?" I lift my hand and wave it around, biting my lip. Oh, come on, Nik, you've never been shy before. Just speak your mind. It's not as if this is a real relationship where you have to impress him. *But what if I want to impress him?* "I've known you for a few years now, and I've learned more about you in five minutes than I have in all that time. You always just seem so … closed off. I like this a lot more than the heavy shield that I always felt like you had up whenever I would come around."

"Doesn't make much sense if we're supposed to be in a relationship and we don't know much about each other, does it?"

"So you'll do it?"

"Mon colibri, you would be shocked at just how much I would do for you."

"You don't know me," I remind him, his confession warming something deep inside me.

"Yeah, I do."

"No, you don't."

He settles back in his chair and crosses his arms. The cocky expression he gives me a second later makes me narrow my eyes, waiting to see what kind of game he's playing. I meant it when I said I had learned more about Shane Kingston in this small time here at my kitchen table than I have since he moved to town. Over two years and he's been some enigma that kept pulling me closer but never gave anything to encourage the pull I felt.

"You work at Rosefield Prep, second-grade teacher for the past three years, got the job right out of college. Only child. Parents not in the picture. Not because they're shit parents but because they had you late in life and you've never been close. You've had one boyfriend, the douche, since you were in high school. You prefer vodka with orange juice but will settle for cranberry if that's not an option. You'll drink until you can't walk but, somehow, can still dance. You're more like a sister to your best friend than she is to her own sister. Your loyalty to her is something, I imagine, anyone you allow close gets. And," he whispers, leaning forward. "When you're about to come, you make this sound that I swear to Christ sounds like a hummingbird is trapped in your chest."

My eyes are just as wide as my mouth, my jaw hanging loose from shock. "How, what… are you kidding?" I rush out.

"Like I said, I know you."

"Are you a stalker?"

If I thought he was the hottest man on this planet before, when he tips his head back and a deep laugh booms from him, I *know* he's the hottest man in the universe. That rusty hilarity getting even richer as he continues to chuckle in the most manly of ways. When he focuses back on me, that golden hue has returned to his gaze, and I melt.

"I mean, I'm thinking I could deal with it if you were," I continue, wanting more than anything to hear that sound again. "I'd just like to know what I'm working with, is all."

"I'm not a stalker, Nikki."

"Oh, well … okay."

"Fuck, you're cute."

My face heats as I choose to ignore him. I stand and collect our dishes, walking to the sink and rinsing everything off before placing them in the dishwasher.

"How do you know all that?" I finally ask, closing the door of the dishwasher and drying my hands off on the hand towel next to the sink.

"Nate's my best friend. He talks a lot. Most of the time I ignore him, but I didn't when you would come up."

"Why?"

He frowns, not answering. I walk to his side and lift my hand to his face to smooth out the wrinkles between his brows. The sensation of his skin against mine making my body burn, drunk for more of the feelings touching him brings. I trail my hand up, raking my fingers through his thick, dark hair. I repeat the motion, bringing my free hand up to mirror the other. The buzz cut at the sides of his scalp tickling my skin. His eyes close, just as lost as I am.

Get the upper hand.

The thought filters through my mind, and without pause, I move my hands to frame his face, giving a twitch of my wrists to tip his face up—going from soft petting to forceful direction. His eyes snap open, hands moving lightning fast to my wrists, holding tightly. I can see he wants to take over, but he doesn't.

"I like how it feels knowing you didn't ignore him."

The fire in his eyes making the flecks of gold come alive. His hold on my wrists just shy of painful. I bend; the position I've got his head in being the perfect angle for me to get nose to nose with him. If he hadn't been sitting, I never would have been able to gain this kind of advantage. I don't think he'll let me have it for long either, so I might as well take what I can.

"You're going to let me get to know you, Shane Kingston. While you're mine and I'm yours to the world, you'll let me in. When this ends between us, I want to be able to look back and know that, while it lasted, I had all of you."

I can feel his rapid breathing against my lips. He doesn't move and his hold doesn't change, but those eyes sure do. Pure golden fire. His nostrils flare in sync with his heaving chest as he continues to search my face.

"C'est un jeu dangereux," he whispers hoarsely.

"What did you say?" I demand, narrowing my eyes.

His brow lifts in answer, not speaking.

"I see I'm going to need to learn French so you can't keep things from me while you're in my life."

I ignore the twinge in my gut at the reminder that his time in my life is temporary, but by some miracle, I keep from showing him.

"I said this is a dangerous game."

"Dangerous is my middle name," I joke, winking at him and still not releasing my hold. "I like dangerous."

His hands flex, my wrists smarting for a moment until his hold relaxes some. "No more ignoring me. We do this; we do this all the way. No way anyone will believe we're together if you're disappearing for weeks."

"You make it sound like it was months, Shane. I had a few busy weeks at work. I didn't disappear."

"And from now on, those busy weeks will always find a little time for me. Always."

A hiccup of air gets caught in my throat. I clear my throat and nod. "Are you going to be able to make everyone—including our exes—believe we're madly obsessed with each other?"

"That, Nikki, won't be a fucking problem."

"Yeah," I murmur, looking at his full lips. "I think you're right."

Chapter 13

Nikki

"NO ONE CAN KNOW ABOUT this being fake," Shane says, his voice muffled by the T-shirt he's pulling over his head.

"Excuse me?"

He finishes dressing instead of answering.

"Shane?"

He sits down on my bed with a huff, pulling his boots on before looking up and leaning back on his hands.

"You're right. I need you just as much as you need me to get someone out of my life. We need to keep this agreement between us. That way, there isn't a chance those someones find out we're playing them."

"I'm assuming you mean I can't tell Ember either?"

He nods, watching me with his stoic expression.

"She wouldn't tell anyone."

"I don't think she would, but if we want to be believable, that means the people who know us the best should buy it too. Otherwise, we're not doing it right."

I weigh his words, pulling my arms across my body. "I don't like keeping things from my best friend, Shane."

"I can respect that, but it's a deal breaker for me, Nikki."

"Son of a biscuit." His face goes soft, and I know he thinks my weirdness is funny. You try working around kids all day and not cussing, and you'll learn all sorts of tricks around it. Weird or not, it's my thing. "If she finds out, she won't be happy."

"Then don't tell her. It's no one's business but ours."

"And when we succeed in getting our exes out of the picture and this thing between us ends?"

He stands, towering over me, and lightly takes my elbows in his hands, not trying to get me to unfold my arms but making sure I see just how serious he is. "Then we'll break up like any other couple but go on as friends."

"Unless you fall in love with me and we end up hating each other."

"Don't worry about me, chèrie." I hear his unspoken words. It's written all over his face that he thinks I'll be the one to fall for him. "Are we agreed?"

"Yeah, boyfriend of mine, we're agreed. Don't worry; I won't fall in love with you either."

"Fuck," he says under his breath.

"What?"

"Nothing. Walk me out?"

I nod, missing his touch when he releases me. I follow

behind him, allowing myself a second to wish this wasn't fake and I could ask him to spend his Saturday with me. Instead, I smile as he opens the door and looks back at me.

"I'll be at Dirty until we open, but Dent should be back so if you can wait to eat dinner until around eight, we can go to the new hibachi place in town."

"Like a date?"

"You want people to believe you're mine, mon colibri, and it's kind of hard to show that off without going on a few."

"I can wait," I breathe.

"See you then," he says, his smirk telling me he's enjoying the fact he can gain the upper hand anytime he wants. He leaves the door open, walks back toward me, and lifts one hand to the nape of my neck. Curling it behind my neck with a strong hold, he pulls me into his body at the same time his lips crash against mine. His kiss bruising, deep, all-consuming, and … branding.

I'm still standing there with my eyes closed and my lips burning long after the sound of my front door shutting stops echoing through my apartment.

Yeah, this is a dangerous game, for sure.

"You're what!"

I hold the phone away from my face but not before Ember's

screech hits my ear, making me wince. I should have put her on speakerphone and saved my hearing, but in my defense, I'm a little rattled knowing I have a date—fake or not—with Shane Kingston tonight.

"You heard me."

"Shane, Shane? As in, the same Shane who is my husband's business partner? That Shane?"

"Know a lot of Shanes, Em?" I laugh, placing the phone on my bathroom counter so I can finish my makeup *and* save my ears from any more outbursts by my overly excited best friend.

"Well, no, but he's *Shane.*"

"Yes, he is," I reply, my voice deeper than normal. I look at my reflection, seeing my lust-filled expression looking back at me.

"When the hell did this happen?"

"A few weekends-ish ago," I hedge.

"Well, that's as clear as mud. Hold on, baby's crying." I hear her phone clatter against something hard and picture her moving around her house in my head. Quinnie's angry cries follow a second later, mingling with Ember's calming sounds. "Sorry about that; she's been fussy with these teeth coming in."

"It's okay. Do you want to let me go?"

She snorts. "Yeah, right. She'll calm down, but this gossip about you and Shane can't wait. I can't believe this is the first I'm hearing of this."

"There really isn't much to tell, Em. We're dating. Seeing where this attraction between us goes." Not a lie. No reason to feel guilty. But I do. I hate keeping things from her. She's been my best friend for so long, and we have no secrets between us. "There's no reason to get all worked up about it, girlfriend."

"Are you nuts?! This is the first guy you've dated at all since that jerk. I think it's more than enough of a reason to get worked up!"

"You're insane." I laugh.

"Are you going to sleep with him?"

"Uh …" I evade.

"You've already slept with him!"

The baby starts crying after her outburst, and I wait for her to calm her before speaking.

"Get any louder and I'm sure the whole town will know. Jeez, Em, calm the crazy down a few notches."

"You know, I'm not blind just because I'm married. I've seen how he moves his body when they're dancing at Dirty. Don't even try to act like you're shocked I'm curious about how he moves off the bar and between the sheets."

"I bet said husband would love to know you're asking about how his best friend can move."

She makes a pfft sound before she snorts again. "Nate isn't jealous like that."

"Yeah, and the sky is brown."

"Whatever."

I swipe another layer of gloss on my lips while my eyes roam over my face to make sure my makeup is perfect. Not even when I first started dating Seth did I put this much work into looking my best. "Do you think it's normal for me to keep comparing him to Seth?" I ask, not liking that it keeps happening but not experienced enough to know if it's normal.

"I wouldn't know, hon," Ember replies, no longer sounding manic in her excitement. "I'm about as well-versed as you are in the relationship department. When Nate and I first started seeing each other, I did the same thing, though, so I think it's normal. Or when you haven't had a lot of experience, it is."

"Or we're just naïve to how all this works."

"You were with Seth for a long time, Nik. Not only that, but you haven't dated since y'all broke up, so I think it's just the natural course for anyone in the same situation. Does Shane know about Seth?"

I wince. I can't tell her just how much he knows, and I hate that. "Yeah."

"If you're worried about it, be honest about it with him. He deserves to have a fair fight with whatever hang-ups Seth left you with. Talk it out and let him show you that he isn't like Seth, the jerk."

"We've already been there," I say softly. "This morning, over him waiting on me to eat, of all things."

"This morning, huh?"

"Oh, hush."

"Tell me what happened."

I replay my breakfast with Shane, only leaving out the talk about our 'relationship' but giving her the rest. Including my near panic-inducing moment about cold freaking eggs. Ember knows just how nasty things got with Seth, so I don't have to go into much detail.

"You know, if it was legal to kill someone, that asshole would be the first person I shanked."

"How do you even know what shanking someone means?"

"I watch *Wentworth* on Netflix; I could be scrappy in prison. Don't think the thought hasn't crossed my mind a time or two with that guy."

"You wouldn't last an hour in prison." I laugh.

"To answer your earlier question," she says, ignoring me, "in situations like that, I think it's normal. You did the right thing by talking to him about it. Letting him know why you had that moment and giving him a chance to ease your mind. Shane's a good guy, Nik. He's going to treat you well."

"Yeah, he is."

"Don't give Seth any power in what you're starting with Shane," she tells me after a moment of silence. "He has no right to something like that. If you're reminded of the bad memories he left you with, you let Shane give you the words to make it good. Holding on to that will only keep you from moving on."

"Easier said than done."

"It is, but you have a few people ready to lift you up if you need it. You know that."

My eyes sting, and I feel even more guilt over keeping the complete truth from her. "I love you, sister from another mister."

"Right back at you, Nik."

"Give my goddaughter a kiss for me, okay?"

"I will. And you call me first thing tomorrow and tell me how the date went!"

I laugh, agree, and wait until she says bye before cutting her off. "Hey, Em?"

"Yeah?"

"If you thought how he moved on the bar was hot, what he can do in the sheets should be illegal."

I hang up the phone but not before I hear her screaming. I'll pay for that, I'm sure, but after hearing way more than I wanted to about her husband's skills, it's only fair.

I almost trip when I walk out of the bathroom and my foot gets tangled in all the clothes I had been trying on before finally giving up on finding an outfit and moving to tackle my hair and face. Why am I making such a big deal about dinner? It's not like this is a real date. Just two people enjoying the mutual benefits of each other's company while having dinner. Right?

This is insane. If I don't drive myself mad with my need for what he can do to my body, I'll do it by constantly worrying about keeping myself on the straight and narrow where this 're-lationship' is concerned. Constantly having to remind myself it's not real will only make it harder for me to actually pretend.

"That's it," I mumble to myself, grabbing my favorite jeans off the floor. "From now on, no more analyzing it as fake versus real." Yanking my pants up and grabbing a loose blouse, I pull it over my head and adjust the neck so one shoulder peeks out bare. "You, Nicole Clark, have a boyfriend, and that's all there is to it. Give it your all, and if anyone is falling, it's going to be him be-cause you're *that* irresistible." I nod at my reflection, happy with my outfit. My long blond hair hanging in loose curls, framing my face. My eyes are bright, excited, and for once in too many months, not worried about a dang thing.

"From this day forward, you're going to give every day your

all and not worry about the reality of your situation with Shane. Enjoy him, let him enjoy you, and take your life back."

I've totally got this.

Chapter 14

Nikki

I TOTALLY DON'T HAVE THIS.

Shane stands outside my apartment, the crappy lighting in the hallway hitting him like a spotlight. He's wearing what I'm starting to realize is pure him. Dress pants, nice shoes, and a black button-down. He's rolled the sleeves up, and his forearms look ridiculously sexy. He always looks hot, and I have a feeling he doesn't even try to be this mouthwatering.

Voices I didn't hear during my inspection of Shane filter through my brain. I watch as he turns his head, and even from the side, I can see his eyes narrow. I'm not sure which of my neighbors is keeping his attention, but there really isn't one who would be better than the other. When he looks back at me, I know he'll have questions about the seedy men who live on my floor.

"You look beautiful, chèrie," he finally says, still not looking any less intimidating than he did when he looked over at the voice.

"You look pretty handsome yourself, starboy."

He shakes his head. Some of the harsh lines leaving when he smirks ever so slightly. "We need to work on that nickname. I'm not a starboy."

"How about pudding?"

"You call me that in public, and I'll pull you to the nearest closet and make it so you can't sit without remembering that I am not your pudding."

"Snuggums?" I question.

"If you're not hungry, you'll keep that up."

I cock my head. "Okay, I'm hungry, so I'll cross that off the list. But just out of curiosity, what would happen if I wasn't hungry?"

A wolfish grin takes over, and my knees grow week. "Then you could call me that bullshit again, and I would spend the night making sure you were pleasured hard but never let you come."

"Well, looks like snuggums just got the permanent marker crossed through it."

"I won't lose sleep over that," he grunts.

He steps to the side, letting me out into the hallway, and I turn and smile at the door while I lock up my apartment. While I wouldn't mind the whole nearest closet option, having him deny me an orgasm after I know just how good he is in bed? Yeah … no.

"How was work today?" I ask, almost stumbling when he reaches out and takes my hand before turning and walking to the stairs that lead to the parking lot. I might have promised myself no more discussing fake and real, but if this is how he's going to act, I'm never going to be able to convince myself that any of this is fake. Dangerous might have been an understatement.

"Easier than last night."

He stops at his jet black BMW, the windows just as dark as the paint job, and opens my door for me. When I'm settled, he shuts the door softly, enveloping me in darkness as his scent fills my senses. I lean my head back and inhale deep, loving the earthy spice scent that is all his. I've never smelled anything better. Ever.

When his door opens, I sit a little straighter, not wanting him to see me all boneless and question me on it. When he starts the engine, the heavy purr makes me press my knees together. His large palm settles on my thigh a beat later, and I look over at him.

"Keep that up and we're back up those stairs."

I gulp, the sound loud in the closed space.

His hand tightens, and I lay mine on top of his. His nostrils flare, and I bet if I looked down, I could see I'm not the only one overwhelmed with need.

"First date," he strangely says, his fingers gripping my leg, my hand gripping his.

"Huh?"

"I don't have sex on the first date."

Bubbles of laughter dance up my throat, and I try but fail to suppress them. I lose his gaze when I keep laughing harder, my eyes watering. Not before I saw his handsome smirk, though.

"That's a good thing, sugar pie, since I'm not that kind of girl."

"Cross that one off too," he demands, no real heat in his words.

"I'll think about it."

"You do that, mon colibri."

When he pulls his hand free, I can't help the whine that escapes. He doesn't call me on it, but when the streetlight illuminates his face, I can see he isn't as immune as he might act. I watch out my window as he drives, the radio on low, and the silence comforting. It doesn't feel like a first date. Probably because we've already gone further than I have ever experienced with another person, doing things way out of order but in a comforting way. I'm glad nothing is normal about us because it makes the usual expectations less daunting. The need to do what I can to keep him interested isn't there. Not having that pressure, well, with that absent, I can be me without worrying about him calling in the morning.

"Have you been here before?"

His question breaks through my thoughts, and I look over.

"Ember dragged me a few weeks ago for lunch. It's really good."

"I heard it was good."

"It's always pretty crowded, though," I tell him, pointing out the windshield at the packed parking lot.

He remains silent, somehow finding a spot right near the front door and killing the engine. He looks over, a playful expression masking his normal indifference. "I happen to know that Lacey is having dinner here tonight. You ready to act like I'm the most irresistible man in the world?"

"Not even a hardship," I scoff, grinning.

"You aren't mad that I picked this place, knowing she would be here?" His question sounds more like a test for me than anything else.

I lift my shoulder. "Why would I be? If you're expecting some jealous outburst, you've got the wrong girl, tiger."

"Tiger?"

"Rawr," I joke with a wink.

He grunts, but I see his smile as he climbs out of the car. Before my hands can curl around the handle to let myself out, he's opening the door and offering his hand to help me. My sandals touch the ground a second before he pulls, careful of my head, and I stumble into his arms, looking up into his playful eyes.

"Keep being fucking cute and we won't make it long in here."

"I'm not doing anything," I answer.

"Dangerous."

Not knowing how to respond, I just blink up at him. He just looks at me, not moving, and then presses his lips to mine. When he leans back, I'm not sure who is more shocked by the impromptu kiss—me or him.

When we get inside the restaurant, I have to mentally remind myself not to look around. I hold his hand with mine while curling the other around his thick bicep, keeping my body pressed tightly against his. Aside from telling the hostess it was just the two of us, his attention doesn't waver from mine. I want so badly to look around, but I resist. Somehow. To the outside, there is no way someone would think this was our first date.

"Right this way," the young girl says before grabbing some

menus and gesturing with her hand to the room behind her.

I give myself a second to take in the room, each of the hibachi cooktops seemingly full of people. She weaves around the room, coming to a stop in the back corner. Shane holds out my chair for me, the one on the end, before taking the other one to my left. I make a mental note to thank him later for taking the spot next to a stranger.

"You've got to be fucking kidding me," someone hisses, not trying to keep their voices from floating toward us.

My eyes go from the menu to the direction where I heard that. My gaze clashes with the angry woman across from us at the U-shaped cooktop. Shane's hand drops to my knee, and I know exactly who that is. I had never really gotten a good look at her because I only saw her through the smoke and darkness of Dirty. I knew about what she looked like in build and such, but I hadn't gotten a good look at her face until now. She's beautiful, no doubt about it, but something is nasty about her that takes all those good looks and dashes them out.

Evil. That's what I imagine is roaring through her veins. Pure, nasty evil.

"Lacey," Shane drawls, nodding his head at the same time his hand starts rubbing my leg to soothe me. I don't let myself analyze that, keeping my eyes on the woman across from us.

She doesn't respond. Her face contorts to an even nastier scowl.

"Hannah," he continues. I see the woman next to her nod.

Thankfully, the only other people at the table seem to be with them, so we're keeping our show to a somewhat minimal audience. My stomach flutters, nervous bubbles making me question the sanity of what we're doing.

"This is rich, Shane," Lacey snidely says to him. "Even for you."

"Don't," the girl next to Hannah says, leaning around the friend between them to look at Lacey.

"Don't what? Him bringing his new slut here was no fucking accident. Just like you, Shane, to parade your toys around. You going to tie her up on the table and fuck her here? Rub it in that you have someone new."

"Your language is atrocious," I speak up, locking eyes with hers, unable to keep the thought to myself. Blue against blue, one spitting fire and the other—hopefully—calm. Shane's grip is the only other thing that registers. I bet I have a bruise, but oddly, I kind of hope I do. What in the world does this man do to my mind?

"Oh yeah, slut? You going to do something about it?"

I lean forward, looking around Shane's body, and make eye contact with the other people sitting with us. Even if they're clearly here with her, her behavior is embarrassing for everyone. They seem to be coming to the same conclusion, looking uncomfortable that they're stuck at a table, and between something nasty. "I'm really sorry for her disgusting behavior. I've never met her before, but please accept my humblest of apologies that you're having to witness something so unstable."

"You fucking bitch," she hisses. "That's my fiancé you have your hands on."

I look from the wide-eyed couple next to us and up at Shane, hoping he can see that I have a lot to say about *that* bombshell. He doesn't look away. I nod once before looking back at her. "Whatever he might have been to you at one point, you weren't smart enough to keep him in your life. Your loss, my gain, and honey ... I won't be stupid enough to let him go. Isn't that right, pumpkin?" I look over at him with my brow arched. I'll pay for that pet name, but right now, whatever that punishment will be is one hundred percent worth it to see the look on her face.

However, the desire in his eyes is telling me he isn't at all upset with my continuing the pet name game in public. His hand leaves my leg, arm arches over my head, and he drapes it over my shoulder.

If looks could kill, I imagine his charming ex would have murdered me a few times. I ignore her, placing my order when the waitress comes over. After handing over my menu, I place my hand on his muscular thigh and lean my head against his arm, turning to look up at him with a smile while I slowly drag my hand up toward his crotch, stopping just shy of the bulge in his slacks. He doesn't outwardly react, but the second I flex my hand against his leg and feel his hardness against the side of my hand, his erection jumps. I know that no one can see, but it makes me feel deliciously naughty.

"Maybe not on a really hot surface like this, but I wouldn't mind the whole tying me up later situation."

Twice in one day, Shane gives me something I have a feeling few others have experienced from him. His full-out, blinding smile as he laughs loudly with his whole body. I feel my own grin grow as I continue looking up at him. When he looks down, his chest still moving with silent laughter, I feel like a little piece of me has just become his forever.

Luckily—or rather, unlucky for me—I didn't have too much time to think about what that meant for me because the second his lips touched mine, I was drenched with the drink that had just been placed in front of the woman across from me.

Chapter 15

Shane

"HAVE YOU LOST YOUR FUCKING mind?" I growl at Lacey.

What the hell did I ever see in her?

Easy. She was easy.

Well, she was easy until she was anything but.

When I heard from a mutual friend she would be here tonight to celebrate her friend Hannah's birthday, I hadn't thought much of it until the plan to take Nikki out had hatched. Never, not once, did I think she would get violent. The hostess, the same one I had stopped by to talk to earlier and make sure we had a seat at the same table as Lacey, rushes over.

"Are you okay?" she questions Nikki, dabbing her with some napkins, not that it does any good.

Nikki, though, doesn't even look fazed. She only spares me a second before answering the hostess, but I can hear the laughter in her voice. Laughter? Fucking hell, does this woman ever do what I expect?

That's about when it all goes tits up.

Lacey's salad hits Nikki in the chest, the ginger dressing and lettuce sticking to her. I stand the second I see her move, my chair tumbling to the ground just in time to stop Lacey from reaching Nikki. No doubt, we've got the whole damn room's attention at this point. Lacey is going nuts trying to get past me. I catch her hand, maybe arm, right in the jaw, but it just pisses me off more.

"Shut your fucking mouth, woman," I demand, my voice hard and unforgiving. Lacey, though, ignores me and somehow gets an empty plate in her hand, swinging it quicker than I can stop it and dropping it on Nikki's head. I've never wanted to hurt a woman more. "You touch her one more fucking time, and I'm not going to hold her back when she's had enough." Do I know if Nikki is the kind of woman to defend herself? Not really, but I have a feeling I'm not wrong.

"You really need a muzzle."

When Nikki's snarky remark hits my ears, I fight back a grin. That's my girl. Fuck, *my* girl?

"He's mine," Lacey snarls at Nikki.

Maneuvering my hold on Lacey, I turn her so that her back is to me and both of her wrists are in my grasp. She tries to kick me but just ends up kicking her own leg.

"Mon colibri, get your purse," I say over my shoulder. "And do me a favor and call the police after you take some cash out of my wallet to cover the inconveniences."

Lacey only gets more animated after that request. I ignore

her, apologize to the staff surrounding us, and feel Nikki's hand reach into my back pocket for my wallet. I don't wait for her to put it back; instead, I lead Lacey out of the restaurant. If Nikki isn't right behind me, she won't be far. I don't like leaving the damage control to her, but right now, all I want is this piece of trash away from her.

When we step outside, I give a little shove and release Lacey. She doesn't stumble but turns and tries to get in my face. I place one hand on her chest to keep her from getting too close. Unfortunately for me, she was able to get one of her nails into the skin on my neck first.

"Has this bullshit been hiding inside since I met you? Because I gotta say, Lacey, had I known you were this fucking crazy, I would have scraped you off long before I finally did."

"You fucking love me, you asshole."

"You're even more unstable if you think that's true."

"Yeah?" she screams. "Then why is your ring on my finger?" She holds out her hand, and I'm stunned silent for a second when I see she's still wearing that damn ring.

"Probably because he was nice enough to let you keep it. Maybe he thought you could buy a new personality with the money you got from pawning it."

Nikki steps up to my side, pushing my wallet back into my pants. Well, saved by the fucking bell.

"You ... you *bitch*!"

"You know, someone once told me you can win more fights with intelligence instead of resorting to animalistic tendencies and words that belong in the garbage." She steps a little closer to

Lacey and turns her head as I feel her gaze on me. I look down only when I know I have Lacey contained. "Of course, those garbage words are pretty amazing when they're coming from you and you're saying them while you're between my legs, honey bunch."

"You call the cops?" I ask, ignoring another of her stupid pet names. Fuck if I'll admit, they're growing on me. Just like all the other quirky things that are one hundred percent Nicole Clark.

She nods.

"I'm sorry our night ended this way," I tell her, not wanting her to think I wanted this to happen. I figured we would show up and Lacey would get the point and see that I was actually not wasting away for her.

She waves me off, shrugging and smiling at Lacey. "Don't be. You're not the one in charge of her rabies shots."

"Fuck, you're cute."

"You know, you don't need to hold her back from me," she tells me, still looking at Lacey, who is red in the face from the yelling we're both ignoring. I glance up at the restaurant quickly and see we've brought an audience out here with us. Looks like we're more entertaining than the chefs tonight. How did I not see this coming? "Drop your hand, Shane."

"Fuck that," I answer immediately with a frown, not understanding why she would want this bitch free.

"Release her, Shane. Now."

"Not a chance in hell I'm letting her near you, chèrie."

"You never called me that!" Lacey screams.

"Shut the fuck up," I grunt toward her.

"Shane, I'm asking you one more time. Be a good boy and let

her go, and I promise I'll let you do whatever you want later for a reward."

I let my hand fall instantly but move to pull Nikki into my arms at the same second Lacey charges, turning so that she hits air and not Nik. Never once did I think that the woman I was trying to protect would be able to move quicker than I could, though. By the time I finish our spin, Nikki's out of my arms and face to face with the woman I stupidly thought I could spend the rest of my life with.

"Touch me. I dare you," she taunts Lacey.

I reach out to take Nikki back in my arms, but again, she evades me.

"I'll do more than touch you," Lacey yells, spit flying from her mouth.

I can feel the animal inside me pacing in agitation while I lose complete control of the situation. Lacey swings, Nikki ducks, and in a move straight out of a kung fu movie, Nikki has Lacey on her back in the grass with one tiny little foot right on Lacey's chest.

"I knew you were stupid for letting him go, but I didn't think you were stupid enough to fall for the good old dare trick. Lacey, is it? Whatever, doesn't matter. Listen to me now because the next time this happens, he won't be able to keep me from you. You let him go, and I will never be as stupid as you. You might have a ring he gave you, but it stopped being more than a hunk of metal and a rock the second y'all broke up OVER a year ago. Stop being a pathetic excuse for a woman sniffing after a man who doesn't want you, and move the heck on."

I hear the sirens, but I'm unable to do more than watch Nikki defend herself—and me.

"He'll always be mine," Lacey gasps, winded from her fall.

Nikki throws her head back, her long blond hair shaking down her back. My hands itch, wanting it in my fist while I take her hard.

"He let you go and didn't want you back. If you ask me, he never was yours to begin with."

"He will be back. Mark my words." For the first time, a little of Lacey's confidence cracks, and I see that she isn't as confident as she would like us to believe.

"Wrong. He's got me now, and I won't ever do anything to screw up what we have. Whatever you think it was you shared, we've got that and then some. You ever seen what it looks like when two people find their forever? Well, open your eyes, sweetheart, because it's right in front of you."

Even knowing she's acting, her words hit something inside me that makes my chest warm and my heart pound. I clench my fists when that sensation gets more intense. Nikki steps back at the same time the flashing lights paint the outside of the restaurant. Stepping into my hold, she doesn't look away from Lacey as she rolls and climbs to her feet.

She wasn't wrong; my ex never was the brightest crayon in the box. She shows everyone watching that when she leaps forward and punches Nikki right in the eye two seconds after the officer steps out of his car.

"Jesus." I look up and see the officer, one I recognize quickly from his connection to Nate, as he frowns down at Lacey, and the other officer with him handcuffs her. "You know, Nik, I thought you might be exaggerating when I heard it was you who called this in."

"Would I do that?" Nikki laughs, curling even more into my side. I tighten my hold, not wanting any space between us. Not letting myself question that.

He just laughs, moving Lacey away from us. I tune him out while he says something into his radio then addresses Lacey. My eyes only for one woman. And the crazy woman just smiles up at me, one red eye and all.

"That was fun."

"Fuck," I whisper, pulling her into my arms and pressing my lips to her eye. I move my hand to the back of her head and press her against my chest while I look over her head as Liam puts my ex in the back of his patrol car.

After he finishes questioning the witnesses, he walks back to us and shakes his head with a grin at Nikki. We had moved to lean against my car while he got his statements, waiting for our turn.

"Haven't seen you around in a while, squirt."

"The school year started back up and I've been busy keeping the youth of America from boredom. How are Megan and the kids?"

"They're great," he answers, his whole demeanor changing at the mention of his wife and children. I don't know him too well, but I know enough through Nate that I wouldn't call him a stranger. "You pressing charges?"

Nikki says no at the same time I say yes. She looks up, studies me for a second, and then nods. She shocks the shit out of me when she looks back at Liam and ignores me as if I'm not even there.

"You'll have to forgive Shane; he doesn't like it when someone messes with his girl. My precious, he's like that."

"Your girl," he repeats, looking at me with lips twitching with amusement, but his eyes hold a lot of questions.

"Thanks for coming," she continues, ignoring the two men at her side and completely clueless to the heat in his stare. "If you don't mind, I'm really hungry, and I was promised a meal before a great night of fun at his place. Do you have something where I can write my statement down?"

Who the hell is this woman?

"Yeah, Nik," he says, shaking his head at her with a small smile. He walks away and opens the trunk of his patrol car, returning a moment later with an incident form. "Fill this out and I'll let you know if I have any follow-up questions later so you two can get out of here. I'm sure Megan's going to want more than I can give her when she hears about this, though, so I'd expect a call from her before me."

Thirty minutes later, we're back in my car. Lacey might have lucked out with Nikki refusing to press charges, but unfortunately for her, Liam still placed her under arrest for disorderly conduct since he witnessed her erratic behavior firsthand—not to mention her physically putting her hands on Nikki with the intent to harm. She won't even spend the night in jail; I'm sure Daddy's princess will have him bailing her out immediately, but there isn't shit I can do about that. I make a mental note to let the bouncers at Dirty know Lacey is officially banned from the club, something I should have done sooner. Had I, then maybe she wouldn't be so fucked in the head thinking I would take her back.

I glance over at Nikki, her hair now dry from the drink, but the dressing from the salad still staining her top. She's wearing a small smirk on her lips, not even fazed by the events of the night.

"Hey!" She jerks up straighter and points forward. "Taco Bell?"

"Do you ever do what someone would expect you to do?"

She giggles. "Never, handsome. Never."

Dangerous game, indeed.

"So ..." Nikki mumbles around a mouth full of her burrito. "You were engaged?"

I finish chewing the bite I had just taken and wash it down with a drink before answering. "Not really."

"Explain that."

"I was with her for a few years. She moved here with me when Nate opened Dirty and I took the job he offered. We'd talked about marriage before, but nothing serious and more me entertaining her when she would bring it up. When I gave her that ring, it was more of a one day we might kind of thing because I was honestly sick of her bitching about it. It was never an engagement ring, and she knew that. I think I always knew we weren't right for each other, and it was easier to dust off our troubles with shiny shit than put up with her screaming all the time."

"You bought her a ring with no intention of marrying her? Harsh, Kingston, harsh."

"Not my finest moment," I agree. "But I didn't lead her on. She knew what it was."

"So what happened? You weren't ready to break it off with her then, clearly, but what happened to end things for y'all?"

I lean back in my seat, looking around the empty dining area of our local Taco Bell. None of the employees are paying us any attention. We might as well be in our own world.

"She fucked someone else."

"Ouch. Been there. I take it she didn't stay with him long?"

I let a grunted huff. "Her. She didn't stay with *her* for long and correct."

Nikki's mouth opens wide, her eyes round. "You've got to be kidding me."

"Do you know any man who would joke about their ex cheating on them with another woman?"

"Well, no."

I lift my shoulder, not saying anything else. What else is there to say?

"When Seth cheated on me, I blamed myself for a long time. He always told me that he felt like he was sleeping with a dead person because I was apparently *that* bad in bed. It took me some time to see things clearly. I know now he was lacking and not me. I imagine it's the same for your situation."

"You know the sad part," I tell her, stopping when her phone rings. She doesn't even look away from me, something that used to drive me nuts with Lacey. *She* never gave two shits about ignoring me when her phone went off in favor of whatever notification came through. "The sad part is I wasn't even that upset. She gave me an out from a relationship that was suffocating me."

"Why didn't you just break it off with her?"

"You know, I don't think anyone has ever asked me that. Maybe I was wrong for not ending it before she had a chance to cheat. I thought I loved her, but after we split, I realized what we shared was never close to that. Sure, at a time I cared about her, but love? No."

Nikki nods, taking another bite.

"I'm sure it's not a shock that she wasn't the most level-headed person."

"Understatement," she snorts.

"She would get jealous. So fucking jealous. I guess it just wasn't worth the fallout that I knew would come if I broke it off, so I just kept on, resenting her more and more with each day that passed. The day I caught her with Hannah, I felt nothing but relief."

"Hannah? You mean the same girl who you said hello to earlier?"

"That would be the one."

"Wow. That's some messed-up stuff. Sounds like an episode of *The Young and the Restless*."

"Welcome to my life."

"So that's why you're single? Because of what Lacey did to you?"

"Partly," I tell her honestly, weighing my words while she

waits for me to continue. "You know what I do at Dirty when I'm not in my office. When I'm working the bar, which isn't often anymore, it's my job to use my sexuality to make the customers feel some kind of rush, the same rush that keeps them coming back day after day. To those women, every time I dance, they think it's some unspoken promise. It's not easy for someone to see the man they're in a relationship with charming other women for a living."

Nikki brushes it off as no big deal, but I've never met a woman who didn't get jealous when faced with that situation I just described. Ever. None of the guys, with the exception of Nate, are in relationships. Dent had a woman for a while, but just like me and Lacey, she couldn't handle him working at Dirty.

"I used to strip," I continue, not sure why I told her that.

"I know." She smirks. "Nate isn't shy about his past. He told Em and me a long time ago about how he knew you."

I narrow my eyes. "That's it; nothing else to say?"

She places her burrito down and tilts her head at me. "What do you want me to say? I'm not like those little insecure girls you seem to be comparing me to, Shane. I don't get jealous. If someone is with me, they have all my trust until the day they don't deserve it anymore. Plus, it's kind of hot."

"Kind of hot?" Is this girl for real?

"The idea of my man working hard for his business, using his body to drive women mad enough that they crave him but knowing *I'm* the one that he comes home to? The only one who gets what he taunts others with. Yeah, that's hot."

"Are you real?" I voice the question bouncing around in my mind.

She giggles. Cute as fuck. "I don't know, honey. How about you take me to one of our homes and find out for yourself how real I am?"

I'm up from the table without having to be told twice. She chuckles the whole time while I toss our trash and grab her hand to pull her from the building. When I have her outside, I spin her body and press her into the side of my car with my hips. I rub my hard-as-fuck cock against her, loving the fuck out of that hum that comes from her parted lips. Her head tips back when I close the distance between our mouths.

Right before mine touches hers, I smirk. "Add honey to the yes column."

Then I take her mouth, kissing her deep. Giving anyone who drives by a show, I thrust my body against hers slowly, driving us both mad. Her nails bite into the skin exposed from my rolled-up sleeves, and when I pull away from her and we're both panting heavily, she tightens her hold.

"I thought there was no first date sex," she gasps, still trying to catch her breath.

"Fuck the first date."

Chapter 16

Nikki

"PLEASE!"

His hand lands against my swollen center again, the sensation stinging through my whole body. I pull at the ropes keeping my wrists bound to his headboard and feel the overwhelming need for more of him cranked up to dangerous levels.

"I'm being lenient, Nicole. Keep it up and I'm going to think you're purposely not following the rules."

What the heck did I do wrong? He drops his head back to my soaked pussy and picks up where he left off. His tongue, mouth, and teeth driving me so high I swear I can see heaven.

Rules, Nikki. Focus.

Sir! Why I can't ever remember that stupid word, I don't know. Probably my subconscious trying to get more of his hard handedness against my skin. Who would have thought I would enjoy being spanked so much?

When his teeth bite my clit again, the emptiness I feel without him inside me becomes too much to handle. I pull at my bindings again, the rope soft but still chafing my skin with all my thrashing.

"SIR!" I scream. "Please, Sir! I'm so empty."

He lifts his head, and I look down my naked body at the man between my legs. His bearded chin is wet, soaked with my arousal. His eyes shining with golden swirls of heat as he looks back up at me. I don't look away. I can't look away.

"You want my cock, mon colibri?"

I nod my head frantically.

"How badly?"

"Desperately," I answer shamelessly. "Sir."

He lifts from his position between my legs, kneeling back between my spread legs. His eyes no longer looking into my face but down at my exposed sex. He keeps looking, breath rushed, and I feel myself growing even more wet from his perusal. When he takes his shaft in his hand, slowly stroking his angry looking flesh, I whine. I'm helpless to keep the sound to myself. I feel like I'll die if he doesn't fill the emptiness.

His free hand reaches over, and the binding on my ankle loosens. He switches hands, not losing a beat in his strokes. When the other ankle is free, I have to fight with my own need to keep my legs where he placed them earlier. Wanting to please him just as much as I want him to please me. The turbulent roller coaster of desire flies off the tracks the second he moves and flips me. He jerks my hips up, gently pushing me up to my knees. The binding on my hands giving me just enough slack to have my arms cross without pain.

At the same time as he grabs a fist full of my hair and jerks my head back, he enters me in one long, hard thrust. I scream, close my eyes, and push back just as firmly as he's pushing in. Just like the last time with him, my mind fogs and I become drunk on the feelings he brings forth with his touch. Each deep thrust bringing me higher and higher.

"Fucking perfect," he grunts, releasing my hair and grabbing both sides of my waist to keep his thick cock deep inside me.

I wiggle but his hold bruises to keep me still. My eyes close as my core clamps down on him; I'm so close but need him to move.

The roaring of my blood rushing through my body is the only thing louder than the animalistic sounds that leave his mouth when he starts moving, and I come instantly. I feel my body trying to pull his thickness back in each time he pulls away, leaving just the tip of him inside me. When I don't think I can take it anymore, he pushes in deep and drops his body heavily against my body. His cock twitches, and his groan of completion vibrates against my back.

"Encore mieux qu'avant[6]," he says against my back, pressing his lips to the space between my shoulders. "Encore mieux[7]."

"That's it," I gasp. "I'm getting Rosetta Stone."

His rich laughter bursts from his lips as his breath bathes my damp skin. I'm sure he thinks I'm joking, but I make a mental note to find the easiest way to learn French as soon as possible. When he pulls out, I miss the feeling of him instantly. He helps

---

6 Even better than before

7 Even better

free my hands, rubbing my arms after the ropes fall loose and kissing my palms before lying down and pulling me into his arms.

"This isn't how I thought tonight would go," he finally says.

I wiggle in his hold, and his arms loosen enough for me to turn. I place my hands against his chest, rubbing the smooth skin while looking into his eyes. His fingers rub circles on my hips. His other arm under my head.

"I'm not complaining."

"No, you definitely aren't."

I mirror his smirk, neither one of us breaking eye contact.

"You were mad outside the restaurant, weren't you?" I ask, voicing the question that had been on the tip of my tongue since we left. I knew he wasn't happy. I could see it in the tense way he was holding his body. "You might say you don't have to be in control outside the bedroom, but that isn't entirely true, is it?"

"It's not."

"Why? I'm not complaining; I just want some help understanding it."

He shifts our hold, rolling to his back and settling me against his side. His free hand—the one not holding me to him, lands on top of mine, pressing my palm against his chest. The steady thump of his heart against my hand soothes me.

"When Libby and I were growing up, we didn't have it easy. I guess, it's my way of making sure I don't ever have to feel helpless. Mama did her best. She worked so many jobs, and I'm sure that played a part in her being weak enough for the cancer to take over. I promised myself the day she died that I wouldn't let anyone else be in charge of what happened to my life."

"That's a lot to take on, Shane. You know it's not a bad thing to share the load with someone every now and then."

The silence ticks by, and for a minute, I'm worried I overstepped. What are the boundaries to this thing? Heck if I know. It just doesn't feel right not to speak up, trying to get him to let me help him see a different way of doing things.

"If you would have told me that a few weeks ago, I probably would have laughed in your face, chèrie. Now, though, I'm starting to think you might be on to something."

"Does that mean you're going to let me take control next time we're getting hot and heavy?"

"Hot and heavy?" I feel him shake his head. "Fucking cute."

I curl into him more. "For however long you'll let me, I'll be here if you need to discuss anything. I don't want you to think that because of what we're doing, I'm not willing to be there for you."

I let my words settle, hoping he hears the sincerity in them and doesn't read them as me being needy. I honestly hope that, if this ends tomorrow, he can still see me as someone to count on in his life. I'm not going to lie, though—just thinking that this could end fills my stomach with a lead weight.

"Nikki." He sighs, pressing his lips to my head. "What the hell are we doing?"

I shrug, the movement awkward with our positions. "No clue, Shane, but at least we're both on the same boat of confusion here in our muddled waters."

Nothing else is said as both of us are lost in our own thoughts. I have to wonder if maybe he's feeling the same way I am right now. Confused. A little hopeful, maybe. Or resigned to the fact that neither of us are really in control while we play this dangerous game.

All I know is, this doesn't feel even a little fake.

Shane

Her body relaxes against me. I keep my eyes trained on the fan, watching as the blades turn, blanketing our bodies with cooler air. Inside, though, I'm on fire. Not because I just came hard—though there's no doubt in my mind that I just came harder than I have ever before. No, I'm on fire because of the tiny little woman who hasn't once in almost a month done what I thought she would.

When I thought she would become clingy and start showing up around Dirty, she went silent and avoided me for three weeks. When I thought she would play games and act coy in her attraction to me, she gave me her awkward honesty. When I thought she would be a meek partner in getting my ex off my back, she fought back against her and *for* me. And when I thought my past would push her away, not wanting to be controlled, it only made her say things that made me question everything I thought about having a relationship and the job that I love.

She's thrown me for a loop, for sure, and I'm not sure what to do about it.

Do I want her? Fuck, yeah.

Do I think I could walk away tomorrow? Fuck, no.

Do I think she could handle my life? Well, if that isn't the million-dollar question … and I'm honestly not sure how to answer it. Not anymore.

And even more confusing of all, I'm actually hoping she's the one in the end to throw all my carefully voiced warnings back in my face.

She stirs, her leg coming up over mine and rubbing the heat of her sex against my thigh, and I wait while she settles. When she finally stops fidgeting in her sleep and I hear my name leave her lips on a breath of air, something shifts inside me, and for the first time in a long damn while, I want something more.

All I know is, this doesn't feel even a little fake.

Chapter 17

Nikki

PULL MY CAR INTO MY spot, smiling and feeling as if I could take on the world. When was the last time I woke up on a Monday—when it wasn't summer break—and felt excitement for the day ahead of me? Don't get me wrong; I love how rewarding my job is. It gives me satisfaction beyond words, but something is completely different today and it has everything to do with my time with Shane.

When he dropped me off at my apartment two weeks ago, the Sunday afternoon after our first 'date,' neither of us seemed happy about parting ways. He walked me to my door, made sure I was safely inside, and then kissed me goodbye. We made plans for the next day, and ever since, it feels like we're slowly becoming inseparable. One thing's for sure—none of the dates we've had since seem to be for anyone else's benefit than our own.

And I've been riding the high every day since.

"Ms. Clark," I hear the second I walk into the faculty entrance. "If you don't mind, I'd like to have a word."

"Of course, Mrs. Worthington," I answer, keeping the smile on my face despite the fact that I know our headmaster has never liked me and this can't be good.

It's early. I'm always early for work. Being late is something I go out of my way to avoid. There aren't any students here, thankfully. I keep my back straight, head forward, and follow the clicking of my headmaster's short heels. Her gray hair is pulled back into a bun low on her head, but it looks so painful, I subconsciously reach up and push my loose hair behind one of my ears.

Her secretary, Mrs. Brown, gives me a sympathetic smile, and I know, I just know, that this isn't going to end well.

"Close the door, Ms. Clark."

My hand shakes with a nervous tremor as I reach out and shut the heavy wood door, enclosing us in silence. When I turn, I see that Mrs. Worthington has already sat down at her desk with her hands folded in front of her. She keeps her narrowed eyes trained on me while I move away from the door and place my schoolbag next to one of the visitor's chairs and sit. My black slacks dig into my stomach, making me hyper aware that I might puke at any moment.

"Do you know why I asked you in here?"

It's on the tip of my tongue to correct her and point out that there wasn't any asking about it, but instead, I mutely shake my head.

"As I'm sure you're aware, your contract with us is very

specific about"—she pauses, one brow arching and lips pursing before continuing—"the way you conduct yourself outside school hours. We have a certain standard that we at Rosefield will uphold at all costs. Do you know how I spent my valuable time the past week, Ms. Clark?"

I shake my head, my palms sweating and my heart pounding. "No, ma'am," I answer honestly, not sure what she's getting at but feeling the dread of what's to follow all the same.

"No, I imagine you wouldn't," she bluntly continues. "I'm going to be very honest with you, if you don't mind?" She pauses for me to respond but clearly didn't actually want the words from me because she continues before I can even get a word out. "I didn't want to hire you. The board, however, thought we needed some fresh, young, and quite frankly, inexperienced minds. I felt differently, but I had hoped you would prove me wrong, and that, perhaps, you could actually give us something here at Rosefield that we hadn't had. It seems, however, that my concerns about your level of professionalism were justified."

"I don't understand," I fret, confusion mixing with my nerves.

"Allow me, then. Did you have an incident two weekends ago? One where there was a very public altercation that ended up with the police being called?"

My stomach drops. Never, not in a million years, did I imagine that I would end up in this situation. I don't *get* in trouble. Not once in my life have I been in a situation like this, and it's completely throwing me for a loop. I don't know what to say or how to convince a woman who has never liked me that I am not the villain here. That what happened isn't what she thinks.

"I can see by your reaction that you're starting to understand why you're here right now."

"Mrs. Worthington, please, it's not what you think," I plead, shifting my body so that my bottom is almost off the chair. I can hear the desperation in my voice, but if she can, she isn't showing any outward signs of it. "I was defending myself."

She clicks her tongue, scorn and something that looks a lot like disgust clear in her study of me. "Tell me, do you think that it's acceptable for you to be engaging in public brawls, food fights, and public displays of affection?"

"It wasn't like that," I attempt again, trying to get her to understand it wasn't some filthy altercation like she's making it out to be. "My ... my boyfriend and I were just trying to enjoy our dinner, and well, the woman who's been causing him some issues happened to be there and caused a scene. Shane, my boyfriend, defused the situation as quickly as possible."

Something that sounds somewhat like a laugh comes from Mrs. Worthington, but her scowl only deepens. "There is zero tolerance for that kind of behavior. Do you know how it makes Rosefield look when a member of our faculty is involved in such ... distasteful behavior?"

"Please, Mrs. Worthington, you have to understand, the only thing I'm guilty of is protecting myself."

She shakes her head, moves from her stiff position, and reaches down. I see her reach into a drawer and pull out some paperwork. When she places it in front of me, the dread that had been climbing and clawing up my spine explodes, and it takes everything inside me to keep from breaking down.

"Do you recognize this?"

"Yes, ma'am," I wheeze.

"And you understand what this is now, just as you did when you signed your contract three years ago?"

I swallow a thick lump of emotion and nod, incapable of anything more.

"It's unfortunate that the board had to learn that I was, in fact, correct in my reasoning for not wanting to bring such a young and inexperienced teacher on because you lack the moral compass of someone more mature, Ms. Clark. However, they've decided to ignore my recommendation of letting you go in favor of a probationary period. Until I feel that it can be lifted, you'll have a board member present during all your classes. Make no mistake; we will continue to investigate the complaint filed against you by another member of staff, and if we find we're unsatisfied with the reality of the events in question, you will be let go without appeal. Do I make myself clear?"

Mutely, I stare at her. There is so much I want to say. Conflicting words trying to push their way past my lips. I want so badly to tell her to take her pretentious position and stick it up her butt, but I don't. Reality is, she's got the upper hand because she's caught me unaware. The fact that my first inclination is to quit should tell me everything, though. Aside from the fact that I love the work that I do here, I *hate* the people I work with. I come here for the kids. As much as I love them, right now, at this moment, I'm not sure it's enough.

"I understand, Mrs. Worthington. I'm sorry for the trouble

I've caused you and the school." The words taste wrong coming out, but until I get my head on straight, I know it's what needs to be said.

"You'll need to sign this letter stating that I've explained why your behavior has put us in such an unpleasant position and that you understand the parameters of your probationary period as I've explained them."

When she holds a pen out to me stiffly, I again have to force myself not to react. I wrap my fingers around the pen, wanting to jam it in her nose, but instead, I sign my name and calmly place the pen down on her desk without speaking.

"Now that we've taken care of that, I think you'll understand that I'm going to have to ask that you use one of your personal days and go home. We wouldn't want the children to be affected by your attitude."

I want to scream at her, *what attitude?* I've kept my mouth shut and not stuck up for myself. I've let her railroad me with her highhandedness. I don't deserve this, but I didn't fight her. Instead of arguing, I wipe my palms on my pants and stand.

Mrs. Worthington doesn't move; her scrutiny follows my every movement, though. I can feel the tears burning behind my eyes. My nose stinging with the effort to keep them at bay. I won't give her the satisfaction of seeing that she's broken a little of my spirit. I don't look at her secretary on my way out. I avoid the main exit for faculty, and instead go out the front doors to avoid running into any of my co-workers. When I get my shaking hands to finally unlock my car, I toss my bag into the passenger seat and make quick work of getting my seat belt on and the car in drive before slowly accelerating out of the parking lot.

By the time I pull in to my complex and park in my normal spot in front of my apartment, I'm a blubbering mess. I managed to keep it together for all of five minutes after leaving the school before falling apart. If you looked up the definition of ugly crying, I would be the picture beside it. My hands grip the wheel, my eyes focusing on nothing in particular as the tears continue to fall. My chest is heaving as I gasp and sputter out my cries. Somehow, I manage to get myself calmed down enough to send a text to Ember even though she isn't the first name to pop in my mind. I can't think about my desire to have Shane here. Not right now. I'm confused enough after everything that happened this morning. No matter how much I want him here, I'm too vulnerable. After I hit send, my head drops to the wheel and I continue to lose myself in my desolation.

"Nik."

I shake my head, my forehead sore, and don't look up when Ember's voice filters through my sobs. I didn't hear my phone chime, unsure of how long it's been since I sent her a text. Knowing my best friend, she probably got here as quickly as she could, though, and it's just the tension in my body that's made me sore and not the time I've spent crying. My back hurts from being hunched over. My shoulders scream in pain from the tension holding my body tight as I cry.

"Nikki, you're scaring me," Ember whispers in a frantic tone.

I just continue to cry, not knowing what else to do and helpless to stop. So many thoughts going through my mind. Where will I live if I lose my job and can't find another right away? My savings would keep me here for a few months, but after that, then what? What will happen when I go to work tomorrow? Am I even *allowed* to go back in tomorrow? Mrs. Worthington didn't say I wasn't, but it was clear she doesn't want me there—heck, it was clear before this that she *didn't* want me there. Can I continue to work somewhere I'm not welcome, no matter how much I love my students? Is this my fault? Did I bring this on because of my harebrained fake relationship plan?

I hear Ember talking, but none of her words are registering while I continue to freak myself out more with the questions that just won't stop. I know I need to pull myself together, but for the life of me, I just can't. My chest is burning, my sobs hiccupping through my whole body with giant body wracking bursts.

When I feel an arm reaching between my hunched over body, I open my eyes and blink through the tears to find a forearm that definitely doesn't belong to my best friend. Do I move, though? No, I continue my pity party for one while blinking through the tears at the hairy, very manly forearm. The arm retreats after my seat belt unhooks, and then I watch as the arm moves under my legs before my body is being shifted. When another arm joins the fun and pulls me out of the car like a baby, I still don't move.

"Get her stuff, baby," Nate's voice calls to his wife, rumbling against my ear as I keep myself tucked close, knowing my two friends will take over and get me into my home. It feels wrong to be in Nate's arms, but I don't have the strength to think about why.

For the first time since leaving the school, something other than my own misery floats through my thoughts as he starts walking, his strong arms around my body, carrying me with no effort. It's not Nate who I want holding me. I feel safe, yes, but his touch is almost unwanted. How messed up is that? I've known Nate for over half of my life, yet his strong arms offer no comfort when I'm craving another's touch. It's my 'boyfriend'—the same 'boyfriend' who's made no secret from the beginning that I shouldn't get attached—who I want.

Right or wrong, I want him.

I almost texted him before Ember. The only thing that kept me from sending a text to him and not her, though, was the reminder he didn't want anything *real,* and my problems are just that … real. Like it or not, wanting him or not, a fake boyfriend shouldn't be the one to dry my tears.

I peek through my eyes and see Ember rushing ahead of us. Nate keeps his silence, holding me tightly as he follows his wife up the stairs like he isn't carrying a full-grown woman. He waits while she uses her key to my apartment to open the door, swinging it open and holding it so that Nate can pass through while tossing the keys into her purse. He walks to the couch and sits down. I wait for him to relax his hold and let me up, but he doesn't. Nate's known for being a little … strange in the things he does for the women in his life, but holding his wife's best friend like a baby needing comfort is a new one.

"Nik," Ember fusses, leaning down over us and placing her face as close as she can. Her concern written clearly all over her face. "Please talk to me. Tell me what's wrong."

"I don't know what to do," I gasp, words finally bursting free as more tears fall.

"Is it Seth? Did Seth do something?"

I shake my head, hitting my forehead against Nate's chin as I do so. I shift my gaze and look at him. "You can let me go." I sniffle, trying to climb free.

"You're fine, sweetheart," he replies gruffly, tightening his arms and forcing me to stay.

"Start from the beginning, Nik. I don't know how to help you if you don't tell me what happened. I'm going out of my mind with the worst possible scenarios," Ember continues, grabbing my hands and holding them tightly.

I sniff, feeling my throat burning, and then my mouth opens and the words start tumbling out. Everything that happened the other weekend at dinner with Shane between us and Lacey. The conversation between my boss and me this morning at the school rushing forth after that. I don't know if she can understand a word out of my mouth, though; my hysterical voice thick with emotion and shaky with helpless desperation. I'm powerless to do anything else but blubber my way through it.

"That bitch!" Ember screams when I stop talking.

"Which one?" Nate asks, still not releasing me.

"I can get up," I tell him, again, my voice hoarse and weak.

"Humor me," he answers oddly. One thing I know is that I just can't deal with trying to figure him out right now.

I look over at Ember and find the expression on her face just as odd as Nate's request. Not having the energy to analyze what the two Reids are up to, I just relax in his hold and listen to Ember while she starts to rant and fume over the two women who have turned the euphoric high I felt as I began the day this morning into a big pile of poo.

"Can she even do that?" Ember screeches, coming to an end of her raging chatter.

"Who?" I ask, not really keeping up with her.

"That bitch you work for! She can't just put you on some ludicrous probation with a babysitter. You're better than that, Nicole Clark. I told you the same thing when you took that hoity-toity job full of insane rules, and I'll remind you now; that whole place is full of snobs who do nothing but look down their noses at anyone they feel isn't their screwed-up version of perfect. The only thing that's good about that place is the kids—well, the ones too young to be tainted by their parents' entitlement. I've seen some of those older kids, and let me tell you, they're just as bad as the adults around there."

I deflate more. "She can, Ember. She's right; I signed my contract knowing there was a morality clause attached to it. What happened falls under that moral turpitude clause. My actions were in public, and even though I didn't start it—or instigate how it escalated—I still played my part by standing up for myself instead of walking away. That, to her and the board, is no better than taunting her. It doesn't matter who is right or wrong. To my boss and the school board, I'm an extension of Rosefield even when outside the school hours, and that's all there is to it."

"So quit," she finally says as if that's the most easy and logical of answers.

A bark of laughter erupts from me. "And do what? Sell my body on the street corner to pay the bills and keep a roof over my head?"

Nate's body shakes with silent laughter.

"No, silly. That's gross. At least, if you're going to sell your body, be a high-end whore and not the kind who stands on corners. Plus, that's illegal in Georgia, and I'm not letting my best friend move to a state that allows it."

This time Nate jars my body when he starts roaring with laughter. He's the kind of person who laughs with every part of their being, and with him holding me tight, my head keeps bouncing against him as he continues.

"She wasn't even that funny," I drone, trying to get off his lap—again. "Seriously, can you let me go? I feel better really. Or I did until your laughing started making me feel like I would be motion sick."

"Just another second," he answers with a smile, his eyes doing the laughing he stopped vocalizing.

I open my mouth to argue, but close it when my front door bursts open, slamming against the wall behind it with so much force that it doesn't bounce back because the doorknob is stuck in the drywall. I blink in confusion at the door, then over at the fuming man standing in the doorway with his fists clenched and his body tense, and then back at my door.

"You're going to fix that," I tell Shane halfheartedly. What is he even doing here? And why the heck is he so angry?

He stomps into the apartment. I look over at Ember to see her smiling like a star-struck teenager with not one ounce of the confusion I feel on her pretty face. I look at Nate next to see him without any hint of the carefree humor he had just moments before. He looks almost … smug? No, that's not it. He's looking up at Shane with something that appears to be real close to a dare written all over his face. When I turn to regard Shane, though, I'm shocked at the venomous ire he's giving his best friend.

What the heck is going on here?

Chapter 18

Shane

MY PHONE STARTS RINGING THE second I step out of the shower. I ignore it and continue drying off, taking my time with my mind on a whole lot of everything. I didn't sleep for shit last night. It didn't have anything to do with being unable to sleep because I was *awake* and everything to do with wanting the company of the woman I could still smell on my sheets. I can't remember the last time I slept as fucking good as I did when she was here with me, and like it or not, I wanted to experience it every time she wasn't here. It's been like that for two damn weeks. If she wasn't here or I wasn't at her place, I couldn't sleep.

After knotting the towel around my hips, I walk into my room and over to the ropes that I had avoided putting away. We've used them so much that they're becoming a permanent fixture to my room. Their reminder today only taunting me with the memory of Nikki's body as she comes apart at my hand. With a sigh, I pick up the ropes, determined to take control over my cravings. Wrapping them up with care, I tuck them back into the drawer on my nightstand. The second my hand pushes the drawer closed, my phone goes off again. With a sigh of annoyance, I walk around my bed to where my phone is charging on the other nightstand.

"What's up?" I greet after seeing the caller on the display.

"It's Nikki," Nate answers, the normal playfulness that he seems to carry around with him completely gone. While it's not abnormal for him to get like this when work is on his mind, something in his tone makes me stand a little straighter.

"What the fuck does that mean?"

"Fuck, man, I don't know. Em just called me in a panic after Nikki sent her a text. I was right around the corner, so I rushed back home. After handing me Quinnie, she was out the door quicker than I could blink. Luckily, my mom was on her way over already, so when she got there, I left her to watch the baby and I'm on my way to Nikki's place."

"Is she hurt?" I blurt as I rush into my closet, not even looking at what I'm grabbing.

"Don't know. Like I said, Em didn't give me much. I called her when I left the house, and she just said Nikki won't talk to her. That she just keeps crying. Fuck, Shane, I've seen that girl upset before, but she's never had trouble telling Em what was wrong. It's not like her to just fucking shut down."

My adrenaline spikes and I start to move on autopilot. I tell Nate I'll be there and hang up before he has a chance to say much of anything. The only thing on my mind is the woman who hasn't left my thoughts once in two weeks. Longer than that, if I'm honest. I don't even pay attention to the clothes I'm pulling on, jamming my feet into my shoes before grabbing my wallet and keys, my phone still held tight in my palm.

As I reach for the front door, my phone rings again, causing my heart to race and my breath to come in short pants. When I see my sister's name on the screen, I feel a little relief knowing it isn't Nate calling me back with more shit. Unfortunately, I know I can't just ignore the call. Libby worries and won't stop calling until I answer. Always and without fail. Doesn't matter what time of the day it is or what I could be doing, she won't stop until she gets me.

"Libs," I say in lieu of a greeting, slamming my front door and locking it without thought.

"What's wrong?"

"Nothing, mon petit ange[8]." It takes a Herculean effort to keep the panic from my voice, not wanting to freak her out. The same panic I haven't felt in a long fucking time—not since our mom got sick did I feel this helpless worry. I hate it. Hated it then and I really fucking hate it now. It's a big part of my control issues—according to the head doctors, that is.

"Who exactly do you think you're talking to, Shane?" she snaps. She hates when I keep things from her, too. Just like when I ignore her calls, keeping her in the dark never fails to piss her off. If I had been of sound mind, I would've been more careful to keep her from knowing I was agitated.

"Liberty," I stress.

"Don't Liberty me, mister. You sound like an animal. All

8   little angel)

growly and stuff. Don't lie to me and tell me you're fine."

"Growly isn't a thing."

"It is *so* a thing."

"Liberty."

"Shane."

I drop into my car and pinch the bridge of my nose before starting the engine and reversing out of my driveway with my phone between my shoulder and my ear. I love my sister, I do, but right now, I don't have the patience. Normally, she would have me smiling and feeling nothing but a break in the normal manic way I worry about mapping out every minute of my day to avoid surprises. Fuck, I hate surprises. Until recently, there has never been another person who could calm the beast of control that drives me.

But, today, all I'm worried about is Nikki.

All I can think of is that she needs me.

All I want is to get her in my arms and let the feeling of her heartbeat against mine reassure me that she's okay.

All I feel is worry for her, and anger that she didn't fucking call *me*. How fucked up is that for all the talk I had about this not being more than our dangerous game?

"Je t'aime, petit ange," I tell her, working hard to keep my voice calm as I recite the phrase I've always used with her. *I love you, little angel.*

"I love you back. As far as I can see and then some. Even when you're being annoying and keeping something from me."

"I met someone," I confess, knowing deep down that I mean those words more than my sister could ever understand. "I met someone, and right now, she needs me. You caught me on the way out the door. Nothing's wrong; I'm just in a rush to get there."

"Is she okay?" she whispers, all that sass and fire doused.

I don't answer. How can I? I wasn't the one she called to her aid. "I don't know, Libby. I really don't know."

I picture my sister's face in my mind, needing something else to focus on other than the unknown I'm rushing to. She's the feminine version of me, so similar in looks that we could pass as twins. Dark hair, dark eyes, and strong features. However, she's delicate where I'm not. Petite to my much taller and bulkier build. When she worries, she frowns and looks like a mad Tinker Bell. When I worry, I break shit and look like a monster. Her whole face scrunches up with her concern in the most adorable way, and mine gets Hulk-like in rage. Control isn't the beast she took from our childhood—worry is.

"Look, Lib, I'll text you later, okay? Just let me get over there, reassure myself that she's okay, and then take care of whatever is wrong. I'll call you tomorrow?"

"Okay, Shane, but I want to meet her," she responds, clearly not happy about the time I'm asking for her to give me.

"Give me until tomorrow and I'll make it happen, okay?" And fuck me, but that isn't a lie. I actually want them to meet. The two of them are going to get along like long-lost friends. Liberty is impossible not to love—unless you're a bitch like Lacey—and Nikki doesn't even have to try for people to want to spend more time with her. She's infectious and fool on anyone who thinks she can be kept at arm's length. Including me. The fact I want them to get to know each other—something I didn't allow Lacey the privilege of for almost a whole year of dating—hits me right in the center of my denial.

Fake, my ass.

"Don't just tell me that and think you can pretend you didn't later on. You always keep the girls in your life from me."

I gruff out a laugh past the burn in my throat. "What girls, Libs?"

"Okay, not girls as in plural. But when you were dating your last girlfriend, I didn't meet her for forever. I don't want to meet this one months or even years from now because you have some weird phobia about me getting attached."

"It wasn't that long," I pause, rolling to a stop at a red light and narrowing my eyes. "And I don't have a fucking phobia!"

"Shane, I mean it. I want to meet the woman whose got my big strong brother acting so out of character."

"Dammit, Liberty. I told you that you will. I promise. Is that good enough?" She doesn't say anything; her silence thick and I know she doesn't believe me. Funny thing is, any other girl and she wouldn't be wrong but not Nikki. I meant what I said; I want them to meet. Probably more than Liberty does. "She's different, Libs. Take it at that and let me go so I can get to her."

A girly-as-fuck squeal comes over the line, and I roll my eyes, thankful for the reprieve from my thoughts because I'm not ready to figure out why Nikki is changing all my carefully constructed rules and plans.

"I'll call you tomorrow," I tell her. We say our goodbyes, and she lets me off the phone without any more arguments.

Living less than ten minutes from her apartment complex, I

pull in the second I disconnect the call from Liberty. All it takes is seeing Nate's truck parked like he rushed in for my breathing to start coming in shallow pants again. By the time I race up her steps two at a time, I feel like my skin is too tight. I see the same neighbor who always seems to be out here, glaring at me from his doorway the same way he always does when we find each other together on the landing. The fear I've had for Nikki since Nate's call, the inability to keep my composure, the anger that something could have hurt her … all of it pours through me, and I can only imagine I look nothing short of savage as I hold his gaze. The seedy looking motherfucker down the hall startles before backing into his apartment and shutting the door quickly. There isn't a chance in hell I'll be able to calm down until I know she's okay, not with this much shit roaring through me. Fucking hopeless. That's what I feel like right now.

My heavy steps to her door echo around me, filling my mind with their thumps. I reach out, grab her doorknob, and open her door with a quick burst of strength. I stand in the doorway with my fists clenched as I scan her small living room area. I'm not sure what I expected to find when I got here, but Nikki curled into my best friend's arms while he holds her was damn sure not one of them. I'm vaguely aware of Ember standing in the middle of the living room, but I can't look away from the woman with tear-stained cheeks and red eyes blinking up at me.

"You're going to fix that," she whispers with no real heat behind her demand.

I march into the room, more tension sliding into my body with each step. Nikki looks from Ember to Nate, and finally, up at me again. I don't move even though my hands are itching to take her from him and feel her against me. Instead, I let Nate know how I feel about finding my woman in his arms by focusing my cold, hard anger directly at him.

"Shane?" Nikki questions meekly, her voice shaking.

"Get out of his lap, chèrie." When she doesn't move, my chest fills with air as my control splinters even more. "Now!" I bark, still not looking away from Nate's eyes.

"I've been trying!" she yells, wiggling and trying to get up.

Nate, the asshole, just arches his brow, cocks his head, and throws down his challenge silently. One I have no doubt he planned the second he called me. He doesn't know the details of my relationship with Nikki, but I played right into his hand. He had no reason to doubt the relationship we've been portraying, but he's not stupid. I've been single for a long damn time, refusing to get close to another woman since my breakup with Lacey until now. I'm not stupid, and neither is he. It's his fucked-up way of forcing me to see things around me even if he didn't know I was resisting the pull before now.

When she finally stands, almost falling from his lap when he continued to make her work for it without help, he leans back against the couch and puts his hands behind his head. Not looking away from me. I shake my head, stepping closer to him and leaning down. He's not a small man, but sitting on her couch the way he is and with me standing, I've got the upper hand.

"I see you holding her again, and I'll fucking rip your arms from your body. Friend or not, Nate."

He looks smug. Yeah, I played right into his hands, and I

couldn't care less.

"It's like that?" he asks after a beat of silence.

"It's past that," I counter, the truth to my words settling deep.

"Understood." He nods, leans to the side, and looks past me. "Em, you know what to do, baby."

Not willing to give Nate any more of my time with his shit, I turn to Nikki. She's standing with her arms wrapped tightly around her stomach—protectively—and I fucking hate it. Her face is blotchy, red, and swollen from her tears—hitting something deep inside me that no one has ever penetrated. Her mascara making her tears run black as a few slip free, only highlight her blue eyes more. Only, they're dull, void of the normal bright happiness that is always there. It's completely gone. Right then, the rest of the mess inside me shifts, and I know I won't leave here today until I get it back where it belongs. The madness inside me no longer without cause, it's focused on protecting and healing whatever is causing her turmoil.

"Come here," I stress calmly, holding her gaze.

She shakes her head, her arms tightening around her. I make myself a promise, right then and there, to do whatever it takes never to see this strong and caring woman like this again. Fuck the rules.

"Nicole." I throw my weight into that one word, hoping to reach another part of her—the part that submits to me every time I've asked her to—just by saying her name in the same tone I use in the bedroom. The one that makes it clear she doesn't want to pick this moment to test the waters by denying what I'm demanding of her.

She moves, her feet shuffling. I tune everything out around us, ignoring the sounds of Ember moving around Nikki's apartment. Ignoring the gaze of my good friend. My eyes only for the woman who I need to reassure myself is okay more than I need my next breath. The one I'm hoping needs my touch as much as I need hers—even if she hasn't come to the same conclusion as I have.

"Hi," she whispers a moment later, her arms still holding herself protectively as she looks up at me.

I scan her face, the small cut from when she bumped her head a few weeks ago just a memory. The redness from Lacey's fist long since faded, luckily though, it had never been bad enough that some makeup couldn't cover it. My gaze drops, taking in every inch of her. When I'm satisfied she isn't harmed physically, I allow myself to take a deep breath and close my eyes as some of the tension leaves my body. Some, not all. A tiny fraction of my sanity returns—again, some, not all—and when I open them again and see her beautiful but sad face looking up at me with a hint of worry, I let go. Years of learning how to hide my feelings from others falls away. Decades of needing to keep surprises from popping up around me no longer important. At this moment, I'm just a man looking at the woman twisting him up in knots, not even bothered by it in the least.

She jumps when I move, but when my arms settle around her body, she melts into my hold. She wiggles her arms out from between our bodies. I don't make it easy on her, not willing to loosen my hold, but when she gets them free and wraps them around my back, clenching my shirt tight in her small hands, I relax for the first time since Nate called me. Her heartbeat races against me. I dip my head, press my lips to her cotton covered shoulder, and continue holding her in silence, just breathing her in.

"What are you doing here?" she asks, her voice muffled against my chest. "Shane," she continues when I don't answer or release her.

I don't want her out of my arms, but I can't just stand here holding her all day, either. I give a little slack but keep my arms circled around her body. She blinks up at me. Fuck, she's perfect. Even looking like she does now, she's the most beautiful woman I've ever seen.

"Why are you crying?"

"I'm not," she lies pointlessly, seeing that her eyes are still full of unshed tears.

"You aren't?" Fuck me, but my lips twitch. How she has the ability to knock me to my knees one second, and in the next breath, make me forget anything and everything … except how much I enjoy this unpredictable beauty.

"Nope. My eyes are just sweating."

"Nikki," I groan, powerless to her charms as my body relaxes even further, and a small grin pulls at my mouth.

"I'm okay," she says immediately, without probing for the re-assurance I can feel with her this close.

"I know that now. Tell me what happened."

A million different scenarios had been pinging around in my mind since Nate's cryptic call, but the last thing I had anticipated was everything she's telling me. On top of my concern for her feelings, I feel nothing but fucking guilt for the part I played in what happened to put her in this position in the first place. All because we were playing that dangerous fucking game.

"I really am okay, Shane. I just had a little trouble processing it all," she assures me.

"I'm sorry." I hold her gaze, wanting her to see the sincerity in my words. I leave the rest hanging between us … I'm sorry for putting her in that position just to put on a show for my ex. It didn't feel right when Lacey started her shit that night, but I let Nikki take the lead, ready to jump in if she needed me—which she never did. It's easy to look back now and play the what-if game by saying I should have stepped in even if she could take care of herself.

"It's not your fault, tiger," she assures me with a wink, trying to lighten the mood by resuming her silly pet name game.

"We can discuss where the blame falls in detail later, mon co-libri," I mutter, dipping my head and placing a soft kiss on her lips before pulling away. Her body gets heavier in my hold when our mouths touch as she surrenders to me. "You scared the shit out of me."

"*I* didn't do anything. I'm still not even sure how you ended up here, Shane."

I shift our bodies so her back is to Nate and Ember and bring my lips to her mouth. I don't look over at the other two people in the room, but I also don't want them to see her reaction to my touch. That soft look that takes over her beautiful face when she yields to me completely. That is mine.

"I'll show you how I feel about not being the first person you called when you needed someone later. When we're alone. Do you understand me, Nicole?" I keep my tone low, for her only, and I'm rewarded a moment later when her face gets even softer than before. I pull her deeper into my arms, pressing my cheek to hers and closing my eyes.

"Yes," she breathes.

"Tell me, did you even think of calling me?" I question, my voice even lower, not willing to give our audience more of a show than they're already getting.

Her breath hitches, sensing the vulnerability I'm giving her by asking that in the first place. She doesn't call me on it, but instead, she nods, her smooth as silk skin caressing my cheek while she confirms. Her arms wrap around me even tighter, pressing our bodies as close as they can get. I harden slightly, closing my eyes and trying to calm down enough that I can let her go.

When I open my eyes and see Ember and Nate on the couch with a bowl of popcorn between them while they watch us with unabashed fascination, I don't even have to keep trying to kill my erection. Nope, they take care of it without trying. With Nikki safe in my arms, what is left of my tension drains from my body, and a moment later, I have to tighten my hold on her as my laughter takes over.

"Our friends are insane, chèrie," I joke, turning her so she can see what I'm laughing at. She joins in, and I lose a little of my anger toward Nate for being here holding her when it should've been me. Not when he's helping put that smile on her face and that brightness back in her eyes just by being the crazy bastard he is.

"Yeah, honey, they are," she answers through her giggles. Her endearment slicing deep and burrowing even deeper.

"Oh, Nate!" Ember squeals.

"Hush, wife. It's getting good."

She takes a handful of popcorn and tosses it in his face.

He just picks up a piece from his lap and keeps his gaze on us. "So this thing is serious?"

"I told you it was!" Ember complains, jerking her elbow into his side.

"I didn't believe you, baby, but now, I'm thinking I do."

"You knew it was happening, Nate," I tell him, sobering at his seriousness.

He nods. "Well, that's true. You see, I'm in a tough spot here, man. You're my best friend, and I naturally don't want to see you get hurt, but the woman in your arms means something not just to my wife but to me, too. She's family, has been since Em and her swapped friendship bracelets when they were scrawny little pre-teens. So let this be your warning … if you hurt her, friend or not, I'll make sure you can't send any more of those dick pics you seem fond of, again."

I give a brief jerk of my chin, respecting the fuck out of him for saying something.

"Right," he calls out, standing and dusting his hands on his jeans before looking over at his wife. "Woman, to the house!"

"But," Ember interjects, looking back and forth between us and her husband. "We're going to miss the best part."

Nate grunts and lifts her off the couch, placing the half empty bowl of popcorn on the cushion. "Which is exactly why we're leaving. You want the best part, I'll give it to you later, but you aren't watching that happen here." He drags her to the door, opens it, and looks over his shoulder, his cocky attitude back and mirth dancing in his eyes. "Wear protection, children. I'm not ready to be a grandparent."

Then they're gone, and I've got my girl in my arms laughing uncontrollably. I'll take that over her 'sweating eyes' any day.

Chapter 19

Nikki

NOTHING IS FAKE ABOUT THIS anymore ... not one thing.

I'm still laughing at Nate's parting shot when Shane takes my face in his hands. The warmth of his palms press against my neck while his thumbs sweep a soothing touch against my cheeks. The look in his eyes, though—that's something I hadn't seen before. Not from him. He's a man who holds his feelings back from others behind his mask of control. I swallow the thickness from my throat and wait, wait for him to lead. I'm terrified this might be the end of fake us, but at the same time, I'm oddly hopeful it's ending for a different reason than us not being together.

"What's going through your mind?" he questions softly.

How do I answer that? If I go with the truth, he might be gone quicker than he came, but... he also might not.

"Nikki, say it."

I know, at that moment, nothing gets past this man. I started this between us five weeks ago. I jumped in, never thinking about what would happen when we fed the attraction flaring brighter than fireworks when we were together. Even during the weeks I avoided him, I fed it. The past two weeks have only brought us closer. Who am I kidding; we're both fools if we believe it's even a little fake. There's no going back now.

"You."

"What about me, chèrie?"

I hold his eyes, the rich brown swirling with both golds and greens, something I hadn't added to my mood index of Shane Kingston yet.

"You're acting like a real boyfriend," I finally say, my voice the barest of whispers.

Bracing myself for the end I'm so sure is about to come to this, he shocks the crap out of me by laughing.

"No, mon colibri, that I am not."

"What does that mean? The mon colibri you always call me."

His eyes roam my face and a tiny smile forms on his full lips. His hold adjusts slightly, allowing him to step closer and tip my head back slightly before he bends down and looks me directly in the eyes. "You mean you didn't look it up yet?" he challenges, looking so freaking delicious with this playful side.

I shake my head.

"It means"—he starts, eyes dancing and minty breath warming my lips—"my hummingbird." He presses a kiss to my lips, quick and delicious, before continuing, his lips moving against mine while he speaks. "When you're in my arms, my touch driving you mad, and you start that hum deep in your throat, I'll never stop trying to make that hummingbird I swear is trapped inside your chest go off. I've never heard anything like it."

Holy crap. What am I supposed to say to that? Nothing. There's absolutely nothing I can say, but tons that I need to.

"The first time I felt that hummingbird vibrate against my naked skin, you became mine, and there wasn't a fucking thing fake about it, Nicole."

My eyes widen. "What ... what are we ... Shane?"

"Speechless?"

"You told me you don't do relationships," I finally wheeze out.

One corner of his mouth tips, giving him a wolfish grin that makes my heart pound even quicker.

"Apparently, I can be wrong from time to time."

I pull myself from his hold and pace my tiny living room area. I look up, see him waiting patiently with that damn seductive grin, and narrow my eyes before looking down and quickening my steps. What the heck does that mean? He can be wrong? Does that mean that we are ... real? Just like that? After all his warnings that I shouldn't want more from him, he is giving it to me now?

"What changed?" I ask, stopping and shaking my head at him, unable to do anything else.

He grunts, raking his fingers through his hair. I study him, the disheveled appearance that I've never once seen, and another piece of the puzzle slides into place. He really was concerned—for me.

"Everything," he finally answers, closing the distance between us and taking my mouth in a deep kiss.

Everything we aren't saying out loud is screamed with this kiss. My hands push between us and hold him close, giving just as good as he is. Our movements are fueled by desperation. Every worry I had before he got here falls from my body, his touch filling the painful holes that had been drilled into my mind earlier. The only thing that matters right now is the two of us.

"Mien," he says against my lips, panting just as hard as I am.

"What's that mean?"

"Mine," he answers without pause.

"Shane, I don't understand. What does this mean?"

His forehead presses against mine, eyes searching, while we continue to hold each other close.

"Earlier, when Nate called, I felt myself splinter, Nikki." He sighs. "There I was, not even sure what the fuck was happening, but knowing that you were upset, I was done for. All it took was two phone calls, and everything I thought I could keep in some neat little pretend box was blown to hell, and instead of the panic I normally would have felt jumping into a tornado of the unknown, I needed you in my arms more than any of that. There I was, the reins of control ripped from my hands, and for once in over thirty years, I didn't give a shit. I cared more about fixing whatever had hurt you than I did about myself."

"Shane," I utter, his words slamming into my heart irrefutably.

"Do you want me?" he questions, eyes searching. Exposed

fully to me.

"You know I do, Shane."

"Then that's all that matters."

"Shane! How can you, Mr. I Don't Do Relationships, sit there and say us wanting each other is all that matters? Our chemistry, our want, has never been in question. This whole thing was built on us wanting each other."

His chest moves against mine as he takes a deep breath then lets it out slowly. "I'm not saying we have it all figured out, but until we do, there isn't any more fake discussing what we have. *That*, chèrie, is all that matters."

"This is insane."

"No, it's just what was meant to be."

"Just like that?"

"No," he answers, earning a frown. He tips his head up and presses his lips softly against the skin between my brows. "Not just like that. I'm not saying we just pretend the reasons that we came together are fixed and gone—we both know it isn't that easy—but from this moment on, we explore us without the bull-shit attached to it. When we go out, it's for us and not anyone else. I think we can both admit it's been like that from the get-go. We figure out the very real us without any rules."

"Real. No rules?" I muse, my heart racing. Is this for real?

"None."

"And what happens when the reasons that brought us together in the first place are finally gone?"

"Then there are two fewer people we have to waste our time thinking about."

I snort. "I don't know what to say, Shane. An hour ago, I was faced with the possibility of losing everything I had worked hard to achieve in my career. Now you're asking me to place the very raw feelings I'm left with into a real us without anything more than that? You made it clear from the beginning that this," I stress, pointing between us, "would never be more. How can you be so sure you want to change your mind now when you were just as sure five weeks ago that we would just be a ruse?"

"Because, Nikki, five weeks ago, I didn't know what I do now."

"And what's that?"

"What having you feels like."

"Now who's playing a dangerous game?" I breathe.

His face gets soft, not hiding the admiration in his gaze. "The best rewards come to those who are brave enough to pick up the dice and roll without knowing what they'll land on, mon colibri," he croons.

Knowing what that endearment means now brings a whole new level of hot damn to the things he says. He was hot when he whispered the French words only he knew the meaning of before, but now, he's downright lethal for my system after explaining them to me.

"Is this when you tell me not to fall in love with you?" I finally ask, trying to lighten the heaviness.

His eyes dance as his hands reach out to pull me closer, and then he throws my heart into overdrive. "No. This is when I tell you I'm going to make you do just that."

Well, holy heck batman.

It wasn't even eleven o'clock in the morning, and here I was answering the door for takeout and preparing to spend the day with my now very real boyfriend. My school clothes from earlier had long since been pulled with care from my body, joining the sweats and faded tee shirt that Shane had on when he got here earlier. My mind still swirling from his revelations about us and what that meant for the future. After basically telling me he would make me fall in love with him, he spent the next two hours showing me a tender side to his lovemaking—no doubt, he was still very much in control of every minute that made up those two hours, but something was different this time—something *real*.

"Your phone's going off again."

I jump, swirl around, and hold the Chinese food bag to my chest. "You need a bell!"

He chuckles, the deep tones not rusty like they had been the first time he was here all those weeks ago.

"Why do you look like that?" I question, squeezing between him and the wall to walk into the kitchen to get the plates.

"Like what?"

"Like a man who didn't just get lucky and wants some."

He steps into the room, and I feel him move behind me, the sweats he had pulled back on the only thing keeping his erection contained as he presses himself against my back. He moves my hair until it hangs over one shoulder and starts trailing kisses up my neck. One hand comes around me until his large palm is pressed against my stomach, pulling me against him. Plates forgotten, I brace against the counter with both hands. He just gave me four delicious orgasms, and already, I want more.

I open my mouth to beg for just that when he holds my phone up in front of me. "*He's* called five times."

"Huh?"

Shane's chest moves against my back. Even though I heard the hardness in his voice, he laughs at me and my reaction to his touch. He knows what kind of power he holds, but he doesn't get cocky about it.

"Your ex," he clarifies.

"So? What about him?"

This time, Shane doesn't laugh. He moves, setting the phone on the counter, and uses both hands to turn me to face him. I don't look away, letting him see the truth in my eyes.

"It doesn't matter, Shane. You can't act surprised that he's stalkerish in his persistence when I never hid it from you."

"Fuck, Nik, I didn't say you did. I just don't get the nonchalant attitude about his calls."

"Well, I've tried for months to tell him to leave me alone. I've tried telling him that he and I wouldn't ever be a thing again. I've tried telling him I had a new boyfriend. Nothing works, so no, I'm not surprised he's still calling."

"This is normal?"

I nod. "Has been for the past six or so months, yes."

"You don't return his calls?"

"Yeah right, big boy." I snort.

"Why?"

"Why, what?"

"Why don't you call him back?"

"I think you need to sit down. Maybe eat something. Clearly, you're lacking sustenance if you're asking me that question."

"Let me rephrase," he says, lips twitching. "Why don't you call him back *now*?"

"Okay, handsome, I'll play. Why should I call him back *now*?" I ask, mimicking his stress on the last word.

His lips stop twitching and his smile forms. Devilish. Yeah, no doubt about it.

"Humor me."

I shrug. The last thing I want to do is have Seth encroach on my mood when it was finally turning around. However, I know Shane wouldn't ask me to do so if he didn't have a reason.

Picking up my phone from the counter, I bring up my missed calls and press 'Douche Lord.' Before I can bring it up to my ear, Shane's hand shoots out, and I watch as one long finger taps the speakerphone button.

"Nik Nac! About time!"

"What do you want, Seth?"

"You weren't at school."

I look up, my confused gaze clashing with Shane's angry one.

"I'm taking some time off," I tell him, not convinced that I'm lying, but I can worry about my job's future after this junk.

"I see. Well, want me to come over?"

"Why would—" I start to argue, but when Shane's devilish grin turns into a cold, calculating, evil smirk, the words trail off.

Then he shocks the crap out of me and mouths, "*Do it,*" to me.

"We can talk, babe. You've got time today without work and all. Didn't you always say that's why you couldn't talk? Always too busy."

Again, Shane's mouth moves. "*Do it.*" I shake my head. "*Trust me,*" he continues.

I close my eyes, take a deep breath, and welcome the pig into the wolf's den. "Sure, Seth. Come on over. We can talk."

The phone is out of my hand, call disconnected, and Shane's mouth is plundering mine. Straight up owning me. I'm honestly not sure at this moment who is the predator and who is the prey, either.

Chapter 20

Nikki

THE HEAVY KNOCKING ON MY front door makes me jump. Shane places his fork down and leans back, waiting and ready. I'm sure his every instinct is telling him to lead, but instead, he's waiting for me to take that role.

"Ten minutes. I figured he would have gotten here quicker than that," he adds, wiping his mouth and standing. He offers me his hand, helping me to stand from my chair. My lunch feeling unwanted in my stomach now as my nerves make me nauseous. "Trust me, Nikki."

"I will. I mean, I do. I do trust you, Shane."

Even through the hardness that he's holding himself, his touch is tender. "Nothing will ever touch you, Nicole. I mean it. You'll see that I'm worthy of that trust with time."

The knocking starts again, this time louder and impatient.

"You ready?"

I answer with a nod of my head. Wrinkles deepen in the corner of his eyes as he smiles a toothy grin at me. I stand mutely when he tugs his sweats lower on his trim hips, his deep V more pronounced and the fact he's not wearing underwear obvious. He shifts, pulls them even lower, and assesses his handiwork. Then he lifts my hands and pulls my fingers through his hair. He looks tussled and well loved, if I'm being honest.

"Kiss me, mon colibri. Kiss me and let your hummingbird purr."

Well, who am I to say no to that? As the knocking starts again, I run my hands through his hair again—without his help—and kiss him hard. When he pulls away, there's no doubt that he's a man who's been pleasured and used. I look down, his shirt swallowing me in size. My nipples hard against the cotton, pressing against the fabric, my piercings only highlighting them more. He rubs his knuckles against the stiff peaks, and I look back up.

"This will be the only time that another man sees what you look like right now. If it wasn't for the point that needs to be made, I would never let it happen, but when he takes a look at you and sees what you give me every time you welcome my touch, he won't be able to deny who and where you belong."

"Nik Nac!" I hear bellowed through the door, breaking the moment, followed by more pounding.

"Go open the door, Nikki."

I nod, walking over and placing my hand on the knob. After a calming breath, I flip the locks with my free hand and pull the door open.

Seth's rumpled appearance is the first thing I notice. Then I see one of the guys from my neighboring apartments. Thing Two, I think.

"Dude, shut the fuck up!" he yells at Seth. No, that's Thing Three. Thing Two sounds like a prepubescent boy.

"Fuck you!" Seth calls back.

I pop my head through the open doorway and give my neighbor a small wave. "Sorry about the noise. Won't happen again."

He looks at me briefly then glares at Seth. "Yeah, whatever."

"Don't look at my girl," Seth continues, ignoring me.

Thing Three just laughs. "Your girl? Right. Tell that to the other dude who got here earlier, dumbass." He flips Seth off then he's gone, door slamming in his wake.

"Hello, Seth," I tell him calmly, ignoring my strange neighbor. I assume he must have seen Shane earlier. "How are you?"

"What did that motherfucker mean?" he snarls, his cold eyes narrowing as he steps closer.

"Who knows?" I shrug, acting clueless even though my nerves are full blown now. "You wanted to talk, so come in and let's talk." I turn from the open door, walking into the middle of my living room. I look over at the kitchen, not seeing any sign of Shane. What the heck?

"Fuck, you look good, Nik Nac," Seth says, slamming my door; his words making me feel as if I'm cheating on Shane.

It takes everything in me not to cover myself more. I know Shane's shirt has me covered, but the way Seth is licking his lips and looking all over my body has me feeling sick. No, exposed. And … so very wrong.

"Look, Seth," I tell him, snapping my fingers when he

continues to peruse my body, eyes lingering on my chest. His eyes come up slowly, and he adjusts himself. Gag. "You wanted to talk, so let's hurry it up. I'm a little busy."

"Doing what, baby?" he questions, his tone sleazy.

"Me."

I'm not the only one who startles at Shane's hard tone. Seth jerks, rocking back on his heels and looks over my shoulder. I almost feel sorry for the guy. Almost.

"Who the fuck are you?!" Seth thunders. Gone is the lazy way he had slithered in moments before as he puffs his chest and stands taller.

Seth loved the gym when we were together. Part of what had initially attracted me to him had been his muscles. I'm not proud of it, but it's the truth. However, seeing him trying to match Shane in height and build, only to fail miserably, makes me see what I hadn't since he started to sniff back around me.

He's let himself go, and honestly, he looks terrible. His hard muscles softer. His abs gone and a small pouch in its place. Even his clothes seem to be too large in some places and too tight in others. For the life of me, I don't know how someone can change so much. Or how I hadn't seen it before now.

"It's real fucking cute that you want to act clueless when I know *my* girl's already told you about me."

Seth's eyes cut to mine, and I see the anger grow. "You told me to come over!"

I shrug, his accusation not mattering much to me since it's true; I had told him to come over—at Shane's request.

"You," Shane continues, stepping around me and placing his

body between me and Seth. The muscles on his back bulging. "You just can't take a fucking hint, can you? I know she's told you about me. Pretty sure she told you fucking weeks ago. I know before that she told you to leave her alone, but still, you kept trying to weasel your way in."

"She's fucking mine, asshole. Has been for years."

Shane's shoulders move, a bark of laughter sounding like a gunshot in my small living room. I push my fingers into the waistband of his gray sweats and press my forehead to his back, gripping the fabric like a lifeline.

"She stopped being yours when you fucked up. Not my problem, though, because of that, she was free to move on. She might have been yours at one point, bud, but I think we both know that stopped being true long before she found you fucking someone else."

"Bullshit!"

"Though," Shane sneers, "I can't for the life of me figure out why you would even think about another woman when you've got the best fucking one right at your fingertips."

I wish I could see Seth's face. The sputtering he's doing now, though, is enough to bring a smile to my face. Shane is *so* getting lucky for this.

"Is that why you're trying to get her back? Because you realized way too fucking late that you already had perfection?"

"You fucking prick. Perfection? Might as well be fucking a corpse."

Shane bellows out a laugh then, easing the all too familiar sting of Seth's words. "Bud, you fucking nuts? She lights up for me. All I have to do is crook my finger and fireworks. Not my fault you don't know what you're doing."

"Fuck you!"

"Uh, no. Here's what's going to happen, Seth. You're going to leave her alone. You won't call, you won't show up, and you'll forget this bullshit of trying to get her back. I'm not a man who shares … anything. I'm being nice right now because I feel like maybe you just weren't smart enough to get a fucking clue before now. I find out you didn't listen, and I can guarantee you won't get my kindness the next time. One thing I'm not is stupid. I know what I've got, and there isn't a chance I'm going to fuck it up like you did. Hear me?"

"She fucking asked me over, prick. Who's the stupid one?"

Shane reaches behind him, gently taking my wrist in his hand and giving me a small tug. "Chèrie, come."

I release his pants instantly, his honey-rich tone washing over me, my body remembering what happens when I do what he says when he's using *that* voice. He isn't the only one in the room who isn't stupid. My feet shuffle until I'm at his side then his arm is around me and my softness is pressed against his hard muscles.

"Have you been trying to get this man to leave you alone?"

"I have," I answer instantaneously, holding Seth's angry glare with a calm one of my own—nerves no match for Shane's soothing touch.

"Even before we were together, correct?"

"Yes, honey," I continue. Seth gets a little more fired at that. I tried, when we had been dating, to give him a cute name. Unlike Shane, who just laughs me off, Seth would get pissed. I doubt he misses the intentional jab.

"And after?"

"You know I did, Shane."

"Well, bud, you seem to be the one here who's confused. I'm trying to enjoy lunch with Nikki, and we have to deal with your calls because, yet again, you seem to forget you no longer have the right to place those calls in the first place. So before you try to use that bullshit on me, let it sink in that she invited you here *after* I asked her to."

"You know what?" he exclaims through clenched teeth, his hands thrown up in frustration. "The bitch isn't even fucking worth it!"

Shane's body gets tight, and I have a feeling he's done playing Mr. Nice Guy. He presses a quick kiss to my temple then I lose his warmth. His arm is gone from my shoulders, and he's on the move. Seth, the idiot, doesn't even realize how badly he's screwed up until it's too late. Shane's hand closes around his neck, and he pushes him into the wall next to my TV with enough force that two of my frames fall off the bookshelf on the opposite side.

"You were doing fine until you called her a bitch. When you leave here, remember this moment because I promise you if we have another run-in, it will end a different way. She isn't yours. Never will be again. Get it through your dumb-as-fuck skull and find someone else to fuck with. Nikki is off-limits—now and always. Is that fucking clear enough, you piece of shit?"

He ends his deadly calm rant with a jerk of his arm—the same arm holding Seth by the neck. His fingers white against Seth's neck and I know he isn't waiting for a verbal answer from him; there's no way he could get one judging by the way Seth's eyes are about to bug out of his head. After another stretch of silence, Shane must get what he wants because he releases him just as quickly as he pounced. Seth wavers on his feet, gasping for breath.

"Get the fuck out of here and remember what I said. You so much as breathe in her direction, and you won't even see me coming before it's too late."

He turns his back, giving Seth an even bigger proverbial middle finger by showing him that he doesn't think he's a worthy threat. By doing that, he makes it clear that Seth is nothing. It's the biggest insult you could have given a man like Seth. Shane's eyes are only for me and mine only for him.

Until Seth proves that he really is as dumb as I thought he was, heaving himself off the wall he had been hunched on to keep his footing while he caught his breath and taking a step forward. My eyes widen, but Shane just smirks.

Then he turns.

I flinch when he steps up, chest to chest … or something like that with the few inches he has on Seth.

"Fuck you," Seth grunts.

"No thanks, man. I got the best thing already warming my bed."

Seth's arm moves, and I cry out, but I should've known Shane didn't need my help. He ducks then comes back up with his arm already moving with him. His fist clocking Seth in the jaw with the force of his momentum blazing behind it. Seth's head jerks back, and he almost loses his footing.

"You won't best me. The next time you think that's a wise

move, I would think twice. Get the fuck out of here."

Seth drools some blood onto his shirt, looks over at me, and then before he can open his mouth, Shane has him by the collar and drags him to the door. He opens it, shoving Seth out. He trips and falls, landing with a bang against the wall opposite my door.

"Last time I'll say it. Nikki's moved on. You're not getting another chance because I'm not fucking going anywhere. You are going to forget about her; do I make myself clear?"

"Fucking crystal, asshole," he angrily says, spitting some blood onto the ground next to him. He looks over at me, opens his mouth, but Shane beats him to whatever he was about to say.

"Try me," he venomously sneers, the words cold, hard, and deadly calm.

Seth shakes his head, climbs to his feet, and starts walking away without another word. Shane shuts the door, engages both locks, and presses both his palms against the door before bowing his head and breathing deeply.

For a man who prides himself on his unshakable control, I can only imagine that—on top of what happened earlier—he's having a hard time with it all. My hands shake, but something deep inside me tells me that he needs me. And I'll do whatever it takes for the man who is quickly burrowing himself deep in my heart to work through the tightness in his stance—wildness in his eyes.

Chapter 21

Shane

THE ROARING IN MY EARS drowns out everything around me. I focus on my breathing, trying to fight the urge to follow that son of a bitch and kill him. If his words weren't enough to piss me off, just letting him see Nikki like that was a testament to my control. I don't want Nikki to see me like this, but she needs to … she needs to understand what happens when things around me start to get unraveled and they tangle something inside me. She needs to accept every part of me or all this talk about making the real thing work will be a bunch of shit if she can't.

By the time I'm calm enough that I trust my handle on things and know I won't chase after that motherfucker, a different kind of concern settles on my shoulders. What if she's scared of me? I can feel myself starting to get worked up again, but before I can get too far gone in my worry, I feel the gentle touch of her hand press between my tense shoulders. I hold my breath and wait to see what she does next. Her hand moves, crossing my right shoulder blade before dipping under my arm and across my chest. I look down, watching as she drags her petite hand across my chest before it settles … right over my racing heart.

And fuck me if that doesn't drain the tension out of my body instantly.

I drop one arm and lift my hand to hold her palm against my chest, closing my eyes as her touch soothes me.

"Shane," she whispers, her mouth close to my back and the warmth of her words hitting my skin. "Thank you, honey."

My eyes close, and I thank my lucky stars I played her dangerous game.

"Take what you need, Shane."

I snap my eyes open, her words slamming into me more powerfully than if a truck roared through her apartment and hit me at full speed with a full tank of nitrous. She can't understand what she's asking of me.

"Let me help, honey," she continues, her other arm coming up, placing her free hand on top of mine. "Take what you need," she repeats. "Sir, please. Use me."

"Fuck," I hiss, powerless to stop myself. I spin, catching her before her hands can fall completely to her side and lifting her off the ground and into my arms. Our mouths colliding, tongues meeting, as we feed the hunger we both have for each other. Our kiss isn't pretty but fuck if it isn't full of enough power to bring me to my knees.

Her hums start, and she rubs her pussy against my stomach.

Her thin panties not hiding how wet she is. My cock throbs and I deepen our kiss, growling against her mouth. She tries to move her hips again, and I pull my mouth away, looking into her dazed eyes.

"Who's in control?'

"You are, Sir," she answers immediately.

My ragged breathing hitches at her words. Needing a second, I release her, keeping my hands on her arms until she was steady enough for me to back away. If I take her now, it will be hard and unforgiving, something she doesn't deserve.

"Go to your room, Nicole. Get naked and wait for me. I want you on your knees with your ass in the air for me. Do you understand?"

She nods. "Yes, Sir. I understand."

"Do it. Don't move until I tell you what to do next."

She turns and stumbles slightly before righting herself and walking quickly the rest of the way. I take my time, needing to calm down. Cleaning up what was left from our lunch, I wash the forks we used before cleaning the table and counters. When the kitchen and her table are completely clean and bare of any reminders of our lunch, I face the hallway, wishing I had a clear view of her bed from where I stand. I still feel out of control and need to channel the turbulence I've felt since the call earlier this morning that brought me here. The same turbulence that grew insurmountably when her ex showed up. I don't want to hurt her—fuck, that's the last thing I want—but I don't think I have it in me to hold back right now. She couldn't have known what she was asking of me ... could she?

Her face filters through my mind. I recall what shifted behind her beautiful blue eyes moments before … it was more than desire. Yeah, it had been there, but it was driven by something a whole lot more commanding.

"She needs it too," I muse on a rush of air.

I don't even give myself a second to doubt what I know I saw in her eyes. My steps silent while I prowl toward her open bedroom, praying like fuck I find her ready for me. When I turn and enter her room, the sight of her with her ass in the air, bare pussy on display between her slightly parted legs, to offer me her body without shame causes me to grab my cock through my sweats to keep from coming on the spot.

I swallow the warm rush of saliva that makes my mouth water, her pussy wet and glistening in the sunlight streaming through her curtains. Walking around to the other side of her bed, I look at her face—eyes closed, lips parted, and hands clenched in the sheets.

"What's your safe word, Nicole?" I ask, her body jerking slightly.

Her eyes open, and she looks up at me without moving anything. "Red, Sir."

Fucking hell. She's perfect.

"I can't hold back, Nicole. I need you to understand that this will be hard and rough. I don't have it in me to be anything less."

"Use me, Sir," she answers softly.

That's all it takes. Just three words and I'm undone. She keeps her eyes trained on me, color hitting her cheeks as she waits for me to do just that.

I reach out, running two fingers down her spine, pausing at the top of her ass, not looking away from her. I can see how badly she wants to move, but she holds herself still. When I move my fingers again, dragging them to her asshole, she jerks slightly before stopping herself and gripping the sheets tighter.

"One day, mon colibri. Not today, but one day you will give me all of you." I softly press against the hole, not breaching, but letting her know without a doubt what I'm talking about. She surprises the hell out of me by pressing back against my fingertips, though, and as much as I like knowing she isn't against letting me take her there, I lift my hand away before smacking her hard against her cheek. "You'll get more when I tell you, Nicole. Remember that," I warn, rubbing the burn from her flesh. The sight of my handprint red against her pale flesh only feeds the hunger inside me. "Look at you, my mark on your skin. If I wanted to mark you, bruise you with my grip, and pink your skin with my strength, would you let me?"

Her head moves as she swallows, answering me on a breathy moan. "Yes … Yes, Sir. Whatever you want."

"Good girl," I praise. "You trust that I won't mark you for pain? That I won't harm you?"

"Yes, Sir."

I lift my hand and give the same hard smack to her other cheek. She pulls her lip between her teeth and clamps down on the flesh. I can see how close she is. I fucking love it. The buzz I feel is better than any drink could give me.

"This time, Nicole, don't hold yourself back. When you're ready to come, I want to hear it. I want to see your thighs soaked with your come. I want my ears to fucking ring. I want your neighbors to hear you, so clear through these walls that they can't help but get off on how much you love what I do to your body. Scream, chèrie. Scream loud and don't hold back."

Her eyes water, not with tears but with her overwhelming feelings, and she nods even though I know she wants to beg me to make my words true now.

"Later, I want you to call that bitch that thinks she's got a dick bigger than mine and turn in your resignation, do you understand?"

Her eyes shoot to mine, and I can tell she wants to argue. It's dirty, waiting for her to be this vulnerable to bring it up, but I know she won't argue when she's submitting to me, a fact I intentionally exploited. I'd do it again and again if I thought it was what needed to be done to protect her. I grab a handful of her ass and squeeze. "Think twice before you open that sexy mouth, Nicole. You'll do what I say, understood?"

She holds my gaze. Instead of fighting me, though, she nods. The blind trust she has in me is something no drug could beat the high of.

"You don't get my cock until I'm satisfied that you've come hard. You want me deep inside this pussy, you work for it."

Then I shift, drop on my knee to the mattress and spank her ass hard enough to earn a scream from her. Her hands jerk above her head, gripping the pillow above her. I alternate, her cheeks bright red, and pull the waistband of my sweats down until my cock is free and painfully hard. I grip the base, knowing I won't be able to hold back if I keep this up. The sounds coming from Nikki with each slap of my hand against her flesh making a little more come drip free from my cock each time the sounds of her pleasure pierce my ears.

I roll my tongue over my teeth, looking from her ass to see that I'm not alone. She was wet before I touched her, but she's drenched now. Unable to help myself, I move to stand at the end of the bed and take her hips in my hands. I bend my body at the same time I lift her ass in the air. Her arms straight, feet in the mattress, and when I've got her supported by my firm grip on her hips, I take her pussy and lick every drop of that wetness up. Not once giving her entrance the attention I'm sure she wants.

She screams every time I suck her clit, flicking it with my tongue while I pull at her flesh. I can feel her pussy as it clenches and flutters against my chin. She gives me what I want, her cries of pleasure fucking loud and echoing around us.

With one more swipe of my tongue, her flavor bursting in my mouth, I lift my face and drop her on the bed. She bounces once before shifting back to her initial position. Ass high, shoulders against the mattress, and hands fisting the sheets. Eager to please. I lick the rest of her wetness from my lips, her scent filling my nostrils, and without missing a beat, I flip her on her back. Her legs drop, opening herself up to me, and her tits bob as she sucks in deep breaths.

I hold her gaze, reaching out to pinch her nipple and teasing the bar pierced through it.

"Do you see how hard I am for you?"

"Yes, Sir," she pants.

"Never, Nicole. I've never wanted someone as much as I

do you." I tweak her nipple again then drag my hand down her stomach.

When my fingertips brush the soft curls on her sex, she whines. I click my teeth and still my movements.

"Don't keep your sounds from me." I lift my hand and smack her pussy. The wetness making the contact louder as it echoes around us.

She cries out.

My cock jumps.

Fuck, she's perfect.

Made for me.

My hand moves quickly before she can brace for it, and two fingers go deep. Her pussy clenches tight, and she screams my name on a whine. Then I curl my fingers and start pumping them. In and out, I drive her higher and higher. Her eyes close, and instead of making her open them again, I look down at my hand. I get closer to her body, my cock painful as I move, and press my free hand right above her mound and under her belly, her softness allowing me more control of what I'm after. When I'm satisfied, I press down and look back up at her at the same time I add one more finger, curling them with a deep thrust.

Her eyes snap open and collide with mine at the same time I hit that spot I wanted to claim. Her wetness gets louder as I pump my fingers, her cries of pleasure not once ebbing. Her eyes are frantic, not knowing what to do with the feelings I'm evoking in her. The panic grows until the pleasure takes her captive, and she screams louder than ever, coating my hand and the bed with her come as she squirts her release.

"Shane, oh my, God! What's happening to me?" she mewls, giving another wet burst from her pussy when I make her go off again. Her eyes roll back, and she thrashes her head against the mattress.

"That's it, Nicole. Come all over my hand," I demand, repeating the movements and driving her back up the cliff. She's powerless, taking everything I give her with nothing but a frantic shake of her head and the delicious screams from her lips.

I take her there one more time, and then I take advantage of the drunk on arousal high she's entranced in and settle my body between her hips. The wetness from her releases against my knees only making me hungrier for her. Before she has a chance to realize my fingers are no longer fucking her pussy, I slam my cock deep and take her hard.

Her hands come up and grab my arms, nails digging deep. I don't stop thrusting against her roughly, but her touch is going to undo the sliver of strength I have on myself. The need to empty myself inside her overwhelming.

"Let go," I bark, panting as I continue to speed up my movements. Her hands instantly drop, and I almost lose it when I see a flash of pain in her eyes. I close my eyes before grabbing her hips and pulling her with me while I fall onto my back—the wet spot now cooling my heated backside. I bend, my stomach clenching as I do, and lift my face up to hers. My hands taking her wrists and holding them at the small of her back while looking into her eyes. "Your touch … I can't, Nicole. I'm not ready to stop fucking you, and if you touch me, it's over before I can drive you higher again. Understand?" I explain, my words coming out ragged.

"Yes, Sir!" she screams, her eyes begging me to move, pleading and helpless for what only I can give her.

"Fuck my cock, Nicole," I demand, tightening my hold on her wrists with one hand while the other rubs her clit.

She moves instantly, rocking and bouncing against the hardness buried deep inside her. Not once does she stop yelling out her pleasure. I keep my eyes on her face, watching as she comes undone again, this time her cheeks wet as she submits fully to the sensations pulling her under.

"One more," I tell her with my mouth clenched just as tight as I feel my balls have drawn. "Soak me, come, and suck me dry with that tight cunt."

"Shane!" she shouts, her walls clamping tight. Her whole body shudders, her full tits shaking, the piercings calling for my mouth.

"Fuck," I grunt, flexing my ass and releasing her hands to grab her hips and lift her up. I feed my cock into her body twice more before pulling her down and hissing through my teeth. With one more flex of my ass, I push myself even deeper and bellow out her name while my vision goes black and I come hard.

Chapter 22

Nikki

I RUN MY FINGERS OVER SHANE'S smooth chest, admiring the contrast of his tan to my paleness. We've been lying here in silence as both of us calm down. He lets my hands roam now. I should want a shower, the stickiness between my legs of our combined releases not exactly the most pleasant feeling, but I'm not ready to leave his arms. Heck, I'm not really sure I'll ever be ready. Pleasant or not, it only reminds me of what we just shared and the monumental shift I felt between us.

Lifting up, I prop my chin against my hand resting on his chest and study his relaxed face. He doesn't move, his fingers continuing their light strokes against my hip. He looks so much younger like this, no hardness in his features, completely relaxed. *I did this to him.* I imagine he doesn't often look this … stripped down. Knowing it's something I get that others might not experience fills me with butterflies.

One golden brown eye pops open, and he smirks. "What is it?"

"Where did you learn French?" I ask, feeling like it's the safer path of questioning than asking if he felt the same shift as I did when we came together.

He shifts, making me do the same. He turns us both on our sides, both eyes appraising me now. "My mother was fluent."

"And you? Are you fluent?"

"Oui, belle," he says thickly.

I blush. I might not remember much of anything from my high school classes, but a fool would know what he just said without help. *Yes, beautiful.*

"If I would have known you liked it that much, chèrie, I would have made it a point to speak it more often."

"Why don't you?"

A flash of pain crosses his face, and I instantly wish I could pull the words back.

"It was such a big part of her. She wanted me and Libs to know her language, to learn about her life before moving to America. Half of the time, I don't even realize I've slipped into that old habit unless someone calls me on it. I guess I don't give that to many people because it's special to me. It's not something I do consciously."

"You should try, honey," I tell him softly. "Let that be part of her legacy and something you pass on to those in your life and one day, your own family, instead of keeping it locked away. She wanted you to take that part of her for a reason, Shane."

He doesn't say anything, but his eyes darken, and I know my words affected him deeper than he wants me to know. Not because he wants to keep something from me; no, I think it's more because he can tell I understand.

"Does your sister still speak it as well?"

He shakes his head. "No. She stopped the day we lost our mom. I doubt she'll ever pick it back up. That part of her died with Mom."

My heart breaks for him, and the pain in his voice is raw. "I would love to learn," I whisper, my cheeks burning.

Some of his pain leaves his eyes, and he smiles at me. "I'd like that."

We settle into silence again, both of us holding our eye contact. I can feel something building, solidifying between us. The same thing I had felt shift while he took what he needed from me becoming even stronger. My body remembering each touch of his while he took me to a place I had never known existed, using my body to channel his emotions from earlier. Not once did it feel wrong but just the opposite. It was as if my body had been awoken, coming to life for the touch that had been made for me and me alone.

"Shane?"

"Yes, Nikki."

"Will you ever let me …?" I trail off, not sure how to put it into words.

He frowns slightly. "Let you what?"

I sigh, holding his gaze and figuring I should just spit it out. "Will you ever let me … take you?"

"Why?"

"I'm just trying to understand you. All of you. I want to know every facet that makes you the incredible man you are. I'm not complaining, just not sure I understand why you need that."

"Would it matter? If I answered a certain way, would that change your mind about us being together?"

I mull his words over. Would it? Probably not, but do I know that? I've never been with a man like him. "I don't know, Shane."

He sighs. "It's who I am, Nikki. I don't like feeling I can't control the way something plays out. I spent the better part of my life growing up with no way to change the things happening around me. I never knew my dad, that choice stripped from me. It wasn't until my mom got sick that I felt a shift in me. I couldn't make her life easier while she did her best to raise us. I couldn't take her sickness away. I was helpless. When she died, something in me did too, and I've needed to let the beast inside me control my life and the situations I found myself in ever since so I never felt any of that helplessness again. Am I telling you no? Not exactly, but you need to understand that I might always need this."

I nod, my heart breaking for him and the pain he's faced in his life, but understanding the whys a whole lot clearer now. "Thank you for telling me."

"One day at a time, chèrie. I can't make those promises right now, but who knows what will happen. Just give me some time."

"Yeah, I think I like that plan."

"Come on. Let's rest and then you've got a call to make."

My eyes widen. "You were serious?" I gasp.

"Belle, I'm always serious."

"But Shane! I can't just quit. I need a job."

"Are you happy there?" he questions.

"Well, no."

"Can you leave the job where you're unhappy at, the one that treats you unfairly, and be okay until you find something else?"

"Probably. As long as I don't have to wait until the end of the school year, I could get by."

"And if you can't get another teaching job right away? Would you be open to something else until you could?"

"Like what?"

He shrugs. "I don't know, Nikki. Anything that didn't sound like you're being paid to get abused by some bitch."

I roll to my back and look up at my ceiling. I could work anywhere and be happier than where I am, sure. I love my students, but he's right; I'm getting a paycheck to basically be abused by those in power at Rosefield. I turn my head and find him studying me.

"Yes, Shane. I could be okay with that."

"Then do it. Jump off the cliff, pull the parachute, and see where you land. Don't let that woman dictate your life. You did nothing wrong and shouldn't be made to feel like you did. Defending yourself is a sign of a strong character and nothing to be ashamed of."

"What about my students?"

His face gets soft, and he pulls me into his body, his arms wrapping around me tight. He places a kiss on my temple, and I curl into his body more, taking comfort in his arms.

"Just the fact you asked that says everything, Nikki. They'll be fine. They'll miss you, I have no doubt, but the beauty of a child is they bounce back quickly. You can't stay somewhere toxic just for them."

He's right. I know he is. Heck, I've been thinking about leaving for months, but I haven't given it serious thought until now. "Ember asked me to help her with the baby so she could get more painting done. I turned her down at the time, but I can ask her if the offer is still there. It wouldn't be a hardship to get to spend time with my two favorite girls and still pay my bills."

"Good, chèrie. That's good."

"I could always apply at Dirty," I joke. He gets stiff under me, and I lift my head to look at him. "What?"

"You've been there, Nikki. You say you aren't jealous, but I don't know any woman who could handle seeing that night after night without it doing damage to a relationship. Let's not rock the boat before we can set sail."

I laugh, and he scowls, only making me laugh harder. "Oh, Shane Kingston, when will you realize I'm not like any other woman around?"

He just tightens his hold on me, and we settle into a comfortable silence. I start thinking about ways to prove to this stubborn man that I'm not the jealous type. He's in for a rude awakening if he thinks his job will push me away from wanting to be with him. No way. Seeing him move has always been the biggest turn-on, and that was before he was mine. For years, I craved him just like everyone else. I never felt jealous of the other women who wanted him. Not once. Now, though, seeing him move and knowing I'm the one who has what the other women crave is a power trip, and I haven't even been back to Dirty since that night. He has no idea what challenge he just threw down.

Oh, this will be fun.

Shane left shortly after we woke up from our two-hour nap. I could tell he wanted to stay, but he had to work later tonight, and I had, apparently, a job to quit. I didn't give myself time to back out either; I called and left my resignation on Mrs. Worthington's voicemail, thankful I didn't have to hear her voice again. I followed that up by emailing my formal letter of resignation to not only her but also her secretary and the whole board. I left out my opinions on their hate-filled ruling of that school and wished them the best with finding a replacement. I also stressed that I expected all my paid vacation hours to be on my final check. They know they pushed me out, and I have a feeling they would rather pay me than keep me on staff. If they didn't, oh well, at least I tried. There wasn't anything of value that I cared to keep from there, and if I was being honest, there wasn't anything in the world worth having to face *her* again to go back and claim it.

Then I put part two of my plan in action and called Ember.

"Hey," she answered, out of breath.

"Did I catch you at a bad time?"

"No, Nate just left."

"Ah, say no more."

She giggles. "So Shane must be gone too."

"Yes, nosy nelly. He left an hour ago to get ready to go in tonight."

"I'm surprised he left at all," she jokes.

"Yeah, yeah. Are you going to stop trying to get me to tell you about our sex life long enough to hear why I called?"

"I'm all ears, girlfriend."

"How about a night out? I feel like Dirty is calling our names," I tell her, smiling at my reflection in the mirror.

"What are you up to?" Ember laughs.

"Oh, nothing," I say in a sugary sweet voice. "Just looking to enjoy some eye candy."

"I'm *so* sure." She snickers. "Let me see if my parents are up for a Quinnie style sleepover, and I'll call you back. If they say no, I'll call Izzy, and we know she won't say no. Actually, it's not Izzy who will demand baby time, it's Axel."

"Sounds good, Em. I'm going to jump in the shower and take catalogue of all my deliciously sore bits and handprints."

I hang up as her gasp and demand that I explain echo through the line. That girl, you never would have thought she was such a little pervert just by looking at her.

The steam from my shower fills my small bathroom. I pull up Spotify on my phone and put on one of my favorite shower time playlists, but before I step in, I look down at my deliciously used body. I can see the faint bruising on my hips from where Shane held me tight. I know my backside is still sore, but when I turn and look in the mirror, I'm disappointed that his handprints aren't there. That man, the things he does in bed should be lethal, hands down.

And … he's all mine, no fake to it. How lucky am I?

Chapter 23

Nikki

"GIRLFRIEND, HOW LUCKY ARE WE!" Ember yells over the pounding beats of "Yeah!" by Usher.

I didn't remember loving this song quite as much in the past as I do at this moment, watching Shane as his body comes alive with the music. Sure, I've been lusting after him for years, but it's almost as if I'm seeing him in a whole new light now that he's mine. I know what the body can do when it's naked on top of me. I know what the man can do when that honey tone takes over his deep voice and he hypnotizes me with passion. The way I see him now, it's a whole new level of wow with the intimate knowledge that I carry. I have no doubt that the women screaming up at him while he comes to life on the bar top are all wondering if he can move just as good between the sheets too. I did. Now, I know I was wrong. He can move even better.

When he turns and faces Nate, doing some hand slap and foot

kick with him, I settle in against the shadowed wall with Ember and feast on the show. My eyes zoom in on our men, both of them working the main bar and dancing together as if they've practiced some routine, playing off the other in favor of hyping up the ladies screaming below them. Shane's got his dark button-down shirt wide open, flapping around with each move of his body to the rhythm echoing around us—making the music feel even more powerful when you're watching the show that accompanies each beat. The taut ab muscles flexing with each thrust and dip of his hips. That V dipping into the waistband of his black slacks makes my mouth water, wanting nothing more than to lick each hard ridge.

"They need a warning when they're acting like this," I muse, speaking loud enough for Ember's ears only.

"You aren't wrong." She giggles, taking a sip of her drink. I look over and frown at her water. She just shrugs and winks.

"You aren't!" I exclaim.

Even in the darkness, I can see her whole face come to life. She's radiating happiness as if someone stuck a light bulb in her butt and cranked it up to full power.

"We found out two weeks ago. I told Nate, after this one, my baby factory is on temporary strike."

"Yeah, right." I snort. "That man was out of control when you were preggers with Quinnie. I told you then, and I'll remind you now; he's got some weird fetish with you being pregnant."

She shrugs, her bright red shirt falling off her shoulder, exposing the top swell of her boob. She doesn't move to adjust it; instead, she turns to smirk at her man while he continues to move seductively. When I look back at her, I understand why she didn't catch the fact that her shirt was about to flash anyone close to her.

"Are they ... wet?"

"Mmmhmm," she confirms, still not looking away.

"How ... when ... aren't they going to chafe?"

Her elbow jabs me in the side, and she has to hold herself up against the wall as she laughs uncontrollably. I frown at my best friend, which only makes her laugh even harder.

"You're something else, Nik. Only you would see some of the hottest moves outside a strip club and be worried about them getting a rash."

"What?" I exclaim, frowning. "It's a valid concern."

The guys jump from the smaller platform in the middle of the main bar, over a laughing Denton's head, and back to the bar top they started on, directly in front of the female patrons still going nuts. The song had, at some point in our gawking, changed to a popular dance song I couldn't recall the name of. I don't remember the guys ever doing their spotlight dances for more than one song, so they must be just as lost in their enjoyment of performing as we are in their enticing moves. An idea sparks in my head, and I make a note to bring it up to Shane. He might not want me to work here, but that doesn't mean I can't help make my man's business a little more successful. Plus, with Nate's growing family, I doubt he would say no to guaranteed income.

"When did they add the wet stage?" I ponder, pushing my other thoughts back until I see Shane later, watching him toss his head back and laugh at something Nate says. The longer strands of hair on the top of his head spray the crowd with water.

"He looks happy."

"Well, of course, he looks happy, chica. He's got the second-best woman in Hope Town," Ember titters.

"Second best, huh?" I jest, ignoring the heat that blooms on my cheeks for being busted speaking my thoughts.

She just shrugs. "He does, though. I've never seen him this ... I don't know, carefree? He always seems so tense. As if he's holding the weight of the world on his shoulders. It's a good look on him. You too, for that matter."

"Me? I'm always happy!"

Her smile gets soft with a hint of sadness. "You haven't been, but that's not important now, Nik. I like the look Shane gives you."

"And that would be what?"

"Contentment."

I look at Ember, and she studies me with a serene expression on her delicate features. She knows me better than I know myself sometimes. I shouldn't be shocked that she came to that conclusion, but hearing it out loud makes me wonder just how unhappy I had been without even realizing it.

"Back to your other question. They added the center stage a couple of weeks ago, but just got the plumbing rigged for that little nugget of wet hotness the other day. I knew Nate was eager to try it out, so I'm not shocked Shane was too."

"That was a good call."

"Oh, you aren't wrong." She giggles. "I make Nate practice his moves in the shower all the time. Something's insanely hot about them moving like that anyway, but you add in the water and plaster their clothes to their skin ... and, well, it's downright sinful.

Every hard inch is in your face, if you know what I mean."

"I think it's safe to say every woman in proximity knows what you mean," I add on a laugh, watching the ladies go a little crazy when the song ends and both Shane and Nate drop back down behind the bar, slapping each other's backs in a manly hug.

"Are you okay with that?" Ember asks, genuine concern in her question.

"With what?"

"This," she says, pointing the top of her water bottle toward the large room before us. "Him dancing, the flirting that's involved in what they do, exposing his skin to capitalize on the fact that these people keep coming and fantasizing about them being more than just a nightlife attraction. I know they don't dance much anymore, just once or twice a week, but it still happens."

"You sound like Shane now," I huff, leaning back against the wall. "He's mentioned his concern that I wouldn't be okay with it. Em, I am, honest. Maybe some other girls wouldn't be, but it's just a big freaking turn-on for me. You've never been jealous of Nate."

She continues to nod after I stop talking. "That's how I look at it. It's like a big game of foreplay between Nate and myself. I just wanted to make sure."

"Yeah," I breathe, moving my head to the side to try to glimpse Shane through the packed room. It still amazes me that, on a night in the middle of the week, this place is full to bursting with people.

"What do you say we go surprise our men?" she coos, tipping her head toward the bar with a wink. "I'm feeling the need to be a little naughty."

I hook my arm with hers, smiling at my friend. "I forgot how horny you were when you were pregnant with Quinnie. I swear, Em, you're like the angel who gave in to the dark side and just wants to be bad all the time when you're pregnant."

"Well, come on, girlfriend, and step to the dark side with me!" She starts walking, pulling me behind her, both of us clumsy with our hilarity as we walk.

It takes us a second to fight through the bodies. I lead the way, pushing people out of the way and making sure Ember has a clear path. I know her new little addition is safe inside her, but I can't help but be protective of her even more than normal with this many hungry women around us. When the guys dance, the men who frequent Dirty looking for an easy lay scatter until they can pounce on the groundwork laid down by the Dirty boys.

"Would you move!" I yell at the tall redhead standing between me and the bar.

"Back off!"

"I hate the groupies when they think they'll actually catch the eye of anyone who works here. Don't you, Em?"

She giggles at my back, and even through the music, I can hear it clearly.

"What did you just say?"

"Uh, move?" I answer with a roll of my eyes.

"Listen here, Barbie. I've been waiting for one of those two to finish up so we could go play, and I'll move when one of them lets me know they're ready."

I toss my head back and laugh.

"Have they actually said they were going to take you off to

some dark corner and give you something every other woman in here is thirsty for?"

"They don't have to say the words, not when they're dancing just for me."

I have to hold in my laughter now. Wow, she's a few screws loose. "Let me try this again. Have you *ever* seen any of them give any more than the dancing they just blessed your eyes with?"

She loses a little of her cocky attitude, knowing that I'm on to her.

"That's not how they do."

"That's not how they do," I parrot. "Em," I call over my shoulder, my best friend wiggling under my arm and popping her head into the space between me and the redheaded Tarzan.

"What's up, sista from another mister?"

"Our new friend here says she's waiting for the two guys who just stopped dancing. Did you know they can let someone know they want some action just by thrusting their hips on top of a bar?"

"Why, no Nikki, I had no idea!" She gasps sarcastically, her eyes round with mirth.

"Gosh, we've been doing it all wrong." I press my hand to my forehead.

"Maybe you should just hike that shirt down and give it a try. I mean, if all we have to do is stand here and blink at them, maybe we can get some action too!"

Ember snorts and almost loses her control over the laughter fighting to break free.

"You don't have what they want," the nasty woman in front of me says with a nasty sneer.

"I don't?" I whine, looking down at the tight black dress I put on. The low cut in the front not extreme. Yet. I move my arms and pull the front down, the straps pulling against my shoulders. Reaching into the built-in bra, I tug my boobs and give my cleavage a little more va-va-voom. Then I run my fingers through my hair and tousle the strands. "Em, I'm not a troll, right?"

"Nooooo," she says with a long drag. "I mean, if our friend is so sure she's who they want, it shouldn't matter. Right, sweetheart?" She looks up at the woman and blinks.

Challenge down. I see the exact moment it's picked up and accepted too. A nasty expression crosses her face, and she steps to the side. I see a few people almost fall over when she bumps into them, my eyes only caring about the spot open right at the edge of the bar now. Just big enough for Ember and myself to fit. Shane and Nate are busy at each end of the bar. When we step up, Dent looks up and opens his mouth, presumably to take our orders, but just smirks.

"Ladies," he croons. "What can I get for you?"

"Two of Dirty's best," I answer with a wink. "Make them both sinfully delicious and a whole lot of naughty, would ya?"

He shakes his head, laughing at us, and quick to cotton on, he turns and rings some bell above his head.

"That's my bell," Ember says against my ear so that the woman drilling daggers with her glares doesn't hear her. I see Nate's head pop up and zoom in on us before a grin takes over and he stops what he's doing right away.

Halfway down the bar toward us, he yells out Shane's name.

"Looks like I'm not the only one who needs a bat signal, mother-fucker!" he bellows with a deep chuckle.

Shane frowns at him before following the finger pointing at us. When he sees both Ember and myself, his frown vanishes and that wolfish grin makes me thirsty … for the promise I can see in his eyes even in the dim room.

"Dent, call Travis if you need backup. He's working VIP with Matt, but they're good with just one back there. We're taking a real fucking long break, if you catch my drift."

Dent mutters something under his breath but nods at his two bosses.

"Step back, ladies."

We do as Nate asks, and so does an arch of bodies around the bar. Then one after the other, they put their palm against the wood, and with a leap, they sail over the edge and land on their feet, right next to each other in front of us.

"Hi," I greet Shane, smiling up at the man who only has eyes for me. I forget about Ember and Nate the second my man's burning gaze is devouring me with intensity.

A smirk slips through that fierce study of his as he continues to silently appraise me, but I only see it for a second before he bends, shoulder gently digging into my belly as he stands and lifts me off my feet. One of his large hands covers the area between my legs where my dress would otherwise be flashing the room, and then he's off—his feet falling heavy and jarring me slightly.

I love it.

Before we get far, though, I press my hands against his butt and push to lift my gaze. When I see the same redhead who had been *so sure* these men would be hers, I give her a wink before grabbing a handful of Shane's firm ass and sticking my tongue out at her.

Childish, sure.

But I win.

Shane tosses me off his shoulder, and I land with a squeal on the soft leather couch in his office. I look around at the rich brown and cream tones of his office, having never been in here before, and smile at him.

"Surprise, pumpkin," I offer, winking at the man breathing hard in front of me. I can only guess what he's thinking. I know his reservations about me being able to handle his job, but if he doesn't see me being able to handle what he does when he takes the stage, he'll never believe I love it.

"What are you doing here?"

"Just enjoying a girls' night. So how's the weather tonight? If I had known it would rain, I would have let you take my umbrella to work," I jest, loving it when his eyes get dark.

"You saw?"

I shift, the ache between my legs growing as I remember how he had moved when the water started to rain down on them. "Oh, yeah."

"And?" he continues his questions, body taut and tense. He's bracing. I hate his ex even more for putting the thought in his head that no one would accept something he clearly loves to do.

"I think, next time, you should take a little more off. It's not fair to just tease everyone with unbuttoning your shirt, sugar lips."

"Nikki," he growls.

"Cross that one off too?"

He doesn't answer; instead, he steps the last couple of feet between us and pulls me to my feet. Even with the tension radiating off him, his touch is gentle.

"The crowd ate that up, Shane. It was so hot seeing you move like that, knowing that your body is mine and not theirs."

Another animalistic groan comes rumbling from his lips. He doesn't speak, so I weigh my words and continue.

"In fact, I think you need to step up the game here. Make that little extreme show something you guys only do on a feature theme night." I tap my chin, trying to come up with a witty name. The second it hits, I feel giddy. "Filthy," I murmur.

"What?" he asks, some of the harshness in his body receding and flowing from his tenseness as he continues to run his hands over my body.

"Dirty Dog gets Filthy."

I see the confusion.

"I've been here when you guys just dance, but tonight, both you and Nate let loose and just had fun. It wasn't hard to see you and think of what you looked like when you were stripping. I'm not saying go buy a bunch of banana hammocks and start doing it again, but who's to say you can't marry both worlds and give those thirsty women one night when Dirty Dog is Filthy Dog."

"You have no idea what you're talking about," he hedges, but I can see my idea has already taken root.

"I don't?" I ask, taking his hand and lifting my dress up until my panties are bared. His nostrils flare, but he lets me continue to manipulate his arm. I press his palm against my thigh, smiling to myself when he has to bend to make up the height difference. Still, he lets me play. I drag his hand up until he's cupping my sex. My soaking wet sex. "I think I know exactly what I'm talking about. Dance for me, Shane. Give me your filthy."

And he does just that; the only thing louder than my screams is the music still blaring in the club below us. That night, I learn just how much fun it can be to get dirty.

Chapter 24

Nikki

"**D**ID EMBER TELL YOU WHAT time they would be ready for dinner?" Shane asks, walking out of his closet while tying his black tie. I lick my lips. When I don't answer, he looks up from his task. "Really?"

"What?"

"I'm tying my tie, mon belle."

That phrase has joined his growing list of French endearments. *My beautiful.* That one started a few days ago, about a week after I made him make me filthy. It doesn't come often, as he still favors hummingbird, but I soak it up each time he croons those two words in my direction.

"It's hot." I shrug. What does he expect from me? Two nights ago, he used the tie he had been wearing at work to tie my hands together and take me hard against his kitchen table. I'll never look at a tie the same again.

"Fucking cute," he mutters under his breath, turning and looking at the mirror behind his bedroom door to finish. "What time are we meeting them?"

I pick my phone up off the bed and smooth the deep purple lace of my dress. "In about an hour? She said her mom was picking up Quinnie at six, and they would meet us at the restaurant no later than seven. Our reservation is for fifteen after."

He nods, giving a little jiggle to the knot he just tied until it did whatever he wanted. Turning, he walks over to the edge of the bed, bends over, and takes my mouth in a deep kiss. When he pulls away and just looks into my eyes, I squirm under his attention.

"What?"

"Liberty is excited to meet you," he answers.

"I'm excited to meet her."

"Though, if she calls me nonstop the next time I've got my cock deep inside you, there won't be family dinners for a long fucking time."

I giggle as last night comes back in a rush of embarrassing hilarity.

"It's not funny, chèrie."

"It's so funny, handsome."

"You didn't think so last night when I stopped fucking you," he returns with a brow high.

I smack his arm playfully. "You answered the phone!" I laugh. "You just pushed in deep, left me tied to your bed, and took a call from your baby sister."

He groans and drops his forehead to my chest. "I had to, Nik. She wouldn't have fucking stopped calling until I did. It was easier to get her off the phone quickly by letting her know I wasn't on the side of the road somewhere and pretending I didn't have your wet pussy hugging my cock so tight it was pure torture not to move when I talked to her."

"Maybe we should have a nice talk with her about calling hours," I joke, not even the tiniest bit serious. Seeing him awkwardly tell his sister he couldn't talk only to get tricked into a makeshift family dinner so she could see Nate and Ember *and* meet her brother's new girlfriend was priceless. He would have agreed to anything to end that call.

"That's not a bad idea."

"Oh, leave her alone." I giggle. "It's cute how she worries about her big bad brother."

"If you knew the kind of pain I was in while I tried to end that call, you wouldn't call that shit cute."

I wiggle, my dress hiking up and allowing me to spread my legs. When his crotch falls against my hot sex, he groans and closes his eyes. "I don't know, Shane. You turned into a savage after, taking what you needed and giving me everything at the same time. If we need to schedule more phone calls during our sexy time, I'm not going to say no."

"Little vixen," he grumbles, smiling and betraying the seriousness he's trying to fake. "One day, you're going to do what I expect."

"I doubt that," I jest. "Kiss me, you fool, then fill my belly!"

His eyes spark, the golden swirls coming to life. "If I fill your belly, we're going to be late."

He kisses me, though, and pays me back for teasing him by taking me right to the edge before standing and adjusting the hardness of his dick then holding his hand out for me. I take it, my blood still roaring through my body, crazed for what he held back from me. I narrow my eyes and adjust my dress before calling him every version of mean I can think of. His gruff chuckles follow me out of his bedroom and through his house. Not once in the thirty-minute drive to the Italian restaurant does he stop smirking either, the big hunky tease.

"Is that her?" I whisper, clutching his hand and looking through his windshield at the beautiful young lady waving in the direction of his car when we pull up and park. "She's adorable." And she is. I didn't even really need to ask because there was no denying they're siblings. The feminine version of Shane, tiny and petite. "She looks like Tinker Bell with brown hair," I continue.

Shane chuckles, shutting the engine off and opening his door. Before he steps out, he looks over at me. "Have you ever seen what Tinker Bell looks like foaming at the mouth and trying to kill someone?"

"What? Of course not. She was sassy but not murderous." I scoff. "You need to brush up on your Disney movies."

"Chèrie, I didn't mean in the literal sense. Humor me," he says with a smirk.

"Okay. Humoring. No, pumpkin, I've never seen that."

He nods, his wolfish grin in place, and steps out of the car. He walks around the back of his car to my door and opens it, offering me his hand and backing away so I have room to stand. I shimmy my dress down, biting my lip when he groans. One thing I've learned about Shane in our six weeks together was I was wrong when I thought he was all about the booty. No, he's made it clear that every single part of my body drives him insane, but when my legs are bare and on display wearing a short dress, he's bloodthirsty for my body. Something I've made no qualms about taking advantage of.

The first day of my unemployment, I purged my closet of all my teacher clothes. I packed them up all neat and tidy, stashing them in Shane's garage at his urging when he watched with laughter dancing in his eyes while I ranted and grumbled about the mean hags who made me resent the job I should have loved. One day, I'll bring them back out, but not until I'm comfortable with the environment of my next teaching position. For now, I'll wear my short skirts and low-cut tops, driving my man insane every time he sees me. Plus, it's not like my new charge, little Miss Quinnie-Q Reid, cares what I wear when I watch her so Ember can get all her projects painted for her next show.

I snap out of my thoughts when Shane shuts the door, his hand taking mine, and starts walking toward his sister. Now, I'm not a tall person, but I'm not tiny either. At five-foot-four, I'm the perfect little pint size to Shane's six-foot-three. However, his sister is *tiny*. When we step up to her, even in her heels, I'm guessing she isn't much over five foot even. Totally Tinker Bell.

"Libs," Shane says with affection painting that one word thickly.

"Hey there, big brother. You going to release her so I can say hi?"

"Maybe. Got a hug for your favorite brother first?"

She rolls her eyes but walks into her brother's arms when he releases my hand and hugs her tight. Her face pressed against his torso, low under his pecs. Her brown eyes smiling at me and open with her happiness shining bright.

Then Shane opens his mouth and wipes that off her face.

"I missed you, Tinker Bell."

Holy Hanson, he was spot-on. If Tinker Bell was a snarling vampire on the verge of starvation and the only available blood was her brother's, that is. Shane's laughter is uncontrollable while he playfully fights her off. His whole body relaxes as he looks at his sister with so much adoration I feel my throat get thick. Seeing him like this, I feel another piece of my heart become Shane's forever.

"Okay, okay," he grunts, taking a jab of her elbow to the gut. Laughing through it, he puts his arm around her shoulder, spinning her to face me.

She runs her hands through her hair, grumbling about her brother and seemingly forgetting I'm even there. My smile grows with his, but my eyes are all for her.

"Dis boujour à ma petite amie, Nikki, mon petit ange. Avec le monde entre mes mains et les deux femmes les plus importantes dans mon monde qui se recontrent finalement, mes jours sont très brillants[9]." he says softly, his sister's eyes getting misty as he continues to croon that delicious language. I have no idea if he's telling her I'm a slob who snores, but it doesn't matter when he speaks his beautiful language. He looks at me, eyes happy and

---

9   Say hello to my girlfriend, Nikki, little angel. My days are brighter with the world in my hands and the two most important women finally meeting

carefree. "Nikki, this is my little sister, Liberty. I'm thrilled as fuck that you two are meeting."

"Holy crap." Liberty gasps, looking back and forth between her brother and me, her eyes full of unshed tears. "Hi."

"Hi," I mimic, smiling and itching to hug her.

"I knew you were different," she continues in awe, whispering so softly that I have to strain to hear her.

My cheeks heat, and I shrug. "I just let him think he's in charge is all."

Liberty, two tears falling, bursts out with the most adorable laugh, pulling out of her brother's hold and slamming into my body with a force that someone so small shouldn't be able to achieve. I rock back on my wedges, wrapping my arms around her just as tight as she's hugging me. I sense something a lot more powerful than her just accepting her brother's girlfriend here, and when I look up at Shane, seeing the same thoughts written all over his face, I hug her a little tighter.

"It's really great to meet you, Liberty."

"You have no idea," she whispers in my ear. "I've waited for so long to see the shadows leave his eyes. Thank you."

It takes so much effort not to let her words show on my face. Right then, in front of Altoberli's, I give another Kingston a piece of my heart.

"Party's here," I hear bellowed from behind us, recognizing Nate's voice anywhere.

Liberty releases me, and we smile at each other. "Before we leave, let's swap numbers and pick this up for lunch next week?" I offer.

"I'd love that."

"Little Tink," Nate jests, and I watch the beautiful Liberty turn back into a bloodthirsty pixie, laughing as she launches herself on Nate.

Ember gives me a hug, looking tired. She's been dealing with morning sickness all week, and I know firsthand from being at her house with Quinnie so much how hard it is for her to do just about anything lately.

"Feeling any better?"

She shrugs. "I'm about eighty percent sure I won't throw up during dinner, but only about twenty percent that I won't fall asleep."

"Well, Em, that's better than yesterday," I joke, smiling when she starts laughing.

Who would have thought that one dinner date with these four would make me feel like I've found something I didn't even realize I had been searching for. Shane pulls me into his side, his scent enveloping me. Yeah, this is what it feels like to be full.

Chapter 25

Nikki

I WALK OUT OF THE LOCAL bookstore with a spring in my step. Having more time on my hands since leaving Rosefield has allowed me to finally tackle my Pinterest boards. I've tackled all the DIY Pinterest projects I had collected over the years, read some amazing romance novels, and got to spend a ridiculous amount of time with my best friend and goddaughter. Sure, Ember and Nate are technically paying me to watch Quinnie while Ember works, but it's hardly work. Sitting with my bestie while she gets lost in her creations and playing with an angel? Not a hardship.

Shane's been busy at Dirty. It took a few more not so subtle hints about my thoughts for a Filthy night at Dirty, but he finally agreed it was a good idea. I could see it in his face when he agreed, though, that he's still worried about me not being able to handle his job and the women who surround him there. A small part of me is worried he might always have those fears. Lacey did a number on him, but I'm stubborn enough that I won't stop trying to prove to him that I don't get jealous. It's hot. He's not humping them; he's standing above them and dancing alone. Knowing that women want him but will never have him is delicious.

Speaking of Lacey, ever since that run-in on our first fake date, she's been keeping a low profile. From what Shane says, he doesn't think that's the last we'll hear of her, and I hate to say, I agree. Seth, on the other hand, moved back home to Iowa last I heard. I guess Shane's just more intimidating, and Seth tucked his tail after their run-in. Even though I got what I wanted, knowing that Lacey is still in town doesn't fill me with gumdrops and rainbows. However, she can keep her crap on the sidelines as long as she keeps her nose out of our relationship.

My phone rings, so I stuff my purchases from the bookstore into my large tote and pull my phone out, smiling when I see Liberty's name on the display.

"Hey," I greet, smiling while unlocking my car and tossing my tote in the passenger seat. "I'm on my way to the restaurant now. Are you already there?"

"Sure am. I got us a booth and ordered you a Coke."

"I'll be there in five, Tink." I laugh, a snort escaping when I hear her feminine growl.

"I'm going to kill my brother."

"Please don't, babe. I'll miss him a whole lot."

She grumbles, and my smile grows. "Order me chicken fajitas with extra rice and sour cream, okay? I got a little zoned out in the bookstore and didn't realize I was running late, but I'm literally five minutes away."

"Sounds good. There's plenty of eye candy having lunch outside, so I have a nice view while I wait."

"What happened to Tommy?" I ask, referring to the guy she told me she had been dating for a few weeks earlier this week during one of our long phone calls.

"Ugh," she gripes. "It seems that Tommy was more interested in Michelle, the girl who lives in the apartment next to mine. He needed an in, and I was the best thing. I'm single and ready to mingle."

"I know some pretty good-looking single guys," I confess, thinking about the younger Cage boys. They're a little older than Liberty is, me as well, but I've known them long enough that—even if I hadn't seen them through high school being great boyfriends—I'm positive they know how to treat a woman. You aren't a son of Greg Cage's without learning how to worship the women in your life. I'll just have to deal with Shane if he has a problem with his sister dating someone who's almost a decade older.

"You'll have to fill me in at lunch," she exclaims excitedly.

I don't remember being that boy crazy at twenty-one, but Liberty has quickly become someone I care about, and I want nothing more than those I care about to be happy.

"Promise."

We hang up, and I toss my phone in my bag and pull out of my parking spot thinking about Shane's sister. We haven't even known each other for a full week, and you would think we had known each other for years. She confessed during one of our chats that she had always hoped her brother would find someone she could form a relationship with. We both agreed that Lacey had *not* been that person. I was shocked to hear how nasty Lacey had been to Liberty, driving a wedge between the two Kingstons that caused Liberty to back away because she was unable to see her brother stuck with someone who made him miserable. Clearly, Liberty is wise for her age to be able to see that and not have the adult knowledge of a relationship's many layers.

She was finishing her degree in graphic design, but her apartment was close to her campus, almost an hour outside Hope Town. It made it a lot easier for her to brush off Shane when he wanted to get together with her while Lacey had still been in the picture. Over the past year and a half of him being single, they had grown even closer. And now, I hope they continue to build that bridge back to what they had been before Lacey's nasty filth got their relationship dirty. Even if I wasn't tumbling head over heels quickly for her brother, I would still adore her.

When I pull into one of my favorite Mexican restaurants, I see Liberty through the window behind their outdoor dining area. She's practically drooling at the men eating and laughing outside. I sneak a look and feel giddy with my luck. What are the freaking odds that the very young men I had been thinking about would be here?

I park, grab my bag, and skip across the parking lot. The guys don't see me, and I don't stop to say hello. I know them through my long friendship with Ember—her family's connection to Cage's going way back before she was born. To her, they're like her cousins. I know it's rude to ignore them, seeing as I'm basically an honorary Reid myself and I've known them forever. I hadn't been to a huge extended family gathering with Ember in years, but the Cage twins look like they grew new muscles each year that had passed since I saw them last.

"Hey," I breathe, scooting into the booth and stifling my laugh when Liberty startles, looking a little sheepish for being caught drooling over the guys outside. "Been a while since you saw a hunky man?" I ask, wagging my brows.

She waves me off, dipping a chip in the salsa. "You might be happily taken, but you can't deny they're worth drooling over."

I hum my agreement, not letting the cat out of the bag that I know them just yet.

"So what's new?"

She leans back and huffs. "I gave some serious thought to murdering my roommate yesterday but decided I was too pretty for prison. Other than that, just studying more than I sleep and eating more than I study."

"Sounds like my college years." I laugh.

"Not too much longer and I can get the hell outta dodge and move back to Hope Town. The day I can move out of that apartment, I'm going to buy myself a gift for putting up with Samantha for the past two years."

"She can't be that bad," I challenge. I loved my roommates. The only time we got into arguments was when they stole my string cheese.

"Last night, I sat down to pee. My eyes were all tired and blurry because I had spent almost ten hours studying for a big test. When I sat down, there was something …" she trails off, looking on the verge of throwing up. "Her asshole boyfriend missed the trash with his used condom, and I sat on it. Lubrication wasn't what was gooey, if you know what I mean."

"Oh, my God. Libs, that's disgusting."

"Tell me about it. I stormed into her room after grabbing the gloves we wash dishes with and threw it right in her face. I was too grossed out to enjoy the fact it stuck to her forehead, the open end dangling right over her mouth."

I make a gagging sound then we both start giggling.

"Enough about my disgusting roommate and sad, single life. How are things with my big brother?"

"Pretty amazing, to be honest. He's got a lot going on at Dirty, but we pretty much spend every chance we get outside of that together. We're going on a little vacation in a few weeks to the mountains. I can't wait to get away, just the two of us, and spend some time together."

"Don't make me gag again," Liberty jokes.

"Did you know he hasn't taken a vacation in over ten years?"

Pain slashes across her face, and I shiver. I knew he wasn't telling me everything when I asked him why he had waited so long.

"Sounds about right. We took a big trip with Mom before she got too sick right after he graduated college. I was still a little bratty teenager, but that was one of the best two weeks of my life."

She gets quiet, and I reach over the table, taking her hand. "I'm not close with my parents. When I was born, they were both in their late forties. Accident of the century, I was. They didn't know what to do with me, never have. When I turned seventeen, they moved to Florida, and I finished high school with no parents. I call them a few times a year, you know all the important dates, but we're basically strangers who share DNA. I won't pretend to know what it feels like to lose a parent who cares, but I have a feeling she's with you every day, Libs, and the memories she left with you will never be able to pack up and leave for Florida."

"Damn, Nik, that's some shit."

I laugh. "Old news, but I don't want you to think that I'm not sensitive to what you and Shane have lost." I lean back when the waiter comes over and places our food down. When he walks away, I look back up at Liberty. "Shane told me you haven't spoken any French since she passed." I keep my voice low, holding her gaze and making sure I don't push her into something upsetting.

She's quiet, moving her food around with the fork. Just like her brother, I can tell when she's deep in thought. They both nibble on their bottom lip and frown with their eyebrows. When she looks back in my direction, I was relieved to see her eyes dry. I had been worried all week about bringing this up in order to ask her for a favor.

"At first, I refused because I was angry she left us. How shitty is that? She was the one who died of cancer, not like she had a choice. Then, over time, I just got used to not speaking in any language other than English. None of my friends know French, so it wasn't unnatural that I didn't continue. Every now and then, Shane tries to force my hand and only speaks to me in French. I can see it hurts him when I refuse to reply in kind. I think now it's more that I'm afraid it will hurt him to actually hear me speak our mother's language again than not."

I shake my head, placing my fork and the tortilla down. I take her hand in mine, holding her gaze across the table. "Sweetheart, he loves you so much, and all he cares about is you being happy. You two and the relationship you have ... it's something incredible. I think the day you give him that gift, you'll be healing something in both of you."

"Maybe," she whispers, her voice thick.

"Maybe," I parrot. "How about ... baby steps?" I offer, giving her a sympathetic smile.

"Baby steps?"

"Yeah. I need some help," I tell her, letting go of her hand and reaching over to my purse to pull out the *French for Dummies* book I picked up before coming here.

Liberty, sadness forgotten, tosses her head back and laughs. "Oh, this is hilarious."

I hold it up to my face, give her my best puppy dog eyes. "Baby steps?" I say again.

She nods, her shoulders still shaking with laughter. "Yeah, Nik. Baby steps sound really good."

The rest of our lunch is full of hilarious banter while my friendship grows even stronger with Shane's sister. By the time we finished our lunch and paid, the Cage boys had already slipped out without us noticing. I make a note to ask Ember when the next big gathering is with all her parents' friends and their kids, vowing to drag Shane and Liberty with me to the next one so I can introduce her to a real man. Without any plans, we leave and head to the local Starbucks and crack the spine in my new book.

Then we take baby steps, and I do my best to soak everything in.

Even if I never remember a word that Liberty taught me, hearing her lyrical voice softly teaching me how to speak the words I was looking for and speaking the beautiful language her mother had wanted her to know so badly was worth every painful second that I butchered it.

Chapter 26

Shane

"I CAN'T BELIEVE WE DIDN'T THINK of this shit years ago," Nate grunts, backing away from the last new stage area we had to install. "I mean, shit, this is what we know."

All in all, we added four new spotlight areas, just like the wet stage at the main bar. Two were in the VIP sections and two more were on opposite corners of the club. With the new theme night at Dirty, we hired a few new guys to take the stage during our Filthy nights, also adding more dancers to our lineup and freeing Nate and myself up to only step in when we want to, not because we have to.

"It's a good idea," I agree, my reluctance in putting more of myself on display and risking Nikki realizing she can't do this because of my job weighing heavily on me. We were a week away from the big night, our first Filthy Friday, and instead of being fucking thrilled that we're about to see a massive spike in revenue, I was terrified that I would lose the woman who I no longer believed I could live without.

"What's crawled up your ass, man?" Nate asks, frowning at me before taking a huge gulp of water. Crumbling the bottle when he finished it off, he tosses it into the trashcan we had pulled to the middle of the room.

"Ember ever give you the kind of shit I got from Lacey about working here?"

Nate barks out a laugh. "You're kidding, right? She loves it. At first, the only issue she had was that bitch Julie a few years ago who worked here. After her, smooth sailing, my man."

"Just like that?"

Nate gets serious, leaning against one of the bar tables and studying me. I can't imagine I'm doing a good job at hiding how stressed I've been with my concerns about Nikki really being okay with what I do. I want to trust what she says, but it's hard when I lived through a relationship that did nothing but show me the negative side of what I do for a living when it comes to having a lasting bond with someone. I know it isn't fair to her, not with the enormity of my feelings for the woman who started out as my fake girlfriend.

"Man, this shit isn't the big bad monster you're building it up to be. I've known Nikki for a long damn time, and I can promise you—just like Em—she wouldn't give a shit if you got on one of these stages and started waving your decorated dick around. All she sees is the man she has that others might want but won't ever have. Stop looking at it like a negative and see the other side of it."

"Yeah? What side, Nate? The only fucking side I know is where my girl goes crazy, stalks my every move, monitors my phone, and then fucks another girl because she wants me to be as jealous as she is. It's all I know, man!"

"One stupid bitch is going to ruin the best thing that has ever happened to you then," he tells me honestly, his expression dead serious.

I run my hands through my hair. "You don't think I know that? I feel like I'm holding on for dear life, just waiting for her to look at me one night while I do my job and her smile be gone. The thought of hurting her is fucking with my head."

"Here's a thought," Nate says, pushing off the table and walking to where I'm leaning against the new stage we just finished building. "Maybe give her a chance to prove to you just how stupid you're being."

"And if I'm right?"

"Then at least you know, and maybe Nikki isn't the girl I've known for over twenty years."

He stalks off, disappearing behind the doorway that leads to his office. I take a look around the club and feel sick. This is why I work so fucking hard to keep everything in line. Surprises ruin everything.

Everything.

"What's going on in that handsome head of yours?"

I turn from the movie I'd been staring at for the past hour, yet not really watching, and take in the woman who has quickly become everything to me. I shake my head, pull my arm around her shoulders, and pull her deeper into my side. Her eyes don't leave mine, but her smile slips slightly.

"Seriously, Shane, you've been quiet since we left dinner earlier."

"There's just a lot going on at work, chèrie. Nothing to worry about." The words taste wrong on my tongue, but I give her what I hope is a reassuring smile.

"Problems with the upcoming Filthy night unveiling?" She shifts on the couch while still within my hold, making it easier to look at me.

I feel her stare, and all it does is make this odd pit of dread I've been carrying since we started transitioning things at Dirty grow to insurmountable levels. The second she put the idea out there, even knowing it would take our 'sex sells' dancing to a new level, I knew it was the right move business-wise. I've just been struggling if it was the right move for me on a personal level—and for my relationship with Nikki.

"Or is it someone else making you get that hulking frown pop out so much on your face," she asks when I continue my silent musings.

"No, Nikki." I sigh, shifting to pull her on my lap. Her legs spread, and her hands curl around my neck. I look up at her, wondering how I got so fucking lucky at the same time praying I stay that way and this girl stays mine. Fuck, I hate having these doubts.

"We haven't talked about Lacey in a while. Are you still worried about her?"

I shake my head. "She won't ever be gone from our lives completely since she lives in town, but she knows she lost whatever bullshit she had let herself think could happen. She hasn't been to Dirty, but I know she's tried a few times. She's not allowed in, and the bouncers know that. She isn't stupid enough to show up here. That's all that matters, Nik."

"Something tells me she isn't done, honey." She flexes her fingers and bends down to look me in the eye. "Especially since the talk of Dirty going Filthy has gained momentum. There's no way she's missed it. I was driving over to Em's the other morning, and they were talking about it on one of the morning radio shows."

"I'm not surprised. We sold out the debut night tickets without marketing what it meant. That doesn't mean she's not going to start her shit."

Nikki giggles, her smile hitting me deep. Fuck, this woman. Just the thought of losing something I had just found makes me feel sick.

"You're crazy if you think that, Shane. Don't worry; I'll be there opening night ready to protect my man from the crazy lovers of past heartbreak."

I lift off the back of the couch, my arms wrapping around her body and pulling her tighter to me at the same time. She melts, her hands shifting to my hair and her face dipping close. I pour everything into the kiss that follows, wanting her to feel everything. We continue to hold each other, our lips moving slowly and deeply. Only it's my hold that feels a tad desperate.

Without breaking our connection, I shift my hold and grasp her ass to support my move as I stand from the couch. Her legs hook around my back the second I stand, causing a growl to rumble in my chest when her pussy presses tight against my crotch. The thin fabric of her yoga pants against my thin and faded sweats does nothing to hide the warmth coming from her. I bet under the layers, I would find her slick and wet, ready for me.

When I toss her on the bed, she doesn't move. My perfect woman, sitting there and waiting for me to tell her what to do. I'm not stupid; I see the spark in her eyes when she wants to ask me to let her lead, but with all the bullshit in my fucking head, I can't go there yet—and if I'm honest, I'm not sure I'll ever be ready. Just the thought of being so vulnerable to anyone makes my skin itch. My control is the driving force that helped me survive the shit in my life. I've become as dependent on it protecting me when I was vulnerable as I have breathing to keep me alive.

Long after I've demanded her to strip and given us both what we wanted, my thoughts continue to race around in my mind. Nikki's heart beats against my chest as she sleeps against my side, close and trusting. My own beats in a slow rhythm that echoes hers in the most lulling tango.

Never in a million years did I think I would know what it felt like to have a woman like her in my life. I had thought, in the beginning, I would eventually feel this with Lacey, but I know the difference now. When you have the real thing, you can see how cheap the imitations you had in the past hold up in what matters in life.

Almost two months ago, the girl I had a crazy-as-fuck crush

on gave me an opening. I didn't realize she would become my everything when we started our fake relationship. Now, I know there was never anything about it that wasn't real. She's meant for me. I was made for her. Two halves of a fucking whole and I know, without her, I'll never have happiness again.

Which is why I'm fucking terrified she's going to run. I lost the ability to control my fears. This woman submits her trust in me and allows me the gift of my control in every aspect that I ask. Her trust is given and comes without question or doubt. How fucked up is it that I can't even give her the same type of respect when she's given me no reason to think she might be like the other women I've known in the past? And I'm not sure what upsets me the most—that she might really be unable to handle my career or that I might not ever be able to enjoy the best thing I know will ever happen to me because I'm too fucked up to give her my complete trust.

Chapter 27

Nikki

"ARE YOU EXCITED FOR YOUR trip next week?" Ember asks, turning to look at me over her shoulder from her paint station in the corner of her studio.

I give Quinnie one more bite of her mushed up and disgusting looking baby food and glance over her mussy brown ringlet baby head to smile at my best friend. "I am. Even though watching my Quinnie-Q-Moosie-Moo is the easiest job in the world, it will be nice to just get away and spend some one-on-one time with Shane, you know? Recharge with some quality time with no distractions before coming back and focusing on getting some applications in at a few schools I heard were hiring."

"You and Shane sound like you're going strong," she muses with a smile, still puttering around with her painting supplies.

Something shifts inside me, the same twinge I've felt for the past couple of weeks. I know he's busy getting everything set up for this upcoming unveiling of Dirty's Filthy night, but he just seems … I don't know, somewhat out of reach.

"He's stolen my heart, Em."

She stops what she's doing at that and turns the smile up, pure happiness. "You love him?"

I nod. "Yeah."

She frowns, turning to give me a contemplative study, leaning against the edge of the counter and crossing her arms. "Why does *that* make you look like someone just kicked a puppy in front of you?"

Quinnie makes a noise, and I give her another spoonful of her disgusting food. She's only eating this stuff sporadically, but I can't wait until she's fully on solids. She sticks her tongue out and blows, spitting some of her mush back out—saving me from having to answer right away.

"He's being weird," I finally admit, wiping Quinnie's mouth and shrugging at Ember.

"Weird as in normal Shane weird, or weird as in something else?"

"I feel like something's bothering him, but he doesn't want to discuss it with me. You know we're together more often than not. I think we've spent five nights, if that, apart in the past month. There isn't anything we don't discuss, but the second we start to change the topic to work or things with the Filthy night, he gets weird. I don't know how to explain it, Em. Maybe it's in my head, but I just can't shake it."

"And you asked him? To see what he says?"

I think back to all the times he's said or done something *off* recently. "Straight out? Not really. He just says that things are a little crazy at Dirty, and that's it. But I know it's not all. Something's there … I just can't seem to sift through what he isn't telling me to hear it."

She moves and comes to sit next to me, giving her daughter a kiss on the way. We both get distracted when Quinnie starts banging on her high chair, babbling the baby words only she understands. Finally, she takes my hand and gives it a squeeze.

"You know what I see when I watch you two together?"

"What?" I ask on a breath.

"I see two people who care about each other deeply. I see a woman who, despite not having the best experiences to move on easily, is doing just that. You trust him to be your happiness, giving him your all, and I love that about you. Shane, while I'm sure had dated before he was with Lacey, has always been more cautious, but he still looks at you like you're the most precious thing to him. The rest of life can get choppy at times, Nik. It did for Nate and me as well, but if you don't come out and ask Shane what's bothering him, you're just doing the both of you a disservice."

"What if he wants to break up?" I question, voicing the one thing that's been bothering me for a while.

Ember chuckles, shaking her head. "Sweetheart, he doesn't want to break up."

I lean back in the chair and look up at the ceiling, the sun's rays making shadows on the stark white surface.

"Tomorrow. I'll talk to him tomorrow. I don't want to stress him out tonight. Not with the big opening. Hell, I had to remind him to get me a pass with the new security crew they brought in to man the door tonight. I don't know, Em. Maybe I'm being stupid and it's just that, his stress."

"Only one way to find out, babe," she smarts, tapping me with her shoulder and laughing. "Why don't you head on home and get ready for tonight? I'm done here anyway. Quinnie can come with me to talk to Annabelle at the gallery."

"I wish you were coming tonight."

"Trust me, you're going to have more fun without me there. Plus, you'll just watch Shane dance then pull him up to the office to take care of what that boy's hips do to you."

I laugh, feeling a little more lighthearted. "Like you wouldn't be doing the same to Nate."

She lifts one shoulder, smirking. "Oh, I would. I made him show me the dance he plans on doing tonight. Since I probably won't get to a Filthy night until after I have the baby, I wanted to get a private VIP show. If Shane plans on doing even half the things that Nate showed me, watch out, girlfriend, because you'll be liable to end up pregnant just by watching."

We both giggle, wiping away tears.

"The crowd is going to go insane, Nik," she continues, cleaning her daughter up after she spits out another mouthful, clearly finished with her lunch. "If we thought the girls ate them up before, you just wait."

"Does it ever bother you?"

"Not really. I mean, sure Nate is flaunting his body and making other women crave him, but at the end of the day, he's married to me. He's coming home to me and Quinnie, and there isn't a woman around who could jeopardize that."

I move my head to agree. "And knowing that they're yours makes it even hotter."

"You aren't wrong, girlfriend," she says, snorting a little with her giggle.

"Shane and I aren't as committed as you and Nate, but I still know he wouldn't stray. Even if he was stripping it all off like he used to, I think I would still feel the same way. He's mine and I'm his. The rest is just a show."

I laugh to myself thinking about how true that last part used to be. I'm so thankful that my fake boyfriend turned out to be, hopefully, my forever one.

I help Ember get the rest of Quinnie's mess cleaned up, and after making sure she doesn't need help with anything before we both head out, I promise to call her later as I head home to get ready for tonight.

Shane left super early this morning. Having crashed at my place, he gave me his own brand of lovemaking all night long, and I didn't even hear him get up this morning. Other than a few brief texts to say hey and chat throughout the day, I haven't wanted to bother him, knowing he would be beyond busy getting things ready for tonight. When they decided to pull the trigger on Filthy, I had no doubt that both he and Nate would be dancing on the first night. They both get off on the high from their spotlight dances, something they haven't needed to do much of lately. They have only filled in here and there when they do, but it was that love of performing and the high from the crowd that would pull them both down equally once in a while to give a show.

I had asked Shane a few weeks ago what it was about dancing at Dirty that he loved so much, and he said much of the same. Stripping was the only thing that he knew after his mom died. He wasn't just trying to finish school, but after she passed, he found himself raising his sister until a few years back when she started school herself. He still very much supports her, but it's not the same now. Still, even though stripping had started out as a way to guarantee a roof over their heads, he loved it.

When it boils down to it, I think it also has a lot to do with his control issues. He can get up there and let loose, blow off some stress, and he knows he is in charge of how much or how little he gives to those watching him. At least, that's how I perceive it. It's also a big part of why I love him. Stripping got him through a big loss but was also how he survived. It's part of my man … the man I love.

Now if I could just get him to let me in the rest of the way and prove that he's not the only one shouldering the stresses of his life anymore. Then, well … then I'll have it all.

The line.

That was the first thing I saw when I turned into Dirty's parking lot. Thankfully, Shane had told me to park around back, ensuring I had a spot right next to his BMW. Following the rest of his instructions, I send a text to Lewis, the head of security for the club, and wait in my car for him to come out the back door and escort me inside.

I set my phone down and pop the visor down to look at my makeup. I put more effort into my makeup tonight than I ever have in my whole life. Shane doesn't care—I know that—and I probably could have shown up in my favorite Victoria's Secret sweats, and he'd still want me. However, this is a big night for him and for Dirty. I want my man to see me and be proud that his woman is there to cheer him on.

After refreshing my lip gloss, I make sure the dark eyeshadow I used to give my eyes a smoky look isn't all over the place, making me look more like a raccoon than seductress, and then focus on making sure my hair looks perfect. I took a while to curl my hair, giving my long blond hair just the perfect amount of body and volume with the carefully constructed waves. All in all, I look less like a schoolteacher and more like a girl-next-door-turned-Playboy-Bunny.

I look hot.

And I know Shane's going to eat it up and hopefully show me how much he loves it from his office while all those hussies that crave him are stuck with just the fantasy of him.

I smile at my reflection. I'm fully aware that it's not normal for a girlfriend to be excited to see her boyfriend basically stripping, but I've been a nervous ball of energy all day. I can't wait to see him dance tonight. There's just something about it that I find insanely hot. Even with all the other eyes focusing on the same man, he's all mine, and I've been drunk on that knowledge all day.

I catch a glimpse of Lewis stepping out from the back door of Dirty, talking into the little device that keeps all the security dudes in contact with each other. I give him a wave, take one last look at myself, and open the car door.

"Hey, Lewis," I greet, smiling at him while shifting to shut the door before pulling the hemline of my dress down. The indecently short little black dress is just inches away from being more of a tank top than a dress.

"Nikki."

"How is the night going?"

"Good."

"You don't talk much, do you, big guy?" I ask, hoping to crack the new staff member.

He grunts, looks me over from head to toe, and then turns to the side with one muscular arm outstretched pointing to the exit he just popped out of.

"That's okay," I continue. "I'm sure you have to learn to keep quiet and all with that little thingamabob picking up all your chatter and all."

I see him shake his head slightly as I start walking.

"How does that work anyway? You can't really hear much, I'd imagine, when you're inside and the music is blaring." He falls in step behind me, still silent. "They haven't started the dances, right?"

"Do you always talk this much?"

I lift my shoulder and smile over my shoulder at him. "Only when I'm excited or nervous."

"Which one?"

I frown at him. He looks less intimidating now that he seems actively engaged in a conversation. Even if he's just humoring my quirks.

"Which one, what?"

"Are you? Nervous or excited?" His blue eyes look so serious; his tone makes me think there's another question he isn't asking me, but instead of asking what that might be, I contemplate his question.

"Uh, both? Excited to see how Filthy does, but nervous that it might not be what I hope it will be for them."

He stops when we reach the door, holding his big palm out to stop me from opening it and leveling me with an expression so intense I don't even think about doing anything except stopping.

"I figured you would be nervous for another reason."

I puff of air comes out when I laugh. "Why? Because my sexy man is going to shake his moneymaker? Think about it, big guy. It's hot."

He opens his mouth but shuts it before saying anything.

"What? Don't stand there, keeping me from getting inside, if there's something you want to say."

"I don't know you well enough to say what I want to say."

"So?" I say with a shrug. "Just because you and I aren't close enough to go get mani-pedis doesn't mean that you can't share what's on your mind with me. If there's something I need to know, I would rather have it now then be caught off guard later."

I had only met him before in passing before a few times, but each time he had been a brick that basically showed no emotion. Heck, I wasn't even sure the guy had any feelings aside from hulking intensity. A handsome brick, but stoic as it gets. So when a huge toothy grin broke through that expressionless mask, I was shocked.

"I like you," he adds to his odd beam.

"Uh, thanks?"

"I've worked in a lot of places like this," he continues, ignoring my confusion. "One thing I've always seen is girlfriends who never last. You might be one of the few who do, though."

"Your confidence in my relationship is really something else," I drone.

"Nothing personal, blondie."

"What brought this up?"

One meaty shoulder goes up. "You know what's going on tonight. Shane's been in a mood all day, and I assumed it was because you were giving him a hard time about tonight."

I narrow my eyes. "Actually, this whole thing was my idea."

Clearly, he hadn't expected *that* because his whole face was full of some comedic level shock.

"No shit?"

I shake my head then look over at the hand still holding the door shut. "It's a good idea; don't be so shocked."

"Oh, I'm not shocked that the idea is good—it's gold. I'm shocked that you would willingly offer up your man dancing even more than he already does."

I wait for him to open the door then walk past him into the dim lit back hallway. Before walking any further, though, I turn to look over and up at the large man. "It took Shane a little while to catch on, but you should just accept now that I never do what is expected of me."

I start strutting off, the big guy laughing without reservation behind me.

When will the men around me finally realize I'm my own woman and not some stupid cookie-cutter mold of the generic model?

Chapter 28

Nikki

*T*HE CHANGES TO THE CLUB were only glaringly obvious to those who'd been here often enough to know how things worked at Dirty. I knew, of course, about the stages they added. The new ones were a little lower than the bars they had been doing their hourly spotlight dances on for the past couple of years to ensure they could spice things up and get *realllllly* up close and personal. I had seen enough hotness in my past visits to know that before they could get closer to the ladies they were hot enough, so I was almost giddy to see how things would change.

A few men I didn't recognize walked around, all dressed in something similar to the dress shirt, slacks, and suspenders that Shane favors. It was another reason I was about to come alive with excitement—knowing that when I told Shane how hot it made me when he danced with suspenders, it became the unofficial uniform for Filthy night. A shiver races down my spine when I think about the sound those suspenders make when they're cracking against someone's skin.

I was so lost in my thoughts that when two hands grabbed my hips and pulled me back against a hard body, I screamed, making a few heads turn in my direction. Then the familiar scent of cologne and hard work hit my nose.

Shane.

Home.

"Scare you?"

I nod, my head moving against his shoulder. When his stubbled cheek rubs against mine, I shiver at the same time his lips press against my jaw. His hands move, arms wrapping around my belly, and I'm pressed even tighter. Something about his embrace makes a chill slice through me. And nothing's pleasant about that chill either.

"I thought you changed your mind about coming," he says, lips pressed against the sensitive skin under my ear. I press my hands against his forearms and rub, hoping to soothe whatever has him acting weird.

"I'm not late, honey," I say, glad that we're not within the main club and I don't have to scream over people.

"You're not on time either. I go on in fifteen minutes."

It takes a little effort, but I get him to release me enough to turn around. My hands curl around his neck, and my head tips back to look up at him.

Damn, he's so good looking.

"What's on your mind?" He doesn't answer, not with words.

However, the worry that I see flash in his eyes is enough for me to know something is really wrong. "Shane?"

His eyes dart back and forth, studying my own intently.

It feels like time stands still. The pounding tunes coming through the doorway at the end of the hallway fade away. The chatter of people walking around the club, nothing but a buzz. It's just Shane and me, nothing and no one else. I'm sure we're only really standing there—both silent, but both saying a whole heck of a lot with that silence.

Mine, I'm sure, is troubled but still hopeful.

His, though … his look is resigned to something close to dread.

"What is it, mon beau?" I ask, using the words for *my handsome* that Liberty had taught me. His eyes flash, but just as quickly as that adoration had flickered, it was gone. "Shane? You're scaring me even more now."

"Fuck." He drops his gaze, and his forehead presses against mine. I wait, my heart pounding, and hope that it's just his nerves. When he looks back up, the intense pull of his features is smoothed out, and he's the same Shane that I fell asleep looking at last night. "Just a little stressed, chèrie. I'm sorry."

My relieved exhale is obvious, and he winces. "You've danced on the bar a million times, Shane. What is there to be stressed about? They're going to eat this up, honey."

He shakes his head, not answering, and kisses me deep—desperately. I eat it up, his strange mood making me feel the same urgency. When he pulls away, he doesn't have that tight look again, but I can see he's still holding something back. The same thing I've felt dragging us down over the past couple of weeks. Not wanting to add to his stress, I make myself a promise to ask him about it when things slow down and we can head home.

One thing's for sure … I don't plan on leaving here without knowing what's got him acting like he's seeing me for the last time.

Shane

We walk into the club hand in hand. Her eyes scan the expanse of the room, a smile curving her lips, and her hand tightens when she does a little jump of excitement at seeing how insane it is in here tonight.

As expected, we hit max capacity in the club thirty minutes after opening the door almost two hours ago. No one knew quite what to expect, but with the buzz and marketing focusing on things getting Filthy at Dirty Dog, one could guess. That excitement had only grown to insurmountable levels since then. Everyone was eager to know what would be coming. Drinks flowing quicker than before, draining a few of our bars to the point that we've had to keep an extra bartender just to run into the stockroom to grab more bottles. We hadn't even had a single spotlight dance, let alone used one of the new stages yet, and people were still foaming at the mouth for more.

When the lights go out and our spotlights take on a whole new level, I imagine that it's going to go from excited to insane in a blink of an eye. Don't get me wrong; I was over the fucking moon thrilled for the success, and I knew that would only grow when they saw what we had planned. But, on the flip side, I had been dreading this night since the day we started rolling out the steps to make it come to fruition.

All I could think about was if I was trading the club's success for my relationship.

With everything in my life, I had a firm grasp on … except what would happen when Nikki got to see just what it was like to have to really share her man with hundreds of horny women. To see what I looked like when I was in character for them and not the me that's all hers. To put it mildly, I had lost control and I was frantic to find a way to take the reins back.

"This is amazing!" Nikki screams, looking up at me with a twinkle in her eye.

Fuck, she's beautiful.

"I need to go get ready," I tell her, my words tasting like the same shit I feel churning in my gut.

That beautiful face just continues to beam. Looking at me like I spun the fucking moon just for her.

"Which stage?" she asks, blue eyes bright.

I point at the two in the middle of the large dance area. The two purposely placed front and center. "There."

"And the best place for me? Do you still want me to stay at the bar?"

I nod, wishing like hell I could just force her to leave. Oh, how I had hoped she would want to watch it from my office. I should have known better.

"Knock 'em dead, tiger," she singsongs, smacking my ass on

her way to the bar. Her ass swaying as she goes.

Instead of running after her like I wish I could, I turn and walk toward my office to take off my pants and go from comman-do club co-owner to black underwear that barely contains my cock stripper. I can only pray that, by the end of the night, I'm able to find a way to take control back of my life … and my future with Nikki.

Nikki

My fingers had just closed around my glass when the lights went from dim to black. Instead of everyone screaming in panic, which would only be a normal reaction to such a sudden shift, they go insane—hyped up on the unknown promise that had been billed high and low.

Then, the beat.

The subtle change of the all too familiar song that got a new breath of life when *Magic Mike* came out. How cliché but how perfect. I turn on my stool, the move much easier now that no one is crowding in behind me trying to order a drink. The pressure of them pushing in had stopped when the lights went out as excited girls looked around for what was coming.

That's when the spotlights start popping on. One after the other, highlighting one stage after the next, all holding one very good-looking man. Until finally, the last two are lit up.

Shane and Nate, both of them in the center of the room.

That's when things go from insane to ridiculous.

The men who happen to be here tonight don't move from their spots near the various bars around the club. All the women rush forward, trying to get the best spot at any mini-stage they can reach, but it's obvious by their numbers that they want the two owners the most.

Nate's cocky self is eating it up, his smirk looking mad with hyper activity.

Shane's eyes aren't eating up the crowd at his feet, though. Not even when Nate starts moving in sync with the other bodies. It takes him a second, but I can see the exact moment he puts himself aside and becomes the man who dances for others. Someone who moves for seduction, looking every bit the man who loves this but with eyes dead.

By the time he had shed everything but his tight black underwear, the kind that looks a whole lot like a Speedo, I'm about to come out of my skin with need for him. My body warring with my mind—my body needing what only he can do to it, and my mind terrified at what I see when those dead eyes search the room at the same time his knees hit the ground and he grinds that magical cloth-covered cock of his in the face of some stranger.

He's just looking in my direction, and I know, had he been able to see me, he would be looking for the sole purpose of testing me for my reaction to what's happening. It's then at that moment that I realize the man I was hopelessly in love with, trusting with every fiber of my being, didn't trust me at all.

It doesn't matter anymore that I love seeing him do this. It doesn't matter that I love every single part of him—good, bad, and ugly. It doesn't matter what we had built up until now. The only thing that mattered was that I had finally gotten the answers I had been searching for. Without a conscious thought, I place my vodka tonic down on the smooth bar top, and I walk through the darkness to Shane's office. The whole time, I know that this moment will break my heart no matter how it ends.

Chapter 29

Nikki

HE'S HERE.

I heard the door open, but even before that, I knew he was coming. I had watched him end his dance and fight through the women to get free. Had he waited like the others, he would have had no trouble getting to his office's doorway without the hands of strangers pulling him back—craving what they had wanted them to want. I watched from the windows above the crowd, the scent of *him* surrounding me. For once, since I met him, it doesn't bring me comfort, though.

"Why?" My voice is just a hint of a whisper. I keep my eyes on his reflection in the glass I'm facing, my heart dropping a little more when he winces. "Why, Shane!"

I spin around, not even feeling a hint of satisfaction when he flinches.

"All this time, I thought we had been moving toward

something solid. The feelings I have for you, everything we've shared, the time together … all of that was for nothing, wasn't it? Because if we had what I thought we did, you would have talked to me before tonight and seen for yourself the truth in my words. Tell me, what did you think would happen? Some giant rage of jealousy because you basically were naked and flaunting your body?"

"Nikki, it's not like that," he excuses weakly.

"Oh, really? Did you not just get up there and look in my direction with fear in your eyes? Because that wasn't the face of a man who trusts what his girlfriend's promised him over and over that she loves. Not one bit."

"You've got to under—"

I cut him off with a shake of my head and the hardest of glares. "No, it's you who doesn't understand. I gave you everything. Not just my trust. For whatever reason, you just couldn't give me the same."

He takes a step toward me, but again, I shake my head, taking a step back until the glass presses against my back.

"I thought we stopped playing games weeks ago, Shane. But that's what tonight was, wasn't it? A test to see if I would be able to handle it? You made me think I was welcome here, but it was all just a big stupid test. If that's where we are in our relationship, then you don't even know me at all. If that's how you feel, then this was never real to begin with."

"Nikki," he breathes, moving again. "Mon coeur[10], please."

"Don't use your French charm, Shane Kingston." I step away

10   my heart

from the glass and walk toward him. Stopping in front of him. His heaving chest just a foot away, tan skin still damp with sweat from his dancing. I don't touch him, just look at him from top to toe, every inch that I love so much, and feel like he's a hundred miles away instead of right in front of me. "Do you want to know what I see when you're working out there?" I ask, pointing my hand at the glass. "I see the man behind the mask you wear when you're doing something you love. I see the drive that put you in that strip club years ago. The young man doing everything he could just to keep what was left of his family together. I see the man he is now, strong and sure, never losing that part of himself. Not because he has to do it to survive, but because he did survive and, in turn, learned how to find happiness in his struggles. I see your strength. Your passion for a better life. I see the man who *owned* me long before he became mine and I surrendered myself completely. I see someone who others could only dream of knowing like I do, but I'm the one who gets that honor. Not once had it even crossed my mind to be jealous that you're entertaining others with your body because I've always known it—you—belonged to me. Just like *I* belonged to you. But even with all of that being said, I deserve better than to have you doubt me in return, and until you understand that … until you can see that when you give someone your heart, you don't have space for something as disgusting as jealousy because the trust you share doesn't even allow it, then maybe it's best that we take some space."

I step around him but stop at his side before I can leave the room, looking up at his pained face. "Tu as mon être[11]." I whisper,

11   you had all of me – roughly translated from 'you have my being'

and like a direct hit, his eyes close, and I know he understands that unless he can give *me* all of *him*, then we're done.

He doesn't stop me. I'm not sure he could if he wanted to, my words doing what I intended for them to do. I left the last part of my heart at his feet while walking calmly through the club. I'm not sure when Lewis joined my side, but sometime between the bottom of his steps and the hallway that takes me to the back parking lot, he fell in step with me. With clear eyes, despite my need to cry like a baby, I look up at him and smile a sad smile.

"How much of that did you see?"

"Don't worry about it, blondie."

"I wasn't jealous," I reiterate, wanting him to know the truth even though I'm sure it looked like something of the sort to those who might have seen the tension.

"I know," he says softly.

"Will you watch out for him?" I'm not sure why I ask, but something tells me he's going to need someone doing it. Nate's his friend, yes, but he's known me a lot longer, and with Ember in the middle of that, who knows what will happen. I just need to know he's going to have more than Liberty to help him sort his head out.

Lewis nods, and I return the gesture. On our way out to the parking lot, we continue in silence. I was in my own head, and he was, well, Lewis. Had I been in the right frame of mind, maybe I wouldn't have lost my mind a second later, but I was a girl with a bruised heart and an unclear future with the man she loved, so seeing the ex that had driven us together in the first place—the same one who had a big part to play in why he's so messed up in the head about this whole jealousy crap—leaning against his car,

I was done.

Gloves off and bell rung.

D. O. N. E.

Lewis moves, speaking in his security thing, but I just don't care anymore.

"When will you get a clue?" I scream, kicking off my heels and stomping over the rough asphalt to her. She looks shocked at first, but then that nasty little sneer takes over her face. "Don't even test me tonight, Lacey. He doesn't want you; he hasn't wanted you!"

An arm grabs my elbow and tries to pull me away, but I'm too far-gone. I pull back, not letting him take me from this woman. Her cocksure attitude dims slightly, but she doesn't back off.

"For months, you sniffed around him and didn't get a clue. You couldn't hold him when you had him because you were blinded by your distrust. Distrust that will sink a relationship. It did with yours then, and it would again if he had been stupid enough to let your claws back in. But he wasn't, and because of that, he found me. Don't even test me right now because I'm over it."

"He'll always be mine!" she yells back, but I hear the tremor in her voice when I pull free from my captor and bump her with my chest, making her fall to her butt on the dirty ground.

I step over her, feet on either side of her hips and look down at her, not even caring if she can see up my skirt. She no longer looks sure of herself. She actually looks scared. I hear Lewis continue to talk, feel him try to take my arm again, and then a bang, but the only thing I care about is this stupid woman.

"He's fucking mine!" I scream. "Even if a day comes that he

isn't, we will always be connected because we're meant for each other. Stop being pathetic and move the hell on!"

Without giving her another second of my time, I step over her and walk to my car, digging my keys out. I open my door, but before I drop down, I look over at where I had just been standing and see Shane next to Lewis. His whole body puffing with exertion and something I don't even have the mental capabilities to handle right now written all over his face. What I do notice, though, is the redness and swelling around his left eye. With nothing left in me, the fight all gone, I just shake my head and get in my car.

This time, *this time* when I turn my back from him, I'm unable to keep the tears away.

"What the hell do you mean you're going to the mountains alone?" Ember screams through the phone.

"Just what I said, Em. I called, and they had our cabin open, so I'm heading up a few days early. I just need to get my head together and figure out if I can stick this out and wait with the hopes that one day he'll trust me like I trust him, or if I need to just cut ties now. He's been calling since last night, and I know he's going to start showing up soon. That's just who he is. It's how he works, and I think it's best we both have some time to sort our heads out."

"I hate this," she complains under her breath. "Do you want

me to come with you?"

God, I love my best friend. I really have the best one in the whole world.

"I'll be okay, Em. If it's meant to be, Shane and I will figure it out."

"I know. I know. I just hate knowing that you're hurting and you'll be there all alone. What if you need ice cream?"

I chuckle under my breath, feeling a little of my heartache easing up a bit. "Then I'll make sure I know where the closest Walmart is so I can buy some if need be. I promise, I'll be okay. If I've learned anything over the past year and a half, it's how to mend a broken heart."

Lies. All lies. What I don't tell her is that I already packed my portable cooler with a few cartons of ice cream and that I've already consumed my weight in a few other tubs while crying over a stupid boy. Truth be told, I don't know if we are broken up. What I do know is that things aren't in a good place, and if they can't change—well, then I've lost something beautiful. That right there, though, is what is causing me the most trouble. I know without a doubt that if Shane and I can't get past this, I'll never find this again ... ever. I'm ruined for another. My heart will always be his, no matter what. And I've struggled with that knowledge since walking away from him last night. But I would be doing us both a disservice if I didn't take this time—give us both the space to figure out where our heads are. Me, I know I deserve his complete trust. Him, he deserves to be able to give it, and in turn, know what it's like to have someone give themselves equally to the other. That's the only way we'll be able to move forward.

And it sucks.

"I love you, Em, but I need to get going. I want to hit the road before lunch so that I'm there before the afternoon rush with traffic. I promise, I'm okay."

"I still don't like it. Remember, I know how to shank."

"You don't need to shank anyone."

"I've been eyeing my toothbrush all morning, Nik. I know what I need to make things happen."

I laugh again because my best friend is the best.

"Keep it up and I'm going to call Nate and tell him you need to be in time-out from Netflix."

"Promise, Nicole. You'll call me when you get there and every damn hour so I know you're okay. I don't want you up there all alone if you need me. Mom already said she would keep Quinnie if I wanted to go with you."

"You told her?"

She's silent, and I know she told me more than she meant to.

"How much did you tell her?"

"Uh, on a scale of what to what?"

"On a scale of she's made for the sisterhood or she's told your dad and he's ready to go kill someone for hurting one of the girls he considers under his protection?"

She might as well have just said what her silence was screaming. "Tell me Emmy at least made sure to hide his guns and anything sharp?"

"I'm relatively sure nothing was within reach, if that helps."

"You know, I feel sorry for whoever your sister ends up with. Now that you're married, Maddox only has her to focus on."

She giggles. "He's even worse now with Quinnie. She's one lucky little girl."

"Excuse me? You didn't exactly feel *lucky* when you were on the other end of Maddox Locke's over-the-top protectiveness."

"True, but she's *my* baby, and I see where he was coming from now."

"Just tell me your dad isn't going to make this even more difficult for Shane? I want him to figure things out because he wants to, not because someone strong-arms him with their scary glares and growling threats."

"HA!" she exclaims. "That's funny. Dad does growl when he's getting all over the top, doesn't he? Don't fret, Nik. Shane's safe from my dad. Plus, Nate took care of that."

I think back to last night, remembering the redness around his eye. I had been too conflicted with my thoughts to put two and two together, but I should have known.

"Are they okay?" I ask in concern, hoping that Shane and Nate's friendship *and* business partnership doesn't get weird because we're … whatever we are.

"You know how it is. Nate loves you like his own sister. You're worried about my dad doing something, but keep in mind, Nate was raised by those very same over-the-top men. Shane knows he screwed up." I can practically see her waving her hands in the air while she talks.

"What a freaking mess," I huff, zipping up my bag of toiletries and tossing them in the duffle bag with my other bathroom products and styling tools. You would think I was moving with the amount of crap I have packed up, but with the unexpected early departure, I basically tossed all my packing lists out the window. What a freaking mess, indeed.

"I love you," Ember says, no longer holding the strong emotional rage she had been exhibiting since I called her thirty minutes ago.

"I love you back. I'll call you later, okay?"

We get off the phone, and I make quick work of finishing my packing. Since I didn't have time to get the provisions that Shane and I had planned to get before heading up later this week, I needed to do about a million other things before locking myself away, so I didn't waste a second throwing all my crap in my car and hitting the road.

I know he'll come after me. After he figures out where I am, that is.

I just need to give myself enough of a head start that I'm able to take some time and figure out what I'm going to do when he does.

Do I settle and take the man who makes me drunk with every mixed drink of emotion, knowing I can love him enough for the both of us ... or do I hold my ground and demand what I know I deserve?

All of him.

Chapter 30

Shane

I'T'S BEEN TWO FUCKING DAYS. Two days of nothing but silence from Nikki. I've called her over and over, left numerous voicemails—so many I've lost track of what I said in the majority of them—and now her phone no longer gives me the option to leave one. I've done nothing in those two days but frantically try to find her and get lost in my own head. One thing I've been successful in, though, is seeing the enormity of what she had said before leaving the other night.

After the first twenty-four hours without Nikki, I knew the one thing I had been too blind with my past to see and, for the first time since my mom died, I knew I wasn't the one in control of my future. There was no way I could take back the reins either because the only way I would ever be able to find a way to ease the torment in my mind was to hand them over to the woman who owns them.

On top of everything being tits up with Nikki, my best friend hasn't spoken to me about anything other than what was necessary for Dirty, and my sister hasn't taken my calls since she found out Nikki and I got in a fight. Like I'm not beating myself up enough? They are the only two people who I had known over the years and could always count on, but it was clear they knew what I couldn't see yet. It was their silence that helped me see what Nikki had been telling me before she left too.

I knew the second I realized she wasn't sitting at the bar anymore that she had seen what I had been struggling with for weeks. I also knew instantly I fucked up. I fucked it all up. And I'm the only one who can put it all back together.

Now I'm stuck in a tailspin, unable to control fuck all, and I can't get a grip long enough to take the steps I need to get it all back. One thing's for sure … I will. All I've thought about for two days—aside from making sure Lacey was taken care of once and for all—was how I would prove to Nikki that she's wrong and I do trust her.

"Fuck," I hiss, punching my wheel when traffic goes from thick to standstill.

When she walked out of the office the other night, Nate was in my face. He must have known something was going on, even if he hadn't been there to witness it, because she couldn't have been halfway down the stairs before he stormed into my office and I had his right hook slamming against my face. All he said was, "I warned you," and then he was gone just as fast as he came. It was as if someone had turned on a switch when his fist connected with my eye—I was rushing through the club, holding up the pants I had hastily shoved on when I rushed to her side just minutes before while I sprinted as fast as I could to catch her before she left.

A lot of good that did me.

Then I had to deal with the Lacey mess, and even though I wish she hadn't shown up, at least I was able to get an order of protection and she wouldn't be back without getting arrested. She might try again, but since her daddy is trying to run for senate, I doubt she'll risk it for fear that he'll finally get sick of her bullshit and cut her off. All that was left with Lacey, as far as I was concerned, was getting Nikki to file for her own restraining order.

I look down at my phone, checking the time on my Waze app and again feel nothing but frantic need to start plowing through traffic.

One more hour.

One more hour and I'll be facing the biggest fight of my life.

One hour until I give her the only thing I know will prove to her that I do trust her. That I trust her with more than what she could ever think to want or need.

Her badly pronounced French words from the other night come back, a ghost of a whisper through my mind. *Oh, Nicole Clark, I'll have all of you again.* There's no other life I can face living if it's not with her in it.

One hour turned into two and my confidence turned into nerves.

I wasn't nervous about what I needed to do—no, I was nervous that she would have used these past two days to realize I wasn't worth the fight. I knew deep down that couldn't be true, but it doesn't take away from the very real fear I have over making myself vulnerable for the first time since I learned how to prevent it.

I park next to her old Toyota and kill the engine, staring at the rustic log cabin that we had spent a whole week searching for on various vacation rental sites. She had known instantly that this was the perfect one for us to get away to, and she wasn't wrong. There wasn't another house around us. The long and winding road that took me up here had been all ours. The closest grocery store was ten miles back, and aside from the five other places scattered over the mountain, we were alone. Of course, that had been something we made sure of in order to have nothing but privacy to enjoy each other wherever and however we wanted—now it would ensure we had a whole different kind of privacy.

The door opens and Nikki steps on to the porch. She leans against the doorjamb and watches me as I climb out of the car, shutting the door and walking toward her. She looks beautiful even though it's clear that she's tired. Her long hair is pulled up on top of her head in a messy ball—one of those bun things girls spend a shit ton of time making sure it looks perfect. Her face is free of makeup, making her look young and innocent with her dusting of freckles across the bridge of her nose. However, it's the redness around her eyes that makes me pause halfway up the steps.

"I figured you would be here tomorrow. I should have known you'd figure it out sooner than that."

"I would have been here yesterday if I could have been."

She nods, a sad one that looks like it takes all her strength.

"Come on," she says softly, turning and walking into the cabin. Her bare feet silent against the hardwoods.

I follow without argument, taking her lead. When she stops in the living room, I wait, not speaking. She points at the couch and drops down in a chair near it, but far enough that she's out of my reach. Again, I don't speak and let her call the shots.

"I don't imagine you would have come all this way without knowing how you wanted this conversation to go, Shane, so go ahead and say it."

I lean forward in my seat, rubbing my hands against my jeans and bracing my elbows on them before looking up and holding her gaze.

"I fucked up, mon coeur. I fucked it all up, and you did the right thing by leaving." Clearly, that wasn't what she expected as shock reigns over her features. "There aren't any words to express how sorry I am that I hurt you, Nikki. Not a fucking one that will be strong enough to even begin to try to fix it. I'll live with that, and hopefully, you'll give me a chance to prove that I'll do everything in my power to ensure I never hurt you again."

"Shane," she whispers, a tear falling free of her eye and trailing down her cheek.

I stop her, continuing with the words I've gone over and over on my way to her. "You were right. I used all the shit from my past to excuse the fact that I wasn't willing to trust you—even though I knew deep down that I could. Fuck, chèrie, I know it's the weakest excuse in the world, but I couldn't see past the only thing I had ever known and because of that, I hurt you. I trust you, wholly and without doubt, and I just didn't and couldn't see it until it was too late."

"How can you be sure? How can you sit there and know this won't happen again? How do you know that you—the man who holds his ability to control any and everything—will be able to trust me without question? What happens the next time I come to Dirty? Are you going to freak out and put up a wall between us again?"

"No," I answer emphatically. "God, no. You have no idea, Nikki. What you said to me that night in my office, you struck something I've never even known I was capable of feeling. The only thing that scares me now is the thought that I might not have you by my side and in my life forever. I need *you* more than I could ever need my control. YOU are more important. I don't just believe it; I *know* with every part of me that without you, it won't ever matter how hard I work to keep control of my life because it won't be worth living."

Her tears are coming faster now, her soft sobs feeling like a whip against my soul.

"Let me show you," I beg, dropping to the floor and shifting on my knees to her.

When I reach her chair, her legs open and I push between them before wrapping my arms around her waist and drop my head to her lap. I hug her tight with desperation and feel my own emotions winning when a huge sob shakes her whole body. My eyes grow damp the second she drops her hand to my head and runs her fingers through my hair. Just having her in my arms, when I had thought I would never feel this again, breaks the dam that had held me together for the past two days.

I look up, not giving one shit when a tear falls from my eye, and hope to God she can see the truth in my eyes.

"Let me give you all of me, mon amour," I plead. "Let me show you what you are to me. L'amour de ma vie[12]," I continue. "Let me show you."

She nods, her tears still falling.

Standing, I reach down and take her own shaking hand in mine, pulling her to her feet.

"Where's the bedroom, Nikki?" I ask, making sure I don't use the voice she's all too familiar with when we're together like we're about to be.

A choppy breath comes out loud in the silence between us, her blue eyes brighter with her tears. She doesn't speak but also doesn't let my hand go as she leads us through the house. Her shoulders hunch slightly as she looks down at her feet. She might be giving me what I've asked, but I can tell she's still holding herself with an air of protection—maybe even preservation—wrapped tight around her. When we step into the large master, the room I had looked at knowing it would be perfect for the way I love to take her, I see it in a new light. The huge wooden frame bed, those slats I had thought would hold my ropes perfectly, now holding a new purpose. When I release her hand and move to stand in front of her, she looks up at me in confusion. I'm sure she had thought

12   love of my life

this would be different. If she's shocked now, she's about to have her jaw on the damn ground.

Despite my earlier nerves, the only thing I feel now is pure, confident calm. I know this is the right thing to prove to her that my words are true. And with each layer of clothing that I strip from my body, baring myself to her, body and soul, I hope to fucking God that she can understand the magnitude and meaning behind this.

After I'm completely naked, I stand and look at the woman who I'll be lost without and give her the one thing I have never willingly surrendered.

My control.

"Vous avez tous moi," I softly tell her. *You have all of me.* "There is nothing more important than that, mon amour. Every single inch of me. Inside and out. Body and heart. My control and trust. It's all yours, Nikki."

Her shuddered breath hitches, and she clutches her chest.

"I'm yours," I continue. "It's up to you what you do with me now."

Then I look down and wait for the rest of our lives to begin.

"Shane," she whispers, her voice thick with emotion. "You … we've … you've never let me have you like this."

"No one has because no one has ever had my complete trust until now. Do you understand what I'm saying, Nikki? I trust you. I trust you with all that I am. All I've ever needed. There will never be a moment in my life when I don't need you more than my desire to control everything. Take me, take us, and please give me another chance to be worthy of your love."

"Oh, Shane," she hiccups through her crying.

Then she's in my arms and her mouth is on mine, taking what I'm offering.

We fall to the bed, her body landing on top of mine and our kiss never breaking. It's hungry, but not in the frantic need that has always been hinting the edges of our lovemaking. No, not this time. This time, we're starving to earn the last thing we hadn't shared before. This isn't just a hard fuck and mutual enjoyment. This is two people becoming something few ever find. Something I almost lost before even knowing I had it.

We shared lust before.

Now we share love.

And fuck if it's not the most beautiful thing I've been too scared to believe I could find.

She breaks the kiss and pulls away to yank her top up and over her head. Her tits fall free, and I groan when I realize she didn't have a bra on. She wiggles against my lap, and I grunt, my cock needing her.

"Why don't you touch me?" she questions breathlessly.

"You haven't told me to," I answer instantly, and the second I see my meaning hit the mark, a new burst of pleasure rushes through my body. Fuck. Never had I thought giving her control of our sex could be more powerful than what we already shared.

"Shane? I don't …" she trails off when I lift my hands and grasp the wood slats above the pillows. "You're serious?" she gasps, wiggling off my lap and staring down at me while I continue to give her this part of me.

"I'm yours."

"Shane," she cries softly.

"Please take me, mon amour. Take me and please let me have the gift of you. I will never take advantage of your trust again, and I will always give you mine. From this moment on, we're equal in everything."

She's crying even harder now, but she still removes the worn sleep pants she had on, climbing back on my lap and looking down at me with her hands bracing against my chest. Her tears fall on my skin and burn a path across my chest. When she lifts one hand and wraps it around my cock, my breath hitches. Then she feeds my cock into her body with a painfully slow glide down. When she's seated fully on my thickness, she loses the ability to keep her emotions somewhat in check and starts rocking and crying, never looking away.

"Je t'aime," she gasps, her whole body shaking as she continues to cry, only now she's smiling the biggest grin down at me. "I love you," she repeats. "I love you so much it hurts."

"Je t'aime, mon amour. Je t'aime."

There's nothing rushed about how she makes love to me. Our bodies taking until it feels like a part of her has filled the part of me that I hope to fuck she feels filling her heart. We might not always have perfect, but I know the second she breathes out her release and collapses on my chest—my cock emptying inside her—that there isn't anything we can't conquer together.

One thing's for sure: I'll make sure there will never be doubt to her or anyone that what we share is as real as it gets.

Epilogue

Nikki

A Year Later

"IT'S ALMOST MIDNIGHT," I YELL at Ember, my drink sloshing over the edge and covering my wrist when I start bouncing up and down. She lets out a little squeal of her own. I'm sure we look like two ridiculous girls, jumping in our heels and making these noises, but I couldn't care less.

"I can't believe this is my first Filthy night!"

"I can, little mama." I laugh. "You've been incubating a human. It's your own fault for making such perfect little girls that demand you sit there and stare at them at all hours of the day."

I'm only half joking too. Ember and Nate make the most beautiful girls. I secretly hope he gets his wish, and she's preggers again soon because she takes care of the baby fever any woman creeping closer to thirty feels just by giving me more goddaughters to spoil. Brookie—or Brooklynn Nicole—had me wrapped around her little finger the day she was born. Which, really, is no different than her older sister. I'm a sucker for the little Reid girls.

"Perfect or not, I'm done having babies for a long time."

I snicker, tapping the side of my glass against hers. "Yeah, right. I give it another six months, tops, before Nate has his way again. Especially if you keep coming to Filthy nights."

"Don't put ideas in his head, Nicole!"

I throw my head back and laugh. "I don't *need* to. Trust me, Em, you might just end up pregnant watching the show tonight."

I can tell she doesn't believe me, but if you've never witnessed the hot factor of these guys getting Filthy for one night, well … you've never *seen* hot. Over the past year, I've been to every single one when Shane danced. He and Nate decided that, being the biggest draw dancer-wise, the best thing to do was to dance once a month. This was the only time our guys got up there now. They no longer participated in the regular night spotlight dances on the main bars either. With Dirty bigger than it's ever been, they've been able to hire even more staff, and in turn, dedicated managers who took over all of the grunt work both of them had gotten tired of doing. They're still here but in a much more relaxed capacity.

Lewis, though, who I now get bi-weekly mani-pedis with, got his very own office and promotion to full-time lead in that department. Shane, after learning from his issues with Lacey, wasn't taking any chances and amped the security here up to levels that rival the Secret Service on nights like tonight when I want to watch my man dance. He does the same for anyone else he considers his personal VIP, though, so it doesn't bother me in the least. It's just the type of man he is. He's let up a lot in the ways that he executes his control, but this is one that I can't fault him on. He wants those he loves safe, and I will always admire and respect that about him. Thankfully, Lacey hasn't even been a thought since that night. When I got back in town from our stay in the mountains, I followed his lead and filed for my own restraining order. Once those were filed, her father yanked her back home to Athens faster than you could say cheap hoe. In the end, we both got our exes out of our lives and won the greatest gift of all.

Each other.

"It's almost time, ladies. You'd better go get to the stage and beat the rush so Lewis doesn't have a heart attack trying to get y'all there," Dent yells over the bar, winking at us both.

I turn, my long hair fanning around me, and smile at Ember. "Are you ready?"

Her own grin is huge. "How close to Nate's Lollipop dance is this?"

"Another universe, Em. Doesn't even come close," I answer, thinking back to the very dance that Nate created as a spotlight regular meant to make his wife melt.

"Oh, my."

"You have no idea!" I start moving, patting Lewis on his big beefy shoulder when we get to his side. "Let's go, you big giant!"

He shakes his head but starts walking. The path clears for him with no effort on his part. He just moves, and people get the heck out of dodge. I'm laughing like a loon the whole time. I'm not sure why it's so funny to me, but I'm not complaining since the big guy gets me to the two main stage's with no trouble and ensures I have a front row spot. He moves to the side after we reach the stages edge and I take his spot, pushing Ember a little toward the other one so that we're both in the middle of the two of them, ready and waiting. I look over my shoulder to see Lewis standing with his back to us, arms crossed, just daring someone to get close. On nights when I'm here to watch Shane, there is never a woman who can get close to me—of course, they can still get close to him from other parts of the round stage, but it's not like he's ever got eyes for anyone but me. And I get drunk off the high of watching him.

Now—a year plus of being together—not even a sliver of doubt exists in his mind when it comes to how I feel about his dancing. I've shown him over and over how hot it gets me after each Filthy night I watch from this very spot, and tonight will be no different.

They've made a few upgrades to Filthy night, so when I see the tiny green light at the stage's floor turn on, I know Shane's under there, ready to come up when the lights go black and the stage floor opens to allow him and all the other dancers to avoid walking through the club floor to take their spots. Huge upgrade that took closing the club for a month to build into the basement but so worth it.

"Brace yourself, girlfriend!" I yell at Ember, the current song coming to an end but still loud. She looks just as excited as I feel, but she has no idea.

Things are about to get Filthy at Dirty Dog.

Placing my hands on the edge of the stage, I widen my legs and brace myself, knowing that in about thirty seconds, my man is going to make my knees weak.

Women start pushing in around the stages. They must have realized how close to midnight we are. I bite my lip and wait, already feeling like I'm about to come out of my skin.

Then the lights go black, and the room goes electric. My ears ring with the level of screaming around me. Then my palms vibrate as the stage floor starts to open, and I feel a whoosh of air come from the basement as the lift starts moving up, filling in the opening and giving Shane an enforced base to move on. I feel his eyes on me before the music changes and the spotlight illuminates him. The hypnotizing beat of Bando Jonez "Sex You" starts and a tingle lights a fire down my spine, heat shooting straight between my legs when I get my first look at Shane.

"Holy hotness," I wheeze, my breath getting stuck, and my head spinning. As much as I'd love to see Ember's reaction to this lovely surprise, I'm not looking away from the warm, desire-filled brown eyes that are locked on me. He's wet. Not drenched, but you can tell he doused himself intentionally. The white T-shirt he's got on molded to his hard muscles like a second skin. However, when I finally look down from that eye feast, I see the one article of clothing *he knows* drives me insane. And I know this outfit was intentional.

So.

Very.

Intentional.

Gray sweatpants should be illegal.

They're dangerous on any man, but when it's my man wearing them … they're lethal.

Especially when they've got just enough wetness from the water he must have dumped over his head to make them press even more firmly against the bulge between his legs. My eyes widen when that bulge twitches, and I shoot my eyes back up to his face. He's got one brow raised and that devilish smirk in place.

Then he starts to move. His body becoming one with the slow and sexy rhythm of the song, his hands lifting his shirt up to tease the audience of screaming ladies with a hint of his hard abs. His eyes never leaving my face. I've seen my share of dancing from this very spot, but something about this one is even more filthy than normal. He usually keeps his dancing a little cleaner, but this … my God.

I moan when he drops to his knees, his crotch right in my face, and looks down at me with something sinful playing behind his eyes. He rotates his hips, thrusting as if he's making love to someone, and I pull my lip between my teeth. If he keeps this up, I'm going to die.

Lightning quick, he tags my wrists and pulls my hands off the stage and places them against his abs, still rolling those talented hips of his. He glances over my head and gives a nod, but I'm too busy trying to figure out how the gray material is holding his cock down when he pulls my hands down and bares the root of his thickness to my eyes. My breath is coming in shallow pants. Good heavens above, he's not wearing anything under there. I know he won't go fully nude, they never do, but when he releases one hand and bares his ass for the women behind him, the screams pick up to unnatural levels. The front of his sweats slipping even more until my eyes feel like they're going to bug out when a good two inches of his cock is showing. I know it's just for me but not missed by those around me.

However, before things can get dangerous for me at the floor of the stage, he moves again and hooks me under my arms, and I'm flying through the air when he stands and takes me to my feet on the stage with him.

Well, this is new.

He pulls us close, his erection hitting my stomach, and starts grinding against me. His hands moving down my back before taking my butt in his palms and lifting me. I part my legs and hook my ankles behind his back. His hips pick up speed, his cock thrusting against my panties, and I drop my head back and hold on to his shoulders as he uses my body to finish his dance. When the last part of the sultry song starts winding down, he thrusts my hips down to his hardness and moves his hands up my back— keeping me secure in his arms—and forces me to look back at him.

"Hey, mon colibri," he says with a breathtaking smile.

"Hey, honey," I moan back.

Then he takes my mouth in a soul-stopping kiss, the music ending and seamlessly transitioning into something else while the ladies around the stages get louder. All the while, he takes me to the heavens with one heck of a kiss, not even stopping when the hydraulics in the stage lift start taking us down to the basement together. The only thing I can feel and focus on is the man who owns my heart. I'm vaguely aware of Ember giggling when the crowd's intensity is drowned out by the door we just dropped down from as it closes again, but I'll talk to her tomorrow about what she thought of her first Filthy experience. If her own sounds of pleasure are anything to go by, though, Nate won't have any trouble getting another baby if he keeps bringing her to these.

I keep my mouth glued to Shane, knowing he'll take care of getting us somewhere private. When he starts walking, his hardness hits my sensitive clit, and I pull my mouth from his and moan deeply.

"Fuck me," he grunts, stopping for a second. I look down and see the passion in his eyes.

"Get me to your office so I can show you how much I appreciate all things gray, baby, and do it quickly." I start licking and kissing a path up his neck, not needing him to speak, and start thinking of all the ways I'm about to do just that.

"How did I get so lucky?" he muses before he starts rushing through the basement and up the back steps to his office. His heavy breathing the only thing I can hear past the roaring and pounding of my need. When he drops me to my feet, it takes me a second to realize where we are. I sway on my heels and look up at his handsome, strong face.

"Je t'aime tellement," he tells me in his lyrical accent that makes my heart soar.

"I love you so much right back, you intoxicating man."

That night, locked away in his office, we spend hours getting drunk off each other—our love something fairy tales are made of—and I know I'm the luckiest girl in the world to have the best not-so-fake boyfriend.

The End

We'll be back for more Hope Town early next year when Liberty Kingston finds out just how sinfully perfect a Cage man can be.

Thank Yous

I always find these to be the most challenging part of writing a story, to be honest. I usually spend a great deal of time freaking out that I've forgotten someone—and after fifteen books, it still happens.

So ... I'll keep this short and sweet.

To my husband and girls with their endless support and understanding when I get so deeply intertwined with my characters and books that I'm locked away for days and days. I wouldn't be able to do any of this without you guys.

To Felicia, the bestest friend in the universe, for ignoring me for hours and yelling at me when I would get all Debby Downer. I would probably still be at the first sex scene in this book if I didn't have you. And ... let's be honest, it's only half as fun when you're writing alone.

To Lara, Georgette, Jenny, Ellie and Stacey. Without the five of you, this book wouldn't be the best it can be. It would just be a mess of typos and hot sex. Kidding, well, not really. I would be lost without y'all.

To my publicist and friend Dani for putting up with me and every single thing that life threw at me that kept this book from you all for so long. She really is the powerhouse behind me that keeps things rolling. Thank you for your support and understanding and most of all, friendship.

A massive thank you to Barbara Hoover for her French knowledge and helping Shane sound like the sexy man he is! I would have a jumbled mix of words, had it not been for you!

To my good friends, Angie and Steve Buckles at Doodles of Pearls – thank you for letting me bring my obsession for you and your business to my world. You guys are amazing and I wish you nothing but the best. For more information on Nikki and Ember's (and my) favorite pearl place, visit: www.doodlesofpearls.com

Last but never least – to my readers. This book is 100% for you. You kept your faith in me during some pretty scary moments in my life and never once gave up, even when I told you this book would be put off for months from what I originally planned. I always knew I had the best readers in the world, but you guys continue to prove it time and time again. I love you all, and I can't wait to continue this ride with you for—hopefully—many more years.